West End Girls 2:

Summer Madness

D0752572

West End Girls 2:

Summer Madness

Lena Scott

www.urbanbooks.net

Urban Books, LLC
78 East Industry Court
Deer Park, NY 11729

ISBN 13: 978-1-60162-286-0
ISBN 10: 1-60162-286-4

First Printing November 2010
Printed in the United States of America

10 9 8 7 6 5 4 3 2 1

This is a work of fiction. Any references or similarities to actual events, real people, living, or dead, or to real locales are intended to give the novel a sense of reality. Any similarity in other names, characters, places, and incidents is entirely coincidental.

Distributed by Kensington Publishing Corp.
Submit Wholesale Orders to:
Kensington Publishing Corp.
C/O Penguin Group (USA) Inc.
Attention: Order Processing
405 Murray Hill Parkway
East Rutherford, NJ 07073-2316
Phone: 1-800-526-0275
Fax: 1-800-227-9604

Acknowledgments

A writer's mind is a fabulous place to visit. It's full of many worlds and people who inhabit those worlds. With open hearts and willing spirits we as writers share those places and people with you. In return we seek approval and appreciation. It's a fair trade, if I do say so myself.

On a more personal note, I want to thank Carl Weber, Maxine Thompson, and Michelle McGriff. Without them *West End Girls* would not be part of a world that's now inhabited and ready for you all to visit, approve and appreciate.

Thanks again everyone for keeping Tanqueray, Unique and Sinclair's story alive. I hope as you read more about the lives of these three girls you grow to love them as much as I have.

Thank you for visiting the world inside my mind. I hope you enjoy your stay.

Prologue

Summer was often cooler in the San Francisco Bay Area than further down the peninsula or inland, but today it was not only cold it was dark and downright gloomy, especially in the West End. Today the West End buried another bit of its future. Today a young boy who didn't have a chance to become a man was laid to rest. While the inner city children played in park fountains and teenage boys walked in the malls listening to the latest hot tunes on their expensive iPods, while urban teenage girls bared their bellies and showed off back tats, Unique Nation wept over the loss of her son Marquis. Gunned down by police in a shootout at the hospital where his sister Cammie, another of Unique's children, lay fighting for her life.

"And all of it is my fault," Unique cried. She'd repeated those words for days despite the comforting words of her sisters, Sinclair and Tanqueray.

True, Unique had turned a blind eye while her boyfriend Curtis molested her daughter Cammie, leaving only Marquis to stand up as the man of the house. Marquis shot and killed Curtis in cold blood. Everyone felt this was Curtis' due justice. Still, Unique would never have prayed for this day to come.

"It's all right Neek. Heaven got a place for li'l G's like Marquis," Tanqueray said, stroking Unique's fresh flat ironed, hair out of the way of the tears so it wouldn't get wet and nap up. Everyone there was taking pictures, so Unique needed to look decent and all that. There was nothing worse than her looking all broken down at a time like this.

Many saw Marquis as a hero. He'd stood up for his family and taken care of business. He went out like a man.

"And you need to know dat," one of the boys said, confirming the street talk that was circulating about Marquis' death. Yes, everyone felt he died like a man. "You should be proud."

"Get away from me," Unique bellowed, pushing the boy away from her as she again burst into tears. She threw the head rag that the boy had laid on her lap onto the floor. She wanted nothing to do with all that gang shit that Marquis had gotten himself involved in.

"Go on now," Tanqueray said to the boy who stood in shock at her reaction to his kindness. He was stunned at the disrespect shown to his colors. Tanqueray quickly hoped to squash any bad feelings that could come up. "She didn't mean it."

"Yes, I did . . . Awww God!" she cried.

The boy nodded as if he'd accepted the apology. None of his crew was watching, so maybe that was as far as it would go. "We gon' watch out fa her . . . fa life," the boy assured her slamming his fist into the palm of his hand and biting his bottom lip. He looked fierce and Tanqueray knew he meant what he was saying with heart. She flashed his gang sign showing her loyalty to his set. He grinned, flashing his mouth gem. True, Tanqueray wasn't from the West End, but who the hell cared at a time like this.

"Much love," Tanqueray added. "Now go on in there and get some barbeque. Mr. Williams got down on that grill."

"Yeah, he did," the boy grinned showing he'd already enjoyed a little bit.

In front of the building the smoke billowed from the grills laden with pork and links. There were plenty of red drinks and alcohol flowing too. The whole neighborhood came together. Even folks from the Palemos, the neighboring hood, braved to cross the lines into the West End to pay their respects. It was a day of truce and very impressive, if Tanqueray did say so herself.

"This was Javina's grandchild. What you expect! We comin'," Mrs. Brown said, when given an option to miss out on the repast.

Tanqueray explained it clearly one more time so she wouldn't misunderstand the situation. "We gon' have it in the W.E. You know folks over there get crazy when y'all cross the line."

"I don't give no care about them folks. The Lord gave me power up and above all them niggardly activities," she said, almost breaking into a gospel song. "We's all one under the lawd." She held up her Bible.

"Yes'm," was all Tanqueray could say.

Folks came through all right. They'd raised over a thousand dollars at the car wash to get a head stone for Marquis. Unique didn't have any money. She lived on welfare in a Section 8 apartment. She had no insurance policies . . . nothing. The County was willing to bury him in an unmarked grave but it just about killed Unique to think of doing that. So they raised as much money as they could. Somebody came through at the last minute with the rest, anonymously. Tanqueray had a feeling she knew who that donor was but didn't say anything to anyone about it.

Just then there was a little ruckus in the living room. Folks were getting a little loud. "What the hell is all that!" Tanqueray blurted upon hearing the uproar.

Sinclair rushed in the room. "Tang, you gotta come out

here. Some nigga up in here with a damn entourage. They got guns and shit."

"Dammit. Always something!"

Unique sat up now, drying her eyes, "Where's the girls!" she yelled thinking of her children now. She had just lost a son and nearly lost a daughter.

Tanqueray mind ran back to the hospital, to the night Unique lost her firstborn child, Marquis. He'd come there to vindicate his sister, Cammie who had early that day been hit by a car. Marquis had come to the hospital to kill a man. He succeeded but in return for his valor was killed by the security guards there at the hospital. Marquis and Cammie both had been taken from Unique in one moment—one unforgettable moment. Unique shook her head at that instant memory and the shame it brought.

Cammie had been hit by a car while running away from her. Cammie's secret had just been discovered and Unique went off. She wanted answers. She wanted the truth to what she heard as a lie. There was no way her man had been molesting her child right under her nose. But apparently the truth was too much for Cammie to say so she ran and was nearly killed by an oncoming car. Even now, today, while they said their good-byes to Marquis, Cammie lay in a coma. Unique fought every day to keep her sanity. Nothing made sense anymore. She could only hope to wake up one day.

"They're safe. Mrs. Newbury has them with her!" Tanqueray said. She grabbed Unique's baseball bat that she kept behind the door and rushed out to the living room behind Sinclair.

Chapter 1

"Hollup Shawty!" the big man with the dark menacing eyes said to Tanqueray, who let the bat be seen and her intent to use it known. He spread his large hands out to block anyone who may try to run up on him. He was all bulked up, as if he'd just walked out of the pen. His complexion was smooth and dark except for the lines that aged his face and the scar that probably had a hell of a story behind it.

One of the local W.E. boys was highly agitated. Maybe it was because everyone had agreed to lay down weapons, yet this man had come all up in the joint strapped back to back. Anybody could tell he was set tight. "Nigga can't just be walking up in here like he own the street. Asked him what set he was wit' and—"

"And I told you to get the fuck out my face punk-ass bitch nigga!" the big dude's bodyguard said aiming the gun right at the W.E. boy's face. It was obvious that the dude was 'somebody' as he had folks guarding his ass. Nobody from the Palemos, the P, had even bothered to come inside, so they must have known who the Negro was.

"Who are you?" Tanqueray asked, feeling Sinclair cowering behind her a little bit.

"I'm Markey," he said, showing nothing in his voice one way or the other. It was as if just that name was supposed to make Tanqueray see past his guns any more clearly. "Senior, I guess," he added. No one had called Marquis, Markey before, or anything remotely like that. He was called Marquis, and so implying that he was a junior Markey just didn't sound right at the moment.

Sinclair stepped out from behind Tanqueray on that one. Even the boy who had jumped bad just a few minutes earlier seemed to back the hell up. Tanqueray lowered the bat just a little and gave the man a good gawking. "Markey? You mean Marquis? As in Marquis, senior?"

"Damn, I didn't know there even was a senior," Sinclair admitted.

"The boy had to have a daddy somewhere," the man said. He smiled. His teeth were perfect and white as if he'd spent the last few months in a dental chair before walking out of those prison gates.

Just then, Unique pushed through the folks gathered in the living room, ready for whatever might jump off. "Marquis?" she said, her voice just above a whisper, tears again rushing from her eyes. She fell into his arms.

Neither Tanqueray nor Sinclair expected Unique to receive this man this way. This man had taken her innocence at thirteen and disappeared leaving her to bear up alone under the wrath of their mother and to face the scorn of society without support. No one would have thought she would have wanted to see him again. No one could have even imagined that Unique remembered what his face looked like, let alone that she cared about him at all. Yet here she was weeping bitterly into his chest . . . and he—he was comforting her.

Tanqueray's heart melted for a half a second before she snapped back to alert. Maybe it was the fact that his goons hadn't laid down their shit that made her worry. Maybe it was the tats they wore and intensity of their faces that kept her on alert. They bore gang colors and markings she didn't recognize as local. They were bringing heat from somewhere else. All she could hope was that the place wasn't hell. However, the closer she looked the more familiar the tats were. She knew them from somewhere. Somebody she knew used to have the same ones. Who?

It didn't matter right now. She'd figure all that out later. In her heart, right now, she knew that it wasn't just the funeral that brought Marquis Sr. from the dead. How she figured that out, she didn't know, but as much as Tanqueray wanted to get off the streets she was one with them. She was street and had a good strong vibe when it came to what was really what. There was something about big daddy Marquis that didn't sit well with her. She was gonna keep her eyes and nose open until he left ,which she hoped was soon because by the looks of Unique's soggy, snotty face she was weak and just prime for picking.

Chapter 2

The scene at the house had just gotten too thick for Tanqueray. It was a bit too serious. She left right when all the church ladies finished piling in. Why the hell they thought Unique was a church girl was beyond her comprehension at that time. "She ain't seen a church since their feet still fell asleep from hanging off the edge of the seat," Tanqueray mumbled under her breath before taking a sip of her drink.

While Tanqueray sat in her favorite spot, she pondered Markey and his gang affiliation. He wasn't tagged with any set, but it was clear he was connected to some tough dudes. She was curious and wanted to ask Finest who the dude was. In a way, Finest had become her man. She was pretty pissed at him right now, but still, Finest was the one to ask as he had his ass all up in the gang, set tight. He'd done some things that Tanqueray was still hearing about. He was going to end up doing some time for sure. But still, he was slowly making his way into her heart. The whole time they were raising money for the funeral he was always cruising by the car wash, pulling in and letting the kids wash his big-ass Escalade. He'd throw in an extra twenty just for shits, you know. He knew it would make Tanqueray smile even though she would fight it. Sometimes he wouldn't pull off until she did. She hated feeling like she did about him. He wasn't any good.

Tanqueray hesitated before dialing the number to Dustin

Sinclair. She had a feeling the rich white voyeur she'd met a few weeks ago and entertained for a few hours, had also come to her family's aid where the funeral was concerned. He told her many times he was taken with her and that she was perfect for his fantasies. Why he was so into her she didn't know, but he was rich and nice and didn't treat her like a ho. So, it all worked for her, no questions asked.

The day that he met her was a rough one. She'd just found out her ex-boyfriend, a damn pimp named Omar, had traded her goodies for a pile of money, as if she was just some ho—a real ho. He'd 'sold her' to a rich white man named Mr. Sinclair for a grip of money. He had some Negro named Cecil, in a penguin suit, coming up to the door to 'take her to the limo' like she was a package. Cecil worked for Mr. Sinclair.

Hell, yeah, I beat that nigga down and ran, Tanqueray remembered, thinking about her and Cecil's first meeting. She smiled thinking about Cecil. He was a pretty cool cat. He seemed to be hard working. He'd grown up in the ghetto, just like everybody else, but he'd made a move and got out. He was now working for a very wealthy man. Sometimes he even got to travel with Dustin Sinclair.

"Yeah, I've traveled with Mr. Sinclair," he answered, the night he was taking her to the hospital to see about Cammie. She and Mr. Sinclair were about to have dinner when the call came that Cammie had been hit by a car and was in intensive care. Cecil was quick to get the car and take her to the ER. On the way, he was working hard to get her mind off the emergency. It was the most he'd ever said to her since their first meeting, which had not been pleasant.

"Must be nice to get out of the hood, mah man. I wish that was me," she had said, looking out the window, noticing the familiar coming into view. She was almost back home now. It was strange how just a couple of bridges separated the mighty rich from the sho nuff po. Looking toward the rearview mirror she noticed Cecil's eyes looking back at her. He had familiar eyes but she didn't ask him who he was related to in the hood or who his mama was. She probably knew them. He hadn't volunteered anything, so in a way, maybe she was right not bringing any of that up.

"You just gotta want it, homey," he had said. "If you can dream it, you can have it. But you have to work for it, if you get my meaning. You gotta earn it proper."

She was thinking about those words now while pondering a call to Mr. Sinclair. Was he truly going to be her ticket out? And what did Cecil mean by proper?

She glanced around for her friend Kashawna. They were supposed to meet for drinks. Kashawna was a working girl, a real working girl, as in nine to five. She was legit, fitting the 'steady job' profile. Even in school when Tanqueray was playing, breaking rules, cutting class and smoking blunts, Kashawna was walking closer to the right side of the line. Once they graduated she took the job that was offered to many of the under privileged kids with decent grades. It was minimum wage, but hell, it was enough to keep them off the streets if they wanted it. Kashawna apparently did. Five years later she was some manager of something. Who the hell knew what position she had. Anyway, she pulled in a fat check, so it was all good. She was getting married too.

"And ain't even pregnant," Tanqueray said thinking about her own life. She was coming up on twenty-five. Well it was a way off, but still, she had nothing to show for her life, except a major hang over. Last night was a humdinger. The funeral was nice and all that, as nice as a funeral could be, short of Marquis' daddy showing up at the repast. Again she thought about his familiar looking tats. *Damn that was straight up freaky.* He only stayed an hour or so, talked to Unique for a while, then left. Unique was in shock. She didn't even beg him to stay. It was as if she didn't really know him or maybe it was as if she had known him her whole life. They didn't even talk much. Tanqueray shrugged wondering how she would have felt under the same circumstances. *Dunno, but at least his being there got Unique out of the bedroom.* Tanqueray was going to ask Unique what they talked about but by the time she'd gotten up this morning Unique had gone to the hospital. She'd spent every day there by Cammie's side.

Kinda late to start being a good mommy though. Ya shoulda been there when that fool was ripping her apart. Tanqueray shook her head at the visual of big ol' Curtis having oral and regular sex with that nine year old child. "Damn pervert. I wish I had known. I'd have killed him my damn self," she said under her breath, accepting Marquis' actions as warranted. "How could Cammie have not told anybody?" She sighed heavily again, realizing the cost of Marquis Jr.'s brave acts.

"Where is Kashawna?" she asked in an undertone, looking at the time on her metro phone. She'd just bought this raggedy thing and already it was showing signs of wear.

Tanqueray wasn't used to all this ghetto shit. She hated Omar with his pimp-ass but at least he kept her in all the latest gadgets and hooked up to all the latest toys and clothes. "But selling me as a whore . . . you done lost me fa sho," she grumbled, not sounding as convinced as she was a month ago when she left him. Right now, she was sober, straight, broke and a little bit horny. None of that was a great place for Tanqueray to be. It had been just a bit too many days between her last hook up and she was getting fidgety.

Just then he walked in. "Ugh," she gasped. It was Finest. What an unresolved problem he had turned out to be.

"Hey," he said, sliding into her booth. She twisted her lips and started to stand but he grabbed her arm and pulled her back down to the seat.

"Hey, what nigga. I'm so through wit' choo," she said, sounding as tough as she could. Finest's name said it all. He had light eyes and soft wavy hair and a diamond inlay sparkling in his pretty, bright-white teeth. He was mixed with something because he was the color of Sinclair. It was for sure she wasn't all black, even though Tanqueray never remembered her mother kicking it with no white dudes.

Javina Nation, their mother, was something that none of her kids had opened their eyes to accept, especially Tanqueray. None of the five children, Larry, Debonair, she, Unique, or Sinclair, had the same daddies, which was obvious. Tanqueray had done that math long ago. Now Javina was dead, so what did it matter anyway. *Let the haters say what they want about my mama,* Tanqueray thought. Truth be known, Tanqueray had to wonder if her mother ever did it for money, considering she never had a job and they did have a house. *Well, until Debonair and his drug-selling ass got locked up and the dope man collected payment by blowing the house to hell!* "Ugh," she said at the memory, although Finest had to think she was making that disgusted sound in his direction.

Finest's grip brought her mind quickly back to the moment. She looked down at his hand around her arm. "We need to talk!"

"About what, nigga? You up here playing me for a fool. Fucking my sister behind my back and—"

"I didn't know she was your sister, and I'm telling you I didn't fuck her. I told you that."

"Then why did you say that? Why did you say you were. . . ." Tanqueray started speaking but stopped. She knew he was lying.

Even when he said it that night she knew. Sinclair was a virgin.
They were close like that, well maybe not close–like that–but
she knew her baby sister, and Finest was too grown of a man
for her. Shit, even Tanqueray had to admit that some of the
tricks he'd pulled on her in the back seat of his Escalade had
been something new for her! She missed his dick for sure.
She fought now to keep the want off her face. She wasn't sure
what it looked like but she wanted to make sure he didn't
see any of it. Kitty was purring hard between her legs and if
he didn't hear it, for sure he was going to smell it soon. He
brought it down in her real quick. But no! She had to drop
him like a bad habit, one she really wanted to quit.

"I was just trying to piss off Malcolm with his punk ass . . .
Ionknow. Look baby," he said, softening his voice.

Finest was a thug, straight up street meat, but when it came
to her she could tell he was going soft. She had him whipped.
It was funny. She could see it so clearly. Never had she gotten
a man so close to the palm of her hand like this. She looked
around and again at her phone. Kashawna had exactly thirty
seconds to get there or she was about to give this nigga a
romp.

"You got anything fa me?" she asked, slowly sitting back
down.

"You know I got you baby. I always do."

"Why didn't you come to the house yesterday for the food,
show some respect? You weren't even at the funeral. My
family was there and my sisters had their support. Hell, even
Marquis' daddy showed up–"

"Little Soldier got a daddy?"

"Everybody got a daddy," Tanqueray said, smacking her lips
after saying the words. "I was just up there alone with nobody
to lean on in my time of need."

Finest looked around. "Waddn't about to be there with all them niggas. I got beef wit'. . . ."

Tanqueray shook her head. "You always got beef and shit. Where's the beef? Show me the beef," she joked, and sort of flirted. His eyes locked on hers. She recognized the look in his eyes. He wanted her as bad as she wanted him. Now she knew he could see the feeling returned. Damn, she had it bad for this nigga.

Finest one! Kashawna zero!

Standing again, she pulled one of Unique's older bags over her shoulder and dropped her broke-ass phone inside. "How did you know I was gonna be here?"

"I seent your friend on her way in. Told her you and I had some business to tend to. She seemed to understand. Said you was missing me."

"That's a lie, Kashawna wouldna told you no bullshit like that," Tanqueray said before breaking into a tell-it-all smile.

Finest draped his arm over Tanqueray's shoulder as he led her to his car.

"Where's the Escalade?" she asked, looking at the sharp, shiny, new black Lexus."

"Draws too much attention. I didn't want our time interrupted."

"Like you know I was gonna give you any time," she said, sliding into the comfortable seat. *Damn, this nig was putting it on thick today.* Tanqueray quickly reached between his thighs as soon as he got in; she wanted to feel a hint of just how thick Finest was.

He smiled. Scooping up her hand he sucked on a couple of her fingers. He smiled again, that diamond sparkling bright, and started the car before sliding on his dark glasses.

Chapter 3

"I wish you had come to the funeral yesterday," Sinclair said to Malcolm. They had been friends forever, until they decided to take it further. Sex ruined a lot of stuff Sinclair figured. Malcolm didn't seem to even want to hang out with her, let alone try finishing what they started a couple of weeks ago on the day Cammie went in the hospital. They had gotten in the shower and Malcolm had felt her up, got her all hot and ready and then—blam! The whole world changed. Cammie was on life support and Marquis was dead. Thinking of that she said, "Marquis' daddy showed up."

Malcolm looked at her, his eyes widening in interest even though she could tell he was trying to hide it. "Marquis gotta daddy?"

"Yeah. Ex con, big nigga, all tatted up and shit. Rough nigga. Came in with his crew—"

"Wow, busted in on them W.E. bitches—"

"Why they gotta be bitches?" Sinclair asked, although she knew why he said that. His cousin Finest was part of the W.E. set and they were on the outs. Malcolm just couldn't get over the lies Finest had told about her. Finest had lied and said they had slept together. It wasn't true but Finest made it sound true. Malcolm believed it and now he was mad at Finest. Hell, he was mad at her too.

"Oh, that's right, you living in the W.E. now so I guess you one of them now. You just changed up . . . just like that. I guess it's easy for people like you to just switch up when you get ready."

"What in the hell does that mean?"

He looked her up and down, "One minute you white, next you black. One minute you hood, next you all bougee and shit. Fuck that. I'm fa real. Real talk here," he said slapping his chest. "None of that sometimey shit."

Sinclair stepped back from him, her face twisted up with anger, "Fuck you Malcolm. I was ready to be your girl and now you clowning me," she balked.

Malcolm sucked his teeth and rolled his eyes.

About that time, a local chick showed up. Her name was Mercedes. Malcolm had once told her that Mercedes was his girl but she'd not seen any proof—until today. Mercedes grinned at Sinclair as if they were friends before she kissed him—tongue and all. Malcolm was digging it too. Sinclair could tell. Her heart began to burn in her chest. She'd never felt anything like it. It wasn't pain so much as an unbearable ache that she had to make stop. This bitch Mercedes had caused it, she knew this much, and Sinclair was going to make it stop.

Sinclair pulled Mercedes off Malcolm by yanking her shoulder.

This time Mercedes wasn't smiling. "What's wrong wit' choo?" she asked, glancing at Malcolm for an answer and then back at Sinclair.

She had innocence in her eyes but Sinclair refused to see it.

"Sinclair, what's your problem?"

"Don't act like you know me bitch!" Sinclair cursed.

Mercedes immediately took a stance that told Sinclair she

wasn't happy with being called out. When she moved her braids back out of her face Sinclair saw her long acrylics. Knowing this was a mistake, Sinclair realized she was in it now with no way out but to finish what she started. She glanced at Malcolm who almost seemed to be smiling. Her face questioned his expression but she got no answer.

"Malcolm, why did she call me a bitch?" Mercedes asked Malcolm.

Malcolm shrugged stupidly before pulling her into his lap. "I guess she's confused about some things baby. Let it go."

"Malcolm, stop! Stop! Tell her who I am." Sinclair ordered.

"And who are you?" Mercedes asked, pushing free from Malcolm's embrace.

"Come on now Mercedes. Let it go. You know Sin is just a little girl, confused and you know . . . She just had some family stuff. She's—"

"I don't know who you calling a bitch but if you think that I'm one because me and Malcolm are a couple, umm. . . ." Mercedes fanned her long nails in Sinclair's face. "Then we need to straighten this shit out. First, I'm sorry for your loss, okay. No disrespect to your family. But second, I'ma have to set you straight on some stuff."

Sinclair slapped her hand out of her face. "You don't have to set me straight on nothing. You and Malcolm ain't no couple. You just a trick he pulled a couple of times. And—"

Before Sinclair could say anything more Mercedes swung on her, tagging her jaw with a closed fist. Sinclair was stunned at first, but then thankful the nails hadn't come out. She jumped at Mercedes taking her down to the ground where Sinclair knew she worked best. She was a wrestler at heart and could generally get down and dirty when 'down and dirty.'

Mercedes apparently didn't expect to end up in the grass

and squirmed uncomfortably under Sinclair's weight. Her mind emptied of logical thoughts and she quickly went into defense mode. All she knew now was that she had to kick ass or have her own pay the price for whatever wild hair had flown up Sinclair's. *If this scrawny bitch thinks she's gonna hurt me, she's gonna have to be schooled on some things,* Mercedes thought, baring her newly applied acrylic nails.

Sinclair quickly grabbed one of Mercedes hands. Mercedes began screaming ahead of time, as if knowing what was to come next. Just as if planned, Sinclair snapped at least three nails off before Mercedes bit her on the arm. "Fucking bitch! You ain't nothing but a bitch! Biting me like a damn dog," Sinclair cursed, slugging at Mercedes face, aiming mostly for her mouth.

Mercedes mind was spinning now like a twenty-inch dub. *How in the hell was this bougee heffa getting the upper hand like this.* Besides that, she'd fucked up a thirty-five dollar nail job. *Oh, you gonna pay for that one, bitch,* Mercedes thought, grabbing at Sinclair's long hair. She pulled at it, hearing the loose strands popping as they ripped from her scalp. Sinclair groaned angrily but didn't stop pounding on her. Mercedes then went for the long braid that hung down her back. She wasn't even thinking about her own fresh extensions. If Sinclair got at those, it would be another good chunk of change down the drain.

Sure enough, Sinclair then grabbed at Mercedes' braids. "Let go! Let go! Yours come off . . . mine don't," Sinclair threatened, pulling on Mercedes extensions with more strength then Mercedes imagined the little bit of a girl having.

"Fuck you," Mercedes said before spitting in Sinclair's face.

"Ew!" someone yelled from the growing crowd.

That was when Sinclair noticed they had drawn a group.

It wasn't clear who was rooting for whom. All it seemed was that folks were enjoying a good girl fight and were waiting for clothes to start getting ripped. This was quickly coming up as Sinclair found a good spot on the front of Mercedes low cut top to hang on to and pull against. She ripped at Mercedes top exposing her bra and then quickly yanked at the tiny clasp in the front unhooking it.

Oh my God, Mercedes thought now, feeling her breast freeing from the tiny bra. It was not the good feeling she got when Malcolm set them loose but more of a mortification that she had never felt before. *This has to stop*, she realized immediately. Mercedes, with tittys loose and flopping, now gained the advantage by pushing Sinclair off and rolling on her before slugging her in the face.

Sinclair began to taste blood as Mercedes began to pound her.

A couple of times Sinclair could have sworn she saw stars. She knew she had been hit in the eye but she kept fighting. She could hear the tearing of her own clothing and the dulling voices of the crowd egging Mercedes on to victory. The tide had turned. She was going to lose this fight. She felt it. Mercedes was crazed now. She was clearly out for pure blood now.

About that time, Sinclair could hear Malcolm. "Mercedes come on. Stop it!" he yelled.

"I'ma kill her ass Malcolm!" she screamed, kicking and swinging as Malcolm held her around the waist pulling her off.

Sinclair felt battered and bloody but in no pain. Her adrenaline was still pumping. She scrambled to her feet ready to take or give more . . . which ever happened first. Mercedes was apparently ready to end this, and she was going to end it the only way she knew how. Bringing her leg up to her chest she pulled her knife from her boot.

Noticing the knife Malcolm let her go quickly so as not to get cut while she swung it wildly. She looked half insane—braids hanging all raggedy, breast hanging loose. Sinclair wasn't sure of all her options and looked for an opening in which she could find a defense of some kind. Her eyes were swelling. Sinclair could barely see the tattoos on Mercedes bare chest. That's when she noticed the nipple ring.

Mercedes egged Sinclair to try it, to charge her so that she could cut her to pieces. Sinclair had had enough. She was done. Unsure of her way out of this alive, she held up her hands while trying to catch her breath. She bent over resting her hands on her thighs. Her blouse, too, was ripped to shreds and her pants were dirty and green with grass stains.

The crowd was loud and pushing against her as if wanting her to run stupidly into the knife that was waving an invite.

Malcolm took a step toward Mercedes only to now have her jab the knife in his direction. He jumped back and so did a couple of other people who were getting a little too close to the action.

"I'ma kill her and then you, ya bastard!" Mercedes screamed. "You fuckin' her?" she asked. "You fuckin' her Malcolm?" Mercedes asked again, now standing wide-legged and vicious looking.

She was past crazy, Sinclair could tell. But now she was after Malcolm and, despite how this all started, Malcolm was her friend after all. What was a fair fight had gotten out of control. Eying the nipple ring that flopped back and forth with each of Mercedes wild movements, Sinclair moved closer. Suddenly, as if reading her mind, Sinclair moved just as Mercedes did. She charged at Malcolm and Sinclair went for the ring. The knife swung. Sinclair caught a little bit of it, on her way down—with the ring clutched in her fist.

Mercedes scream was blood curdling as she clutched at her breast. Blood spurted everywhere—like Dracula's mother's milk.

Chapter 4

Finest and Tanqueray drove down the peninsula not talking a whole lot before he pulled into a Radisson in Santa Clara. They were way out of the way this day. She had to wonder what the big deal was about today. Sure he was in sore need of some 'make up time' but he was really pulling out the stops. He got out first and went in the office, coming back promptly with a key. He swung his head in a motion that meant for her to get out of the car. He looked a million bucks and even if he only had a few thousand on him, that was fine with her today.

She had on her sister's clothes again. They were Wally World specials, but Unique knew how to shop well. She didn't have much money and so she made it go a long way. She was just shorter and a little smaller than her, so everything fit kind of funky, but oh, well—beggars couldn't be choosers. Tanqueray was used to designer threads but each week that went by she was getting further and further from that lifestyle.

They entered the room. Tanqueray was normally pushier about what order their dates came in and all this gentleman-like behavior was unusual. She normally would have a cigarette, some *drank* and something up her nose by now, but she was playing along, seeing what the Negro had in mind. He tossed the keys in the chair, pulled her bag off her arm and tossed it over there too before pulling her into his tight embrace and full mouth kiss. They went at it hungrily, as if it had been months instead of maybe a couple of weeks or so since their last encounter. He pulled her leg up around his, stroking at her thigh and squeezing at her butt. She pulled at his hair, allowing him to kiss her face and neck.

"You got something for me?" she finally whispered in his ear.

He looked at her.

"Yeah, I do," he answered swinging her over on the bed.

She fell back. He climbed on her tearing at the thin fabric of her cheap blouse and filling his mouth with her small breasts. She purred and arched up for him to enjoy it to the full. Slowly he inched down her body, unzipping her short skirt, which she quickly wiggled out of. She'd bathed in all of Unique's smell goods this morning so she knew Kitty smelled good. It was a good thing too, because he was down in it with quickness, eating away as if he'd not had lunch. She held his head in place when he reached the spot. He raised her hips sliding his tongue in deep.

"Shit!" she screamed out the first time she came. It was sharp and intense and quick, as if her battery needed another jump.

Rising up he unzipped his pants and pulled off his black shirt and wife beater. His tats were dark against his untanned chest—two F's, one on each pectoral muscle. He sucked his teeth as he slid from his pants.

She grabbed at his endowment, sliding forward on the bed until she was even with him. He pulled her hair while pushing her head forward. He was in need and by the looks of things, about to explode. She smoked him like a Cuban cigar. Normally, Tanqueray felt this act was only for men but this time even she enjoyed it as he twisted at her nipples and cooed like a baby, hunching his hips forward as if working inside her lower half instead of her mouth. He was quickening his pace and about to cum when she pulled off.

"Fuckin' cunt," he called her.

He was sex crazed now. Tanqueray was sure of it, as he had never called her that before.

She moved back on the bed as he stalked forward toward her, grabbing her ankles and spreading her legs far apart. His member was dangling stiff and nearly blue with need. He thrust into her without words. She could have sworn he hit the back wall. She cried out, but he paid her no mind as he slammed into her.

"Don't ever think you can get away from me," he said rising up and pulling her legs over his shoulders. His hips wiggled as he found his stroke, as if breaking concrete with a jack hammer. Wham, wham, wham! He went at her tender walls.

She grabbed the head board and hung on for the ride with her eyes wide open. She was a little scared because he looked crazy as hell with his brows all furrowed, and biting his lip. She wasn't even sure he was enjoying himself until finally he took a deep breath and his stroke changed to a quick, quick, slow pace and then a deep slow one, as was his common stroke when he felt real good. He grunted as he came, releasing his hot emissions inside her, while he slowly released her legs. He lay on top of her as was his normal 'after love' thing to do.

She rubbed his back while he purred—satisfied. She didn't come but was scared to tell him. He might want to do her again and she wasn't so sure she wasn't bleeding the way he was tearing up shit. Just then she felt his hands wandering down below. She squirmed in the slight discomfort of his fingers entering her anal cavity—one, two, three fingers.

"What are you doing?" she asked reaching down there and taking him by the wrist. "That hurts," she said.

"I know it does," he said, in an evil tone. "I want you to turn over."

"Hell, no, Finest. You ain't getting ready to do that," she said, pushing him against his chest.

He rose up and attempted to wrestle her over to her stomach. She reached up, trying to cover herself with the sheet, but he fought her. Finally she kicked his thigh just missing his jewels. He stopped for a moment to regroup. She jumped up from the bed and started for the bathroom, but he grabbed her from behind and bent her over.

"I said you are not ever gonna leave me, or fuck another nigga, or nothing like that Tang. This here is mines and I'm claiming it today," he said, entering her rectum.

She screamed out in pain but he didn't stop. He didn't enter her fully but just the head was enough to send her over. As much of a ho as everybody always thought she was, there were things she didn't do, and this was one of them. Finest was taking her virginity, her innocence, her dignity, so to speak.

Soon he found a rhythm and Tanqueray noticed the pain wasn't as bad as before. *Damn, nig knew how to bust the back door too,* she thought. Fear and shame turned to pleasure as he inched his stiffness in a little deeper, carefully and almost tenderly while pleasuring her anally. He stroked her hair and kissed her back, teased her gold pubic hair with his fingers before sliding two of them inside her. She began to convulse inside.

"I'm cumming," she whispered, scared to really admit it.

"I know you are baby. This is what love feels like," he whispered back before pulling out.

Immediately she had to release herself and rushed into the bathroom. He followed her in and turned on the shower.

"Get in when you get finished," he told her not even caring that she was taking care of her business. It was as if they had been together for years. He was beyond comfortable with her.

"I. . . ." she began, but couldn't even lie. A shower was more than what she needed right now. Her mind was spinning. She was out of control. This nigga had her mind and that wasn't good.

Is this what being turned out felt like? she mused. *Had this hood figga turned her out?*

She stepped in the shower to find him all soaped up and smelling good. He had soaped up his dick and it was bobbing and weaving. He soaped up his hands and lathered her body. His strong hands felt good on her back and shoulders.

Damn . . . this felt like love, she thought.

He kissed the back of her neck and then turned her around pinning her between his arms that he pressed on the shower walls behind her.

"Look here, Tanqueray," he said as if tasting her name. Up till the night at the hospital, the night that Marquis was killed, he didn't even know her name. She had only told him her stage name—Sugar. Why not? There was nothing between them but good fucking and good drugs right? He'd beg her to tell him her name. Now he had it, and apparently felt that he had her too.

"I'm a businessman and can't always be with you like this," he said. "But you gotta know how I feel."

She nodded.

"I want you to be mah gurl. And being that, you gotta be here for me. You gotta be everything I need when I need it," he said.

She opened her mouth to state her needs, but he quieted her with his finger to her lips.

"I know your nose be getting hungry and I got that. I

know your pussy be feining this here," he said grabbing at his thickening member. It was as if hearing his own words he was turning himself on. "And I want you to know I got that too," he said. "You just gotta do what I ask you to do. I mean, sometimes I may need your help and you gotta be there for me. You gotta be wit' me on thangs okay?"

The water was warm and relaxing. Before Tanqueray could argue about being her own woman, she felt her head nodding, giving into his dream of what he believed ghetto love to be. She had never loved anyone before and doubted if she loved Finest, but he was feeling her for sure. If he was going to take care of her needs while she figured out her next step in life . . . then fine.

"You mah wifey," he said, almost in a question form, grinning, showing off that diamond.

She felt her face smiling. Her brain was still all mangled up. She needed a drink, some blow. She needed something. She sure as hell didn't need any more fucking, but the way he started groping at her she could tell that was what she was about to get. He kissed her mouth pushing his tongue nearly down her throat. She slowly put her arms around his waist, holding him tight while he grinded his hips against hers, raising the heat. Reaching around her, he turned off the water.

"I got something for you," he said then.

Finally! she thought, following him naked back to the room. She sat on the bed while he dug around in his pants pocket.

"I got you some raw shit. Just like you like it," he said, taking out the small envelop of white powder.

Every ache, pain and sore spot eased up as she realized how high she was about to get. He could have whatever he wanted after she filled her nose. She reached out greedily for the envelope.

He snickered while watching her prepare. He handed her a twenty to roll up.

Up the nostril.

Her head went back. She squeezed the burn.

Up the other nostril.

The high was instant and intense. Whatever he'd cut into this blow was fantastic. She fell backward writhing in its aftermath. In the blur she saw him snorting a line before he lay on top of her. That was all she remembered before awaking a few hours later to the sound of him re-entering the room. He had someone with him. Quickly she pulled the blanket up around herself but surely he'd had an eye full.

"Hey, baby, didn't know you were awake. I brought my homey with me. We need to talk some business, okay?" he said pointing at the big dark skinned brother.

He smiled. He had his four front teeth gleaming with mouth candy. He wasn't Malcolm's brother Floyd, Finest's usual partner.

"Finest, I need to get dressed. Can he like go out for a minute," she asked.

"Nah, girl we won't be long. You just stay right where you are. It's all good with choo fine ass," the guy said. Finest snickered.

"She fine as all that," he bragged motioning for her to pull the blanket down and give the guy a free show. "Come on nah, we talked about that. Ain't nothing gonna happen to you. This is my friend," he said moving over to the bed and wrestling the blanket from her, exposing her nakedness.

She attempted to cover herself.

"Oh, shit! Her pussy is gold just like you said too," the guy cackled. Finest was high as hell and apparently so was the other guy.

Tanqueray was sober now and this was nowhere near funny. She'd been naked in front of men before. Hell, she was a stripper for years, well before she met Omar last year. But she got paid to show her shit. Nah, this free peep show wasn't funny at all.

"I'd like that on me for a minute," he said.

"You got money nigga. Ain't nothing free up in this camp."

"Waaaaait," Tanqueray barked.

Finest laughed, and then put on an innocent face, "I'm just teasing baby. I wouldn't make you do that. Not unless you wanted to," he said, raising the innuendo.

"Hell, nah," she balked, stepping off the bed, grabbing up what was left of her blouse, panties and skort before storming into the bathroom to dress. She didn't care what the guy saw at that point. She was assed out and didn't even care.

Once she got in the bathroom she sat on the toilet lid pondering the mess she'd gotten herself into. *Tang, this ain't getting you outta nothing. I thought you were trying to get outta this life.* She shook her head and again thought about Mr. Sinclair. She felt sick, but then again she'd been feeling sick for days.

Soon she heard the hotel room door shut and peeked out to find Finest and the other guy gone. Rushing over to her cell phone, she called Mr. Sinclair.

Chapter 5

Unique hadn't really thought much about big Marquis since the funeral. *No, that was a lie.* She'd done nothing but think about him. He just showed up and left like that. At first she thought it was a dream, like all the other dreams she had of him since she was a girl. She'd done nothing but dream about the boy who had turned her into a woman before her time. He was the boy that made her feel things that she was too young to feel. She'd done nothing but dream about him since the day he took her virginity in that abandoned building. *Nah, get it right Unique. He raped you. What Marquis Sr. did was nothing better than what Curtis did to Cammie. It was wrong on so many levels.* But still, his showing up to bury the son he'd never met had touched her deeply.

After she fell into his arms, he stayed for a minute, ate a little food before getting a signal from his boys that it was time to leave. He never seemed to be the kind of man who could stay one place too long. But during his time there in her home she took him in . . . she stared at him while he ate. She looked for resemblances to Marquis, her son, in his face and in his eyes. They were there . . . they were there strongly.

Just his being there comforted her for a moment. In a way she felt as if God had answered her unuttered groaning for peace. Now if only Cammie would wake up. She couldn't even bring herself to accept that she'd lost two of her five children in the same day.

Unique sat at the hospital next to Cammie's bed. She had prayed yet again for the deliverance of her daughter. Guilt consumed her and she wasn't sure if she could make it through this one. She'd been through a lot but this one was about to take her over. She thought about her mother. "Is this what you meant when you told me I didn't need any kids? Is this what you wanted for me, to lose them one by one?" she asked aloud. "You always hated my kids mama . . . you always hated me," Unique cried, burying her face in her hands.

Just then she felt something touch her hair. She looked up thinking it was Cammie coming out of her coma, but no, the child laid still. She looked around to see who could have touched her but there was nobody in the room. It was quiet and empty except for her and Cammie and the machines that aided Cammie's breathing with their swooshing noise. A chill came over her. Something or someone touched her head. She looked around again. *Am I crazy?* she thought. Something touched her head. That she knew. Standing, she gathered her purse. She was a little shaken and wanted to get out of there for a minute.

"Well, Cammie, baby, mama is gonna go home for a minute. Everybody is there waiting for dinner. I'm making your favorite too. Gonna save some for you," she said, smiling now at the thought of Cammie's love for food. Never again would she yell at her or fuss at her for eating. Never again would she scold her for finding comfort in eating. Unique's eyes burned. There would be so many things that would change between her and Cammie once Cammie came home.

Leaning over the bed she kissed Cammie tenderly on the forehead. "I. . . ." She choked up. Again today she couldn't say the words. How could she even say those words to a child that she had treated so badly? How could she ever tell Cammie she loved her after what she allowed to happen right under her nose. "I'm sorry," was all she could say. Unique knew she had done the unforgiveable where Cammie was concerned, even worse then what her mother had done to her.

After her mother found out what she and Markey had done, she beat her with a belt and insisted she have the baby she found herself pregnant with. Unique wasn't given a lot of choices in her life except one, to love her child. Marquis Jr. that her child. He made it easy for her to forget the bitterness of her mother's actions. He made it easy to pretend that what she felt for Big Marquis was alright.

What Cammie would never know was that Unique was not going to do the same with her. Had Curtis impregnated her, that baby would be destroyed. There was no way Unique was even thinking about allowing Cammie to live the life she had. Unique felt her life had been confused and shortchanged of all that was good because of her mother. "I was turning into my mother Cammie, and I'm so sorry," she whispered, feeling the words vibrating off Cammie's forehead where her lips touched it.

Marquis Jr. had killed Curtis. He shot him dead right there in the hospital waiting room. While everyone wondered what, why, when and how things in their life could have come together in that hospital ER, Marquis Jr. answered it all with several shots from a stolen gun. That was right before the police killed him, leaving the biggest question in life for Unique to figure out. And now Marquis Sr. was here. Was he the answer? Had he been the answer to all her life's questions?

Leaving the room, she headed to the elevator that let out in the lobby right off of the emergency room. Exiting, she heard the commotion. It caught her attention, especially the familiarity of the voices. Reluctantly, and against her best mind she stepped closer to the area where everyone coming in had to wait for hours to be called. In this neighborhood, unless you were shot and the cops brought you in, or you were white and here by accident, you were not going to be seen in any reasonable timeframe. That was Unique's thoughts on the matter.

The waiting area was full of black folks, all in an uproar. She couldn't help but wonder what the hell was going on. All these young people in ER at one time seemed odd, especially since there were not gang colors flying and no cops, no guns. Just then she saw Malcolm, a friend of Sinclair. She called to him.

Malcolm's eyes were wide when he looked at her and he rushed over to her right away. "Unique! Who called you?"

"Didn't nobody call me," she answered, her stomach tightening suddenly.

"Oh, shit," he groaned, running his fingers through his mop. "I thought Sinclair had called you. They took her in a while ago."

"She's here in the hospital!"

"No, I mean yeah. She was fightin' and—"

"Fighting!"

"She got cut a little bit," Malcolm admitted.

Unique didn't wait to hear the rest. She rushed up to the window demanding someone come talk to her.

Chapter 6

Sinclair's arm was stiff. The cut wasn't all that deep, but deep enough to require stitches and would probably leave a scar. She'd taken some of the pain medication the doctor had given her in the ER. She had a prescription, but was sure it was going to cost a fortune. Unique was supposed to add her on to her welfare case, but she was dragging her heels about doing it so Sinclair had no insurance at all. She'd be eighteen soon and SOL for sure unless Unique did something on her behalf really soon. Sinclair was getting hit daily with life's realities. Ever since her comfortable life—the life that fed her dreams and goals—went up in smoke, Sinclair was forced to think about what was to come next.

Still she had no real answers.

"And why? Why do this? Why you fightin'?" Unique whined the question. "I don't want to have to start worrying about you too. I'm already dealing with so much," she added.

Sinclair glared at her. She hadn't intended to give her such a dirty look, but it just happened. "Didn't nobody tell you to worry about me. I can take care of myself." That was a lie and Sinclair knew it, but she also knew she was going to have to start working on a plan, and working on one *quickly*.

"Like today, and what you did to that other girl," she whispered as if Sinclair was now in some serious trouble or something. She hadn't started the fight and, if anything, she was going to be the one pressing charges.

"Crazy bitch pulled a knife on me!"

Just then Malcolm pulled back the curtain. "They said I could come in."

"And why is that? What lie did you tell them?" Sinclair snapped, jerking her neck from side to side.

"None, Sinclair. I told them I was family. Look, I thought it was gonna be a clean fight."

"Bullshit! Fuck you! Clean fight," she hollered holding up her bandaged arm. "Waddn't no clean nothing! Buncha male ego bullshit while you set there jacking off." When Unique patted her arm, she flinched and jumped. "Damn Neek that hurt. Watch out!"

"Sorry, sorry," she said nervously.

"Sinclair I told you about Mercedes way back. I told you I was seeing her."

"Then why. . . ." Sinclair looked at Unique and then changed her mind about putting her business out there. Her eyes were burning but there was no way she was going to cry. She wanted to ask Malcolm about their times together. She wanted to ask him why he had touched her and held her and acted as if they were going to be together.

Malcolm hung his head shamefully as if knowing her next question. "'Cuz," was all he answered. "Because I care about you . . . like that," he answered. "And I didn't want you fooling with Finest's ass . . . like that." He stood up straighter when he said that as if that was his true defense, protection of her dignity.

"Whatever," she answered schooching off the table and throwing open the curtain completely. She looked around for any signs of Mercedes. She had heard her in there hollering when she first came in. "Where is she anyway?"

"They had to admit her. She had some complications."

"Yeah. Whatever. I got some complications, nigga!" Sinclair growled roughly. "You going home, Unique? I'll ride with you."

"Yeah, I was on my way. Cammie is still . . ." she hung her head.

Sinclair's heart gained a pound or two and she hugged her sister tight. "She'll wake up when she's ready. She'll wake up when she's ready to get over Marquis. She knows Unique. She knows everything and if I was her, I wouldn't be wanting to wake up to none of this shit either," she said, glaring at Malcolm over her sister's shoulder.

He shrugged and shoved his hands deep in his pockets.

"I'm sorry I missed the funeral yesterday Unique," Malcolm said now.

Unique hung her head and then smiled warmly. "It's okay Malcolm. A lot of people didn't come. Folks all gang affiliated and shit. Everybody scared. But not my Marquis, he wasn't scared of nothin'," she said sounding proud.

The gangs had divided the peace for years. Boys with wife beaters and menacing hatred tattooed across their chests, meted against boys with gold implants in their teeth and anger tucked hidden in the waistbands of their exposed shorts. *Guns, bats, and sometimes worse*, Sinclair thought, remembering the grenade that took out her mama's house. The gangs were scary, but fear was something you couldn't live with, simply because there was not going to be any life there in the ghetto without it.

Sinclair knew Unique knew that. She could see she had been working on her brave front since the day it happened. Since the day Marquis died right here in this very hospital, Unique had struggled to be brave. At the time she had just started seeing this guy, a social worker type. She was finally getting happy and things were looking up for her and her

kids. But since that night, nobody knew what Unique was
doing to put things behind her, short of coming to this place
and sitting by Cammie's side. Over the last few weeks that's all
she'd done. So as far as Sinclair was concerned, Unique's
bravery was just a front.

"Well, you know I'm not in that . . . " Malcolm began. Then
as if hearing his own lie he stopped speaking and cleared his
throat. "Anyway Sin, Mercedes is okay. Just her . . . ." Malcolm
circled his own breast area. "Her shit is all tow up, and they
had to fix it and make sure it didn't get infected."

"Well, I am sure you are the only one concerned about that
heffa's titty. I'm sure not," Sinclair huffed as she pushed past
both Unique and Malcolm out of the ER area and through
the lobby to the outside of the hospital.

"I got my mama's car. She said I could take you both home
and then come back and pick her up later. If y'all want a ride,"
he offered.

"No!"

"Yes."

Unique and Sinclair spoke at the same time.

Finally Unique sighed heavily and stared at Sinclair as if
mentally trying to reprimand her. Sinclair recognized the stare;
she remembered how her mother used to do that. "Fine," she
agreed, following behind her to Malcolm's mother's car.

Just then, Finest pulled up in his Escalade. "Get in," he
barked at Malcolm.

Sinclair rolled her eyes. "Yeah whatever. Get in Malcolm.
Your boss is calling you."

"I'm about to take them home. Catch me there," Malcolm
explained acting as if he hadn't heard Sinclair's sarcasm.

"I said get in!" Finest yelled. "We got some business!"

"What kinda business Malcolm? You don't have to go

nowhere wit' him," Sinclair said, backing down off her initial thoughts. Finest was bad news. Business with Finest could mean jail time, or worse. Sinclair thought about the boy that she met while riding with Finest one day. They called him So and So. He was just riding, while Finest handled some 'business.' He ended up dying from an overdose of something bad. Yeah, riding with Finest was not always a good idea.

"Look, Little Bit, you need keep your little pink ass outta this."

"You don't know nuthin' about my ass so . . ." Sinclair puffed up. Malcolm gave Sinclair a confirmation that she needed to shut the hell up.

"Malcolm." Finest rolled his eyes before glancing around Sinclair to Unique, "Sorry for ya loss," he said quickly. "Malcolm. We got business," he said again through gritted teeth.

Malcolm looked at Sinclair and then pulled open the back door to the Escalade.

When it opened, Sinclair could see plenty of folks in the back. All of them looked fierce, angry and violent, with wife beaters showing. Whatever Malcolm was getting ready to get into wasn't good.

"Malcolm, don't go," she begged, pulling at his pant leg.

Without looking at her he shook her loose and slammed the door. The Escalade sped off.

Chapter 7

Malcolm was running to trouble; Unique knew that. Finest was no good, no good at all. She knew by the way he wore his gang attire, he was set tight. What was worse, he carried with him a mixed message. He had mouth jewelry like those boys in the W.E. and yet, he wore the wife beater and tats like the dudes in the P. To Unique that meant he was one who followed the money, wherever it took him. Those kinda thugs were the most dangerous of all in her opinion. How Tanqueray ever got hooked up with the likes of him was unknown to Unique, but Malcolm, Malcolm had no choice really, he was blood related.

Unique's attention was brought back to Sinclair who sat there on the bus growling and rumbling in her frustration over Malcolm leaving with Finest. Without a ride, they got on the next bus to pull up heading in their direction.

"Don't know why you acting all crazy about them leaving together. Them niggas gon' do what they gon' do. Just be glad you ain't with him or you'd be all messed up and involved. This way, if he gets shot, it won't be that serious. Just be glad you just friends."

Sinclair raised her bandaged arm slightly. "We are more than friends Neek. Can't you tell that? Me and Malcolm . . . we've gotten serious. And if he got shot I'd be devastated. I love Malcolm can't you see that!"

Unique smacked her lips and turned her head slightly, chuckling under her breath. "You don't know what serious is and love . . . phsst paalease."

"I do know. I know what it all means!"

"All you know is that you got your ass whooped and got cut by some crazy heffa that apparently Malcolm likes more than you. You ain't his girl because a real man wouldn't let his 'girl' go through what you went through just to prove her feelings, Sinclair. So if you done started fuckin' Malcolm, that's on you! But listen here, you done wasted something precious on a friend and. . . ."

"Please! You're not one to talk," Sinclair said clearly without thinking.

It was true though. Unique had allowed men to do many things worse than what Malcolm had done. Unique had allowed a man to molest her child right under her nose and for what? Love? Her eyes welled up with tears and she quickly gathered her bags and moved from the seat next to Sinclair.

"I'm sorry Neek. I'm sorry I didn't mean it," Sinclair begged, moving next to her in the new seat she'd found. Unique pushed her off the seat, causing her to yell out in pain when hitting the floor of the bus.

"Hey, y'all quit that!" the driver yelled. He didn't use the loud speaker since the bus was basically empty.

Sinclair sat on the bus floor for a moment before slowly pulling herself up and sitting in an empty seat across from her. Unique regretted her actions, but not enough to apologize. Instead, she pulled the cord.

"This ain't even our stop," Sinclair mumbled. "Why you getting off in the P? What am I supposed to do? I thought you was gonna get my prescription filled and shit. What am I supposed to do?"

"I don't give a damn," Unique said, holding her head high and exiting the bus as soon as the back door opened.

Chapter 8

Malcolm's heart was beating, but he was in it now and there was no way out. He thought about Sinclair, begging him not to come, but he also thought about his pride. This pride would not allow him to leave. Finest appeared so fearless right now donned in his dark hoodie pulled over his head and that dark Ninja mask. They were on a mission to collect money owed. In the last few weeks since he'd been working with Finest he'd made more money than he'd ever made hustling bootleg movies. Sure this was dangerous, but it was working out a lot better. He knew soon he'd have enough money to make it out of the ghetto.

He'd planned to take Sinclair with him. Sure he hadn't told her that or that he was fucking with Mercedes, so there was no way she could have known. But hell, a man needed things and Mercedes was the go to girl. She had been there when he needed what Sinclair didn't know how to give. Mercedes wasn't the kind of girl you marry but she was the kind of girl you fucked. She was good at what she did too. The thought of Mercedes brought a smile to his lips despite the fact that he was never going to get at that again, not after all that went down between her and Sinclair.

Hell, Sinclair was just going to have to get with the program. *A man's got needs*, Malcolm thought, realizing how much he sounded like Finest. Finest would cut anything that twisted a hip. That was before he started messing with Tanqueray. Since fuckin' with her, he'd slowed his roll a lot. Malcolm found that hella funny too, considering what everybody knew about Tanqueray. *Maybe it wasn't true*, he pondered for a second. *Maybe Tang waddn't really a ho like everybody said. Whatever.* Tanqueray was hella fine. She had those tight little tits and slanted eyes. She looked mixed a little bit, but her hair wasn't pretty like Sinclair's. Sinclair was surely mixed with white even though nobody had ever seen her daddy, not even her.

"Let's go," Finest said, interrupting Malcolm's reverie.

Malcolm quickly covered his face with the black Ninja mask. They had pulled up to the spot where the niggas that owed money hung out. Finest had given them the instruction. They weren't going to ask any questions. These niggas were about to get the hell beat out of them. Knowing Finest, there was going to be some shootin', even if it was just in the air. It seemed so much like TV when the guns started poppin' and crackin'. Everyone would scatter and run for cover. Finest would shoot one in someone's general direction to make his plans and intents clear. Then they would bogart in and take the cash. It was easy. Malcolm hadn't used his gun yet but he was ready just in case. With all the women in the place, nobody really wanted to get shot and so far nobody had been. Malcolm wasn't sure if Finest would really kill someone or not. He seemed serious enough though.

Pop! Pop!

"All y'all niggas get down!" Finest called out, followed by the familiar screams as they busted in the door. "I'm here for my fuckin' money, ya punk-ass bitches!"

Malcolm went behind the register, pushed two buttons and the register opened. He scooped out the cash. Floyd,

Malcolm's brother, hit the back room with two other goons. There would usually be some shooting in there too but they normally came out with fists full of money and drugs. Like clockwork, they came out with hands full and within two minutes they were back in the Escalade and out of the area— clean.

This was business as usual.

The adrenaline was pumping and Malcolm never stopped to think if what he was doing was wrong. All that was on his mind was getting out of there without a bullet in his ass.

They reached Vallejo in record time and unloaded the stash. Finest would always cut shit fair. He was good about that, even though in general he was a prick of high order. He knew better than to mess with a man's money. These niggas riding with him were no joke. They were like hybrids. They were from dudes Malcolm only half recognized. His brother had said that some of them dudes were the W.E. and the rest from the P. Malcolm was still kind of fuzzy on what side they were riding for, if either.

This whole gang shit had gotten confusing. Even his brother had put some jewelry in his mouth which was not what those in the P normally did. It was as if they were wearing two colors, or better yet, formed their own set. Maybe they were a new gang. Didn't matter, 'cuz whoever it was they were working for paid a lot of money for their services. Nobody had gotten killed yet, so Malcolm was cool with all of it.

He'd heard a rumor that Finest had killed somebody and didn't even blink. There was something cold inside Finest that would sometimes come out, so Malcolm sometimes believed what he'd heard. He just hoped that Finest wouldn't kill again, at least not while he was in the car.

After splitting the money, Finest would bundle the rest of

it up. They would all then get in a different van and ride out
somewhere and drop the money off. It was a different spot
every time. The dropped off money was like a deposit for Da
Man, whoever the hell that was. Malcolm never asked nor
cared. After the drop they'd all get in another vehicle. It was
usually something big but causal looking. That car or SUV
would be waiting there and it was always something that took
the attention off of them. Then they would all ride back to
the hood with the music banging, as if they'd been out for a
joy ride.

When Malcolm got back home, he was planning to call
Sinclair and see how she was doing. Maybe she'd come stay
over. She used to stay over all the time back when they were
friends. Now that things between them had changed maybe
she wouldn't stay over. *I need her with me,* he thought to
himself, feeling tense and tight inside. He'd used Mercedes
over the last couple of months. She was more than willing
and able to ease his mind and body. He didn't want that to
be what Sinclair did for him. He cared more about Sinclair
than just having her for a booty call. That's what he needed,
something more than a booty call. Maybe now after a few of
these runs he was starting to feel like a grown ass man, a man
in need of a wifey, someone to come home to. Finest had
Tanqueray. It was obvious he'd gotten back in her drawers.
Despite his determination to collect the money and get the
job done tonight, he looked calm and collected. A couple of
weeks ago he was ready to jump down every body's throat for
nothing. But clearly he'd gotten his needs handled tonight.
Floyd had told him that Tanqueray was the one fixin' his shit.

Yeah, Malcolm knew now, he needed Sinclair to fix things
for him.

Chapter 9

Leaving the hotel room, Tanqueray walked past the registration desk to the front of the hotel. She'd called Mr. Sinclair. Of course she'd not gotten him directly, his assistant took the message. It was all good because within a few moments Cecil, his chauffer, was en route, confirmed by a return call.

"Be out front," Cecil had said.

Cecil was an Oreo big time but they'd come to an understanding about things. Of course he would never understand that she was not a whore because Mr. Sinclair gave her money for her time spent with him. But they never had sex—ever.

She'd not even seen him since the night of the incident. Even that night, after he'd watched her bathe and all that, he never touched her. She would have let him of course, not because she was a whore, more because he was a nice man. He wasn't like the other white men that Omar used to try to get her to be with. They were all hands and shit. She'd do a lap dance and still that would never be enough. Sometimes she'd show them her tits and still they would want to suck on them or slap her ass a few times. Mr. Sinclair just wasn't like that; he only liked to watch.

The two of them were about to start a conversation the last time they were together but it all got put on hold by the call that Cammie had been admitted to the hospital. By the time the night ended, life had changed so much that she'd not put that conversation back into her mind. However, tonight she would hear what Mr. Sinclair was going to say. Maybe he was going to make her the same offer she'd gotten from Finest in the shower, the request to be his number one. Maybe tonight Tanqueray would have to choose between thug love and true security outside of the ghetto.

Omar lived outside the ghetto, true. But life with him was a prison worse than the one that her brother Debonair was facing. Omar was a pervert and nasty in his ways. Sure, he kept her looking tight and definitely kept her nose right, but what she had to do for it made her sick sometimes. He was a freak with some strange fetishes. Tanqueray thought about how he would have her piss on him sometimes and how he would get into her pussy, eating her out like she was a sloppy joe. Finest was never like that and just the thought of him between her thighs made her wet.

"Tanqueray," Cecil called after whistling for her. She frowned at his summons before rushing over to the car.

"Don't be whistling at me like I'm some damn dog," she huffed.

"Get your ass in the car. He's waiting," Cecil said under his breath. He knew better than to get buck wild in front of Mr. Sinclair. Their first encounter was disastrous and almost ended with Cecil losing his job. It was that night Tanqueray realized how much clout she had with the rich white man in the limo who even now sat in the back seat eager to see her. She grinned wickedly at Cecil and climbed in the back seat.

Mr. Sinclair's eyes lit up as soon as she slid in the seat next to him. "May I kiss you?" he asked immediately.

Tanqueray was taken off guard as his request was blunt and out of the ordinary for him.

"I'm sorry," he then said. "I just missed you so very much and, and you look so much like her," he added.

"Mr. Sinclair. Who is this, *her*? You 'bout to make me jealous of *her*. You've said that more than once," Tanqueray teased flirtatiously. It wasn't that she didn't want to kiss the handsome man; it was more that she wanted to know who she was competing with. Shantel—*the bitch*—now lay in her place in Omar's bed. She now wore Tanqueray's pretty things, so yeah, she wanted to know who the *her* was Mr. Sinclair refered to. Life was all about rotations and so Tanqueray wanted to know whose place she was taking.

"A woman I loved once," he answered.

How could she remind him of a white woman? Tanqueray's heart jumped into her throat. "Loved? Was she your wife?" she asked with what was left of her voice.

"We were lovers. Well, I loved her," Mr. Sinclair admitted. "And no, she wasn't my wife."

Tanqueray stared deep into his dancing green eyes, deeper than she wanted to at the moment. In his eyes she saw something familiar but couldn't put her finger on it. "Did I tell you my sister's name is Sinclair," she said, hoping to ease up the awkward tension that was growing between them. She reminded him of a black woman he loved once. Just that thought made Tanqueray a little nervous.

"No, you didn't, but you also didn't answer my question," he smiled slyly.

"And that was?"

He leaned in close. "For permission to kiss you."

Tanqueray smiled and nodded, allowing him a tender kiss on her cheek.

He was precious and at that moment she knew she wanted him to fall in love with her. Maybe it would change her life if he loved her. Maybe it would be good for the both of them. Either way, being with Mr. Sinclair was a way out of the life she'd been living, an easy way out at that.

She thought about Cecil's words now "you gotta earn it." Was this what he thought she was doing now? Working her way out through the use of Mr. Sinclair? How could she explain to him that she wasn't—but was—but wasn't. Looking toward the front of the limo, she caught Cecil's eyes in the review mirror. She couldn't read them, but deep inside didn't want to. Who knew what Cecil really thought about her?

And who gave a damn, really?

Chapter 10

Sinclair got back to the apartment. Unique had finally given her a key. For a while there she was locked out sometimes, but now that it was clear she was going to be staying until she was eighteen, Unique broke down and gave her the key. Plus with all the back and forth to the hospital to see Cammie, and all that, everybody would be in the street if she didn't give somebody else the key.

The old woman a few doors down sat with Gina and Apple most of the time while Unique was gone. She felt bad for what had happened to Marquis Jr. Unique used to call her just a nosy ass, but things between them had apparently changed over the last few weeks. It was almost as if she was filling a maternal need in Unique's life. Sinclair didn't like that idea. Nobody would replace Mama in her life and she wasn't about to allow that woman to get that close to her. Sinclair was determined to keep her memories. Of course now with the house they all grew up in, gone, and being replaced with a new one, lots of memories were fading.

It had been a minute since she'd checked on the progress of the new house. After finding out indirectly that the house didn't even belong to their mother, her interest in the replacement of it faded just a little. Everybody said the house belonged to some white man, apparently the one who was coming by in that big white limo watching it get built.

In the early stages, when the big trucks were there, he came to watch them move the dirt and remove the debris. He'd just sit there with his Black bodyguard/chauffer, watching, eating snacks from some expensive deli while all around him starved until—well, until the first anyway. That was just how it was.

Sinclair never really put feelings on her life there in the P until that white man sort of moved in. It wasn't until he came that she noticed how poor everybody was. Maybe it was because she knew she would be leaving and just figured this life to be part of the journey. Maybe she just didn't think that hard on it. Either way, when that white man came it all started to come together in her mind. She started noticing the haves and the have-nots and, frankly, she wasn't sure which one she was anymore.

Once she was tempted to ask him for some of that good looking stuff he was eating. She missed eating good food. She would always get in on expensive stuff at school. Her friends would always bring fancy lunches and all that. When her lunches started getting thin, right before Deb went to jail—right before summer—she would just act as if she wasn't hungry. Her friends would always push their food on her and man, she was more than happy to finally give in and chow down on that expensive stuff.

The white man and his bodyguard/chauffer would sit for hours sometimes, as if it was truly entertaining watching that dirt get shoveled. Well, maybe she was no better. She would stand there as well, watching the trucks scoop up her life and throw it away.

When she lived there on that street, before her brother Debonair had gotten his dumbass self locked up, she attended a predominately white school in Pinole. Pinole was way outside their area. Her mother had put her in that school to make sure she got better books, better teachers and basically a better education with a chance to get out of the ghetto. After Deb went to prison, all those chances at better were gone. Sinclair wasn't sure how she felt about it either, but watching that man enjoying his simple pleasures she once again wanted for what she had coming to her. She wanted a chance to have better. She wanted a chance to get out.

But now, as the summer rushed to an end, nobody seemed to care anymore about the house way over in the Palemos on Appaloosa Street. It was as if the memories there had been carted away with all the rubble. Sinclair continued to think back to when the construction started. All the folks were standing around watching the crane scooping up piles of her life and taking it away as if it was truly something to watch.

Sinclair had moved to the West End after the house went up. The West End was another ghetto even worse off than the one she had grown up in. At least in the Palemos the old folks kept wisdom in the air. The West End was full of young crazy folks who loved to fight, kill and keep up a bunch of drama. Nonetheless, this woman a few doors down from Unique was one out of the norm. That was for sure. Her kindness was unusual. She was a church lady and maybe that was why. She read her bible and always seemed to be trying her best to live what she read. One day Sinclair figured she'd need to take a peek into that book and see what it was all about, but for now, she just figured it was a book of magic words directed to the old.

After dropping off her gear, Sinclair headed to the woman's door to pick up the girls. Who knew where Unique was? She'd gotten off the bus near the Palemos, so who knew where she was headed.

Gina and Apple were happy to see her, although their eyes

seemed darkened. They hadn't smiled much over the last few weeks. Their worry for Cammie was obvious. And now they saw her arm all bandaged and they seemed even lowered in spirits. It was as if there could be no hope for their safety, what, with everyone getting hurt.

"Come on," she said to the girls as they hesitated before gathering their things.

Mrs. Newbury smiled at Sinclair. "God bless you and your family, chile," she said—as always.

"Thank you Mrs. Newbury," Sinclair answered, ushering the girls out of her apartment and down the hall. The loud elevator announced a visitor to the floor. When the door opened the big, dark, menacing-looking thug that claimed to be Marquis' father stepped out. Sinclair tried to hide her intimidation but couldn't. He was a scary looking bastard. It was obvious to her that his bulk was prison-made and his jailhouse neck tats added to her thoughts. His face had only one scar, so that meant he was tough and hadn't had much trouble while on the inside. Either that, or he gave others their fair share to stay off him. She'd heard about prison life. Debonair did nothing but cry on the phone now that he had been moved down to Soledad California Men's Facility. Sinclair didn't even want to think about how he was making due—with his pretty self.

Debonair was older than Tanqueray, who was the oldest of the three girls. He was handsome for a man with soft features. He had long lashes and long hair that he wore relaxed. He didn't look like any street thug she'd ever seen. That was why she was surprised to learn he'd been hustling drugs for so long and had gotten caught owing so much to Da Man when he got busted, which was why the house was blown up.

Wonder what happened to Gold Mouth? Sinclair thought of

the ugly man with all the gold fronts that demanded, from her, the money Deb owed. Malcolm and Finest stood up to him one afternoon when he came by to threaten her. *He'd already blown up the house. Hell, what else did he want?* But it was cool. Finest and Malcolm told him to get the hell out of dodge and apparently he did. She'd never seen him again.

Sinclair's thoughts about Deb and Gold Mouth left when the big man smiled at her. His teeth were white and pretty. *Yes, he was somebody big in prison. He was too well groomed to have been anybody's bitch.*

"Unique here?" he asked. His voice was deep and rumbling. It was quite affecting.

Sinclair felt heat running through her body. Gina and Apple must have felt it too as they stood close beside her. "No. She's not here. She got off the bus in the P somewhere," Sinclair said, probably telling too much. Surely by the time he got to the P, Unique would be back here, so it was cool.

He nodded. "Can I wait?" he asked.

"Nah," Sinclair snapped before catching herself.

He frowned. "Why? You scared?" he asked.

"Nah," she lied. "But under the circumstances, we don't let men in the apartment anymore. That day of the funeral was an exception," Sinclair said, hoping he fell for it. She was using her East Bay diction now, the one she used in the white school. She could switch it up on a dime when called for. It was a talent she planned to master once she left the ghetto. Yes, Sinclair was going to get far. She had plans.

The big man seemed to ponder her words for a moment. "What happened to my son?" he asked.

Gina looked up at Sinclair. She hadn't been there for the repast so it was obvious she had no idea who this man was. The girls had stayed at Mrs. Newbury's until the apartment was empty of people. It was just something that Mrs. Newbury felt would be the best way to handle it. "Your son? You Marquis' daddy?" Gina asked. At eight she was quick. Fast was more of the word for it, but at this moment, she was just being quick.

"Yeah, baby, I am," he answered her, sounding almost soft in his tone.

"He got shot!" Apple said. "He shot Curtis and then the cops shot him," she added relating the incident that took her brother's life.

"Hmmph," Marquis Sr. nodded knowingly. "That true?" he asked Sinclair who nodded. "Hmmph," he repeated. Taking in a deep breath he let out what seemed to be many thoughts, imaginings and future plans about the life that he may have envisioned while behind bars—life with his little man when he got out.

"How'd you find out about Marquis?" Sinclair asked him.

"You hear thangs when you locked up. I heard about Larry's sister having a baby. I did the math. I knew it had to be mines. You know, she was fresh when I got at her . . ." he stopped and glanced down at Apple and Gina, deciding not to say anymore about "getting at" the thirteen year old Unique.

Not caring about a time she could not really remember, Sinclair was surprised that anyone knew her oldest brother Larry. She asked, "You know my brother Larry?"

"Yeah, we hung out in the same clique. Shame he had to go out like that. He was all right. He just talked too much."

Sinclair nodded as if understanding street life better than she really did. "I didn't know him real well."

"Nah, 'cause you was a baby," Marquis Sr. smiled again. "I remember you too."

Sinclair was taken by his ruggedly handsome smile.

He then noticed her bandage. "What happened to you?"

"Got cut," she answered. "Fightin'," she mumbled, hoping Gina and Apple weren't paying too close attention.

Marquis Sr. laughed. "Fightin'? Li'l Bit, who you trying to take out?" He laughed even heartier now. "And don't tell me it was over a nigga. Please!"

"No," Sinclair lied.

His head went back in laughter. "Yeah, it was over a nigga. Girl don't you know that wasn't even worth it. He wasn't worth it. If he let you get cut, he'll let anythang happen to you."

"No, he won't. This was my fault. I shouldn't have . . ." she paused looking now at Gina who was paying close attention. "I don't want to talk about it. Look Marquis, I need to get inside so I can take my pain meds and—"

He nodded and pointed at her arm. "Better watch that shit. Damn doctors'll turn you into a crack head."

"I ain't no crackhead!" she said chuckling at the thought.

The moment grew tense now as Sinclair stood waiting for him to leave. There was no way she was opening the door with him standing there. Not that men truly weren't allowed in the apartment, but under the circumstances, there was no way this man was getting in there.

He seemed to catch on and finally backed away. "Well, let me go," he said pushing the button for the elevator. When it opened, he stepped in.

"Bye, Marquis's Daddy!" Gina called. He waved as the elevator door closed. "I didn't know Marquis had a daddy," she then said.

"Everybody's got a daddy," Sinclair said. She opened the front door to the apartment, thinking about the fact that she had no idea who hers was.

Chapter 11

Unique entered the old church. She'd not been there in years. Pastor Williams was there laying out prayer books and apparently getting ready for the night's service. His nappy gray hair was sparse on his head. He looked older than she remembered him looking, but he was humming. That she remembered about him; hFe always hummed.

She had no intentions of staying long but she did want to see him. She was hurting deep inside and wanted some peace. She wanted to know that she hadn't killed her child. She needed to know it wasn't her fault.

"Hello, chile. You scared me," he said turning and seeing her unexpectedly standing there. "The last person I thought I'd ever see in my church was one of Javina Nation's children." He chuckled.

"Why? Was my mother wicked?"

He smiled slightly, weakly, as if regretting his words. "No. It's just—well, your mama wasn't much of a churchgoer. You know that."

"No, I guess she wasn't, but then again, we kids kept her plenty busy with all of our badness."

"Y'all waddn't bad kids, especially you Unique. You . . ." he let his words trail off before coming back to the conversation. "If I remember correctly you was about the quietest one, short of the baby. But then she was just a baby." He laughed again.

He was a stocky man and given to laughter easily. He had joy in his eyes. Unique could see that.

"She's a woman now. I mean, she ain't got no kids but—"

"Don't take kids to make you a woman Unique," he interjected as if aiming for a direction in this conversation.

"I know that fa sho," she answered. "But I done loss my child to death and I don't feel much like nothing no mo'. I . . ." Unique's lip trembled. "I feel . . ." she hesitated.

"Give me your trouble," he requested of her now, reaching out for her.

How did he know she needed to take his hand? How did he know she needed to feel the power of God? She grabbed his hand tight hoping for a miracle, hoping to feel something magical.

He began to pray aloud, asking for such a miracle. "Amen!" he screamed. "Amen!" he screamed again.

"Amen!" Unique screamed back. She was still hoping for a surge of power to come through their tightly clasped hands. She wanted it. She needed it.

"Do you need Him? Tell Him you need Him!" the pastor yelled out.

"I need you! Jesus I need you!" she cried out. "I need you!"

"This child of yours is in pain. Tell ya father you in pain, chile!"

"I'm in pain! Lawd I'm in pain!" she yelled. Tears began to flow like water now. She couldn't control them.

"Heal her pain—" he began. Unique pulled away and fell to her knees.

"No! No! Lord, heal my child!" she wept. "Heal my child!"

The pastor then squatted down to her. "If you believe, she shall be healed," he whispered. Unique looked up into his eyes which were the color of dark coffee. His face was calm and serene. "If you believe in Him, you will get both of your children back," he said touching her head and closing his eyes. "In the name of God! Amen."

"Amen," Unique said now, closing her eyes. She believed him. She wanted with all her heart to believe him and she did. How she would get little Marquis back she had no clue but she believed.

After drying her eyes and praying again with pastor Williams, Unique quickly ran out of the church headed back to the hospital. She was in hope of a miracle now and wanted it to happen without further delay. She wasn't expecting to see Marquis Jr. at the hospital, standing in the ER where he died, but she was expecting to see Cammie smiling at her. She was expecting that with all her heart.

The bus seemed to be waiting for her. She jumped on, dropping coins in quickly as if feeding a hungry lion. Her eyes must have been wide with fervor as the driver just stared at her without asking any questions. He must have sensed her urgency.

Within moments it seemed she was back at the hospital. She left the bus, ran inside to the elevator and up to ICU.

"Hello Ms. Nation. You're back already?" the friendly nurse said, smiling.

"Yes! I'm back on an angel's wings!" Unique told her trying to calm her nerves before heading into Cammie's room.

Sliding into the chair next to the bed, she could see that Cammie was still sleeping. Her heart sank with disappointment. "I just knew you'd be up and waiting for me baby. I just knew it. I guess God don't think I deserve it yet. I . . ." Unique began to weep bitterly. "I don't know what else to do. I went to the church and I prayed. I don't know what else to do." She covered her face sobbing. "But don't give up. I'ma keep on praying. I'ma pray until you wake up fa sho," Unique promised.

"I love you Cammie. I love you with all my heart. I love you and I loved Marquis. I love Gina and Apple and I'ma change. I'ma change fa sho. I done prayed and I'ma keep on prayin' until you wake up," she cried, laying her head on Cammie's leg.

Just then she felt something touch her head. Jerking her head up wondering if it was the same strange phenomena from earlier she was stunned to see Cammie's dark eyes looking at her. "Cammie. Oh my God, Cammie."

"Doctor!" she screamed, darting quickly from the room.

Chapter 12

"Where the hell you at!" Finest barked in her ear. He sounded tense.

She glanced over at Mr. Sinclair who seemed less than concerned about her taking a call while in his presence. They had reached his mansion in Sausalito and he was handing out orders to his staff, one being to run her a bath. She was excited and couldn't wait. Mr. Sinclair loved to watch her bathe in the huge sunken bathtub.

"Tell me bitch!" screamed Finest.

Tanqueray was too busy listening to what Mr. Sinclair was planning to listen to Finest's little tirade. The bath was to be run in the master suite. *Oh, something new,* she thought, smiling broadly.

Mr. Sinclair noticed. "And some fresh fruits on a tray would be nice too," he told Cory, his butler.

"Very good, Sir," Cory said, smiling at Tanqueray.

Everyone on his staff liked her, well, except Cecil and even Cecil had a soft spot for her, she could tell. He just felt she wasn't good enough and hell, he was probably right, but it didn't matter. *Not everyone did what was best for them, ya know.*

Turning her attention back to the phone she interrupted Finest's tantrum. "I'm visiting a friend. You didn't come back so I left. And what I tell you about calling me a bitch," she mumbled that part under her breath.

"I can call you whatever I want, bitch. I went out and got some money fa us. I come back to this expensive-ass room and your black tail is gone. I'm sitting up here wantin' mah shit and you got yo ass somewhere's else. Who I'm supposed to fuck now?"

"What?"

"You heard me."

"Shit! Fuck ya self." Tanqueray hung up. Finest's ringtone played again instantly. She pushed the ignore button and then turned the phone off.

"Everything okay?" Mr. Sinclair asked.

"It's all good," she said, smiling brightly. She felt good and safe and happy. She felt different with Mr. Sinclair than with Finest, that was for damn sure. Yes, Finest had her jones on overdrive. He could look at her and she got naked, but there was something missing there. Mr. Sinclair gave her something deeper, something deeper than the flesh. Mr. Sinclair made her feel good inside. He made her feel pretty. He made her feel as if she was as beautiful as she remembered her mother being.

Javina Nation, her mother, was a beautiful woman, and everyone always said she looked the most like her. Men used to love Javina and gave her a lot of attention and gifts. Tanqueray admired her mother and wanted to be like her. Mr. Sinclair made her feel that way.

Holding hands they walked up the long spiral staircase to the master suite. Pushing open the door, the room took her breath away. The color scheme was black and white accented with smoked glass. The walls were covered with black and white pictures of still life in thick expensive looking silver frames. "Wow," was all she could say.

"You like it?" he asked.

"Oh, yeah," she purred walking over to the huge round bed and pushing it for firmness. Turning back to him, she saw he had closed the space between them.

"I know I usually watch you undress, but tonight I want to do it. Will that be okay?" he asked.

"Sure," she answered bubbly. It wasn't as if she had much on, only a ripped up halter top and a skort. Finest had taken care of her thong. He'd torn that to shreds. But thank goodness she was clean. She'd showered at the hotel. Usually when he picked her up she was stank and full of cum and cocaine. Tonight, the cocaine had worn off, and the cum? Well, it wasn't like it usually was after leaving Finest.

"Why were you at the Radisson?" he asked, pulling the string that held her breasts inside the top. It fell loose, leaving her exposed. He took in a deep breath as if trying to contain himself.

"I was with a friend. Is that all right?" she asked testing his tolerance and freak level. "I mean, it was a man."

"Did he pay you?" Mr. Sinclair asked. He unzipped her skort and pushed it down over her hips. It fell to the floor. He again smiled at the fact she wore nothing underneath. Her gold pubic hair was nice and shiny too. He stared at it as if seeing it for the first time.

"No. He didn't. I was there because I wanted to be."

"Is he your boyfriend?"

Tanqueray hesitated.

Mr. Sinclair did too, his hands poised on her hips.

"Dunno," she answered.

"Does he know about me?"

"No," she answered.

"I like that. I know about him but he doesn't know about me." He smiled, again looking down at her pubic area. "I like your gold pubic hair," he said, apparently noticing she'd touched up the color.

She'd dyed it back when she was a stripper. Everyone loved her gold hair. She had never regretted dying it. It used to get her hella tips when she was stripping. The crowd loved it so she kept it gold. *One never knows when one could find themselves on the stage again.*

"I was a stripper."

"Ahh, one day you'll have to dance for me," he said.

"I could do it now."

"No. Right now, I want you to bathe," he said pointing at the tub. She smiled and nodded, heading toward the sunken tub.

"Are you going to get in this time?" she asked him as he stood watching her get comfortable in the bubbles.

Just then the door opened and the tray of fresh fruit was set on the small table. The kitchen attendant left quickly without looking one way or the other. "They never knock?"

"Why?" he asked. "We are all voyeurs. We all want to see what someone else is doing, right?"

"Voyeur? What's that?"

"Somebody who gains pleasure from watching other people," he paused before speaking, ". . . especially watching them have sex." He giggled naughtily.

Normally Tanqueray found giggling men gay-sounding but on Mr. Sinclair, it was sexy.

"Are they gonna watch us have sex?"

"No. But I would like to watch you have sex some time, maybe with your boyfriend."

Tanqueray choked on her laughter. "Are you kidding me? Me and Finest?"

"His name is Finest?" Mr. Sinclair asked, bending down to scoop up some of the warm water in his hands and pour it over her shoulder. The bubbles melted away and she noticed he caught his breath again when her breasts were exposed.

"Yes. Finest. He's a street thug. I don't think he'd be into that."

"What about Cecil?"

Tanqueray burst into louder laughter then. "He hates me."

"No, he doesn't." Mr. Sinclair said. He repeated what he had just done, since Tanqueray teased him by covering herself up again with bubbles. "He's just being that way."

"Are you hard Dustin?" she asked him, calling him by his first name. She'd noticed how excited he seemed to be at the sight of her breasts. He blushed but didn't look at her directly. "You never have sex with the woman you pay to spend time with you?"

He hesitated before shaking his head. "Sometimes I let them touch me. But . . . "

"Touch you. You mean like give you head or something?" she flirted. She was game, and funny thing was, she wasn't even high. Maybe this was what being turned on felt like because, truly she was hot and bothered. Reaching deeper into the water, she felt Mr. Sinclair rub her thigh. Yes he was up for it. Shaking the water from her hands she quickly dried them on the towel he provided.

He stood and began to unzip his pants but she stopped him.

"I'll do it," she said patting the side of the bathtub requesting him to kneel beside it as he had been.

He obeyed. Still red-faced in blush, he giggled again as she unzipped his pants.

She didn't know what to expect as she'd never done a white man before. She's only done the lap dancing and maybe let them give her pussy a sniff. But never had she smoked any of them before. Omar was pretty clear about not doing that and she was glad.

When she pulled out Dustin Sinclair's hard member she didn't notice too much difference between his and Finest. Finest was mixed with something, Tanqueray knew that because he was real fair and had soft hair and all that. He also had a white dick. But because there was black in there, Tanqueray never really put two and two together that perhaps a white man's dick would look the same as his. Anyway, she took Mr. Sinclair between her lips and began smoking him good.

He hummed and purred stoking her hair softly. "You're really good," he purred. "Oh, yeah. You're as good as . . . " he paused. Tanqueray looked up at him. Their eyes met again and again the strange sensation hit her. Perhaps it hit him at the same time as he suddenly removed his shirt. "Continue," he said softly.

She did.

He moved his hips now getting fully into the act. "Please ask your boyfriend to come over. I have to see you have sex," he purred.

She nodded while sucking harder on him.

He seethed now. "Yes, I have to watch you cum."

She gently squeezed his balls now that he'd pushed his pants down all the way. "God, I wish someone would come in right now and watch this. It would be so much better."

At that Tanqueray pulled off. "You are really a freak," she laughed.

"No. No. I'm not really. I . . ."

"It's all good. Get my cell phone and let me call that fool," she requested sounding full of play.

Quickly, Mr. Sinclair, with his pants and shorts down around his ankles, rushed back into the bedroom and retrieved her phone.

She called Finest.

"What bitch!" he barked as soon as he answered. He was obviously still pouting.

"You want to do something new?" she asked grinning at Mr. Sinclair as if they were both planning some devilment.

"Any money involved?" he asked.

"Money?" she said aloud. Mr. Sinclair nodded heartily.

"Yeah."

"Okay, I'm down."

"I gather you forgive me now."

"I love you bitch, of course I do."

Chapter 13

Cecil wasn't ashamed of his life. He wasn't ashamed of any of what he'd had to do to get out of the ghetto. True, he'd not seen his mother in ages, and had ignored her phone calls many times. She was such a reminder of a place he didn't want to be anymore and a way that he didn't want to live.

And now there was Tanqueray. Why now? Why her?

He often wondered why Mr. Sinclair had taken him under his wings long ago as a protégé, teaching him many wonderful things about a life that, up till now, he'd only been allowed to enjoy crumbs of. *Had it been a kindness or a cruelty?* Cecil often wondered as he moved along the freeway in the fancy car. He popped in a jazz CD and settled in the seat. He'd been driving this Bentley now for about two years. It felt like it was his car. So many things of Mr. Sinclair's felt like his.

He had full reign over the house, the kitchen and the vehicles. If he needed anything he had but to mention it and it was his. He even got a salary with which he had rented a small apartment in a good part of the city. Mr. Sinclair didn't know about that apartment—or at least he hoped he didn't. That apartment was his private haven. It was there he entertained his friends and women he would meet on occasion. Between his cousin Omar, the pimp, and Mr. Sinclair, the John, women were not an issue for Cecil. Some of the women were cast offs of Mr. Sinclair, but Cecil didn't care—not really. It wasn't as if he had to pay them like Mr. Sinclair did.

Omar was a true thorn in Cecil's side. But then if he was being honest with himself, he had to admit that it was his fault that Omar was even back in his life. He knew what Omar was. He was a pimp. But Cecil also wanted to please Mr. Sinclair. Maybe deep inside he also wanted to touch a little bit of the familiar too. Once involved with Omar, Cecil quickly became trapped between Mr. Sinclair's penchant for black women and Omar's greed.

It started out with Mr. Sinclair wanting to "entertain" a black woman once or twice a month. "Why would I know where to find black women," Cecil had answered when first approached with the possibility of supplying Mr. Sinclair with 'company'.

Mr. Sinclair just laughed at the comment. That's when it hit Cecil what Mr. Sinclair thought of him. Perhaps he truly saw that 'boy out of the ghetto but ghetto still in the boy' thing. But Cecil was not ghetto. He'd been set free from that life and that meant all the expectations of it, right?

He wanted to comment harshly to that wicked chuckle that came from the backseat but instead he said nothing. He pondered the request. At the time, he'd not made any contact with folks from his past. He'd avoided the streets he grew up on. He stayed clear of all that mess. But, every now and then, a "little bird" would offer him some information about people he knew. That "little bird" had reported to him that Omar, his first cousin, had moved up a bit and was living out in the East Bay where the white folks lived. He'd started an escort service where he pimped out fairly decent looking hoes. He was told that the business was doing well—if he was interested. At the time he just rolled his eyes and ignored the whole thing but filed it away. It's a good thing he did.

"I might," he finally said to Mr. Sinclair who had since

busied himself with the view outside his bayside window. He caught his eyes in the rearview mirror. "I might know where to find a woman you could . . . entertain," he said offering a dramatic pause. Mr. Sinclair smiled.

That was all it took. That and one call to Omar. Cecil called his mother who called her former sister-in law, who called Omar's daddy, who gave up the number.

Within hours, Cecil pulled up in front of Omar's condo in the limo. That was the evening car of choice for Mr. Sinclair. He stepped out fully dressed in uniform to greet the female who would be visiting. She was pretty enough. She had large breasts and small hips. Her smile was bright and her hair long. Most of her assets were probably false but that was fine for what her intentions were.

Two grand was what Mr. Sinclair paid for this evening on the town. Two grand of which Omar told him later, the woman got only about two hundred. What a deal and a racket for Omar. It was one that Cecil eventually decided he needed to get in on. Maybe Sinclair was right. Maybe Cecil still had a bit of the street hustle in him.

But now there was Tanqueray. There was something different about her, something that was all the way bad.

Omar had actually been bedding this woman. She was his woman, or so it seemed. Cecil wondered what had happened why he was passing her off to Sinclair.

"She's a bitch. She thinks she's better than all the other hoes in my stable . . . yeah, that's it . . . she thinks she not even a ho!" Omar had laughed. "Can you believe that?"

"Okay," Cecil had said as if he understood the logic.

"Yeah," Omar added, clearing his throat, as if realizing that Cecil and he were never going to be fully on the same page in regards to hoes and such. "Anyway, she's been embezzling

from me," he went on, sounding totally disgusted now. "And
I need her to be taught a lesson."

"So this is 'teaching' her something?"

"Yeah," Omar said.

That night Tanqueray taught them all a lesson that Cecil
would not soon forget. She made it clear she was not a whore
by trying her best to kick his ass. It was embarrassing and
revealing at the same time. For the first time since this all
began Cecil was forced to see a black woman in a new light.
It wasn't the best light, but still it was a new one. Since that
time, Tanqueray had done nothing but confuse him. It was
clear Mr. Sinclair favored her over all the rest.

But do I want her too?

Shaking his head of that crazy thought, Cecil pulled into the
P. His stomach tightened at the stench that he was probably only
imaging that he could smell through the rolled up windows.
Double checking the address, Cecil could see the young light
skinned man standing out front. He was cold-looking and
a little hard around the edges. It was clear he was a thug—
nothing more. Again Cecil's stomach tightened.

It was clear Omar didn't know about this young thug or he
wouldn't have asked Cecil to do what he had asked him to do
the next time he had Tanqueray alone.

Yeah, this whole Tanqueray thing was getting messy.

Maybe all this had to do with the fact that Cecil was having
a hard time dealing with the thoughts he was having about
the things he shouldn't know.

Cecil had taken Mr. Sinclair to his attorney's office. It was
there he found out about the trust fund. He didn't understand
it all but he got this much out of what he'd found out from
the secretary there. He'd had a few dates with her and she was
apparently pretty impressed with him. She had started telling

him Mr. Sinclair's confidential business matters. It was just yesterday, or maybe a month ago, who knew anymore. The pain was so sharp it could have been an hour ago as far as he was concerned. Anyway, this woman . . . Cecil realized then he didn't even remember her name. It was strange to think about spending so much intimate time with someone you didn't really know. Anyway, she told him about the money Mr. Sinclair planned to give to Tanqueray. Money that was part of what he was supposed to inherit! Now he was going to be splitting it with this tramp! This whore! This hood rat Tanqueray! Why? What did she do that was so different from all the others?

Cecil was going crazy over that question. He couldn't sleep wondering why Tanqueray had moved into Mr. Sinclair's heart like this. He was going nuts trying to figure out how to stop all this nonsense, that is, until Omar called. He was wondering why Sinclair hadn't needed any girls lately. Mr. Sinclair was obviously his best paying client.

"Because of Tanqueray," Cecil told him in a huff.

"Who?"

"That bitch Tanqueray," Cecil divulged.

"You've seen her?"

"Of course I've seen her. I pick her up and bring her to him. Whenever he wants her . . . he gets her. Whenever she wants him . . . she gets him." Cecil knew what he was saying and the response he was going to get from that news.

Omar flipped, just as expected.

"So you're the driver, huh?" asked Finest, breaking Cecil's thoughts, bringing him back to the bleak realities of his life. Cecil looked him over as he stood with the passenger door opened.

"Yeah, get in the back," Cecil said coolly.

Chapter 14

Tanqueray lay on Mr. Sinclair's big bed waiting for Finest to enter the room. When he did, he looked a little nervous. She could tell he'd never been in a house this beautiful before.

"Girl you always into some freaky shit," he said to her, noticing Mr. Sinclair at the small table in his robe enjoying the fruit.

"Ah, hell, nah . . . I am not doing no dude," Finest bucked.

Mr. Sinclair shook his head in his attempt to correct him, his mouth filled with grapes.

"Ain't nobody doing no dude. You gon' do me. He's gonna watch." Tanqueray explained.

"Ah, hell, nah . . . Tanqueray what's going on here? What you been doing with this dude. You been doing him?"

"No," Mr. Sinclair answered quickly. The guilt showed on his face.

Tanqueray was sure Finest saw it.

"No," Tanqueray confirmed. It was true. She'd not done him—he'd done her. "He is my friend. He watches me take baths and stuff. He's a voyeur," she added, winking slyly at Mr. Sinclair.

After she had gotten out of the tub earlier, she had stood naked before Mr. Sinclair dripping wet. "I know you want more than that," she said.

He smiled. "No. It wouldn't be right."

"Why?"

"I can't tell you why."

"You gay?"

His brow furrowed. "No."

"Married?"

He shook his head.

"Then why can't we do it," she asked.

"Why do you want to? You don't even know me. Wouldn't you rather do a black man?"

"I've never done a white man," she said.

Mr. Sinclair smiled.

"That's what she said too," he grinned. "You are so much like her. Gosh! You. . . ." He looked around. Naked now, he padded into the bedroom to the intercom. "Cory I need the camera," he said. Turning her, he pointed to the bed. "Get on the bed and spread your legs wide. Cory will come in and film you," he said. "Touch yourself," he instructed.

Tanqueray obeyed. Moments later, Cory entered with the small camcorder. Tanqueray could see he was used to this, as he had no comments or response to her lying there masturbating on the bed. Nor did he seem to react when Mr. Sinclair pulled the dildo from the cedar chest.

"Don't worry. It's brand new. I bought it for you." He smiled.

Tanqueray, noticing the large size of the fake white penis, stopped what she was doing for a second.

He looked at her, his face twisting slightly. "Don't stop," he said. "I'll bet this is gonna feel sooo good," he purred looking at the toy. "I've heard its one of the good ones."

Cory didn't stop the camera as Mr. Sinclair climbed on the bed between her thighs. "Relax," he said then, moving her hands and replacing them with the dildo which he had switched on. It began to vibrate. Knowing just where to move it, Tanqueray laid back and enjoyed the sensation. He stroked her inner thighs and belly as he used the toy on her—in her. He was well trained and soon she felt the orgasm starting. It was mild but it was there.

"Really good baby," he whispered. "You're beautiful when you cum," he said. "You look just like her when you cum . . . gosh you look just like her when you cum."

Tanqueray could not speak. She just watched him as he seemed to enjoy giving her pleasure as much as receiving it.

He pushed her ankles to where her knees came up more exposing her openness to him. Again he used the toy on her. She came again, this time with a little more intensity. *He was good at this*, she thought. Never had she done anything like this before for a man. Lap dancing was one thing, this was totally something else.

"Wonderful!" he said turning to Cory. "Did you get it all Cory?" he asked. Cory pulled the camera down from his eyes smiling.

"Yes I did."

Smoothing back his hair, Mr. Sinclair caught his breath. "That will be all Cory," he finally said. "Let's call your boyfriend again," he suggested then, sounding giddy.

Now Finest was there.

Tanqueray had to admit that she was getting into all this. She was amazed that she was still stone sober. She'd not even had a cocktail.

Finest slowly undressed and moved over to the bed, watching Mr. Sinclair out of the corner of his eyes all the while. Despite his apprehensions, he was rock hard. His member was bobbing and dancing its familiar dance. Tanqueray took it between her lips, licking and sucking on it.

"Damn girl you act like you in a movie," Finest purred

pulling on her hair roughly while working her mouth as if it was her lower half. His pace quickened as he often did before he came. But instead of coming in her mouth, he pulled her off and turned her around mounting her doggie style. "In case he don't know how we do . . . now he know," Finest said, referring to Mr. Sinclair as if he were a novice.

True, with Finest it was always good. She came fast and with an intensity she never knew she could feel. He was wonderful in bed and she always enjoyed every minute of it. Although she'd just been entered less than an hour before with the large dildo, Finest, made it all feel fresh. He had her moaning loudly along with guttural grunts and pants. Reaching through her thighs she found his nuts and squeezed gently pulling them from his body hoping to make his hard on last a little longer.

"Yeah, baby! Yeah," Finest said, pulling nearly all the way out and slamming back in again and again. He tugged at her dangling breasts hard and roughly bit her on the back of the neck. He then pulled her hair to raise her head. "I want that ass. You know I do."

"No . . ." she whispered back. "No. Not in front of Mr. Sinclair," she begged.

"Then you better make this pussy sing to me," he growled, pulling out and turning her over. He entered her quickly pulling her legs over his shoulder.

She heard Mr. Sinclair sigh slightly. That's when she noticed he was jacking off in the chair. He was enjoying this show a lot. Finest musta heard him getting off as he glanced over there.

"Yeah, mah man, it's singing to me! It's mah pussy . . . got that," he said, thrusting even harder into her while in a stare down with Mr. Sinclair.

Maybe his jacking off was turning Finest on. Tanqueray

didn't know, but he kept watching as Mr. Sinclair tugged on his member. The faster he pulled the faster Finest's stroke became. Tanqueray watched both men, one fucking her vicariously through the other. It was ultimately arousing, exciting and turning her the hell on. Soon Tanqueray began to cum. Both men seemed to feel it in the air and reacted in kind by stroking their sexes faster and faster. Finest's was inside and Mr. Sinclair's at his own hand—both men groaning and enjoying the sex.

"Stop, stop!" Tanqueray cried out as the orgasms took over. They were intense nearly to the point of pain, but Finest didn't stop. Deeper and deeper he drilled, harder and harder. Maybe it was because she wasn't high, who knew, but this orgasm was different. It was . . . it was ecstasy. She began to quake and cry out, tears streaming down her face.

Mr. Sinclair called out as he came in the hand towel that he quickly pulled off the table. "Oh, Tanqueray—God yes, it looks so good. You are so beautiful!"

Finest said nothing as he was now caught up in her multiple orgasms that came and came. She'd never done this before. Her muscles were contracting as if she was having a baby. She knew she was on fire inside because she could feel her own heat. Finest's strokes were shallow and quick, he was about to cum. He was cumming for Mr. Sinclair. That she knew. She grabbed his hips and pulled him deep inside her. Finest cursed her, closed his eyes and gave into the hot release. He continued to pump in his emissions and soon felt firm inside her again. It was emotionally overwhelming. In her mind, she imagined Mr. Sinclair inside her, his green eyes dazzling as they did while he pleased her with the dildo, and she came for him. When she opened her eyes she saw Finest in all his beauty and again she came for him.

She hadn't realized that Mr. Sinclair had moved over to the

bed until she felt him stroking her hair. Finest slowed his pace enjoying her body writhing beneath his. He came again with a grunt, but continued to stay connected to her as she quivered. Mr. Sinclair kissed her forehead. She was amazed now that Finest had allowed him to get so involved in their intimate moment. "I love you," she said now, directing her comment to the both of them.

"You two were great. I hope we can do this again," Mr. Sinclair said softly. "What would you like for dinner?" he asked.

Finest looked down at Tanqueray. Together they burst into laughter.

Chapter 15

Sinclair had taken the last of the vicodin pills and was feeling the pain lifting in a good way. She was feeling real good. She was high.

There was a knock at the door and she had to admit that she'd not even heard the elevator. "It better not be Marquis' daddy," she barked, looking at the clock. Gina and Apple were asleep and who knew where Tanqueray was. *Heffa waddn't ever home*, she thought regarding her sister. "Who is it?" she yelped.

"Malcolm!"

She clicked opened the three bolts and then pulled the door open as far as the chain. "What choo want! I'm so mad at you I could scream."

"You look high as a muthfuck. What you on?"

"Stupid ass! I'm not high. I took those pain pills for my . . . my arm that your bitch girlfriend cut up."

"She's not my girl," he said.

Sinclair sucked her teeth. Her eyes were heavy and she was indeed high as a kite. Was this the feeling everyone wanted to have? She wasn't sure she liked it, but had to admit it was better than feeling pain. Pulling the lock off, she opened the door and let Malcolm in. "You got nerve coming here. I was gonna forgive you but then you left with ummm . . . ummm," she stammered.

"Finest. Yeah you high," Malcolm said.

"Yeah, Finest. Where did you go?"

"Nowhere," he said.

"Lyin' nigga, but whatever," she fussed, moving back into the apartment. She flopped on the sofa. Malcolm sat next to her.

"I'm sorry Sin," he finally said.

"Oh, yeah. Well prove it."

"How?"

"Tell me I'm your girl. Tell me I'm your only girl, Malcolm." Malcolm smiled at her. "You are so crazy."

"Tell me you are gonna break up with Mercedes and I'ma be your only girl," she slurred.

"You high as hell."

Her eyes crossed, but she could still see Malcolm sitting there for a moment or two longer before she could only dream about the two of them walking hand and hand in the summer sun.

Sinclair woke to find she was alone on the sofa. Gina and Apple were watching TV. It was around 9 A.M. She looked around for Unique, but she still wasn't home. She didn't even think that Tanqueray was there—*was she ever?* Sinclair smacked her pasty mouth. "Man those pills are strong," she thought aloud.

"What Aunt Sin?" Gina asked not turning her head away from the TV. They had cereal in bowls in front of them.

"How y'all got food? Yo mama been home?"

"We know how to get food," Gina said rolling her eyes a little bit as if to say "duh."

"You act like we're babies."

"Yeah, I guess you would know, huh," Sinclair said, moving her stiff body from the sofa. Her arm was starting to ache a little bit. She was out of vicodin. This wasn't good. She was hoping Unique would be home so that they would talk about getting her a medical case opened so she could fill this prescription. The liaison at the hospital said she only had ninety days before she would get billed for that ER visit. At that moment Sinclair wondered about Mercedes and how she paid for stuff. Sinclair wondered how she would pay for her injuries. But, then again, judging by the stretch marks on her saggy titties, she probably had a baby and was getting medical stuff paid for. *Some people had it easy,* Sinclair thought before realizing that Unique had nothing coming easy. *Nah, welfare was not the way to go.* Sinclair quickly revised her mind.

Did you see Malcolm here?" She asked.

Gina's head shook to the negative without turning from the TV. "Waddn't nobody here. . . . you was dreamin'," Gina said.

"Yo, mama call or aunt Tang?

Again her head shook.

"Damn, I guess they got me up here playing mama fa real. I got thangs to do. I can't be watching y'all all day."

"You don't have to watch us. We can stay with Mrs. Newbury."

"Nah, I don't want you down there wearing out cha welcome."

Apple smiled while gulping down her mouth full of cereal. "No. Mrs Newbury said she wanted to raise us if our mama ever got tired. We could stay there."

"Oh, really? That ol' bitty trying to be slick. She's gon' take you from ya mama."

"Yeah," Gina said nodding. "She ain't slick. But she does cook some really good food."

"I'd run away if she took me," Apple chimed in.

"I'd go away with Marquis's daddy," Gina said. "He wouldn't hurt me like Curtis did to Cammie. He would protect us because he's big and strong."

"Right," Sinclair chuckled. "Ain't nobody going nowhere

with Marquis's daddy. Matter of fact, I don't even want you talking to him if you see him around. He's trouble. I can tell."

About that time her cell phone rang. It was Malcolm. "Hey," he greeted.

"Why you leave?"

"When?"

"You were here last night weren't you?"

"You high?"

"Nah. I took my pills and you came to the door . . ."

"You high as fuck. Yeah I came and then I left after I got what I wanted."

"You lyin'," Sinclair balked.

"Yeah, I did. I got the choochie and split. You was all sleep and shit so I just took it. Ask anybody."

"You lyin', nigga!" Sinclair yelled, looking at the girls and then down at herself. She seemed intact but who knew. She didn't know how she was supposed to feel after sex. She hadn't ever had it.

"Yeah, you was all relaxed. It was real good," he said, snickering a little.

"You lyin', nigga. I knew you wasn't here. You lyin'," Sinclair said now, realizing that she had indeed been hallucinating.

"Anyway, what you doing right now. I wanna see you."

"I'm not your girl."

"Well, Mercedes sure ain't. She got an infection in her titty. They may have to take some of it off. The black part the . . ."

"Her areola? They may have to take it off! Shit!" Sinclair groaned at the thought of that kind of surgery.

"She's mad as hell too. Gonna kill your ass when she gets out of the hospital."

"No, she ain't. I'ma rip her other saggy ass titty off if she come fuckin' with me," Sinclair boasted.

Malcolm laughed. "Oh, you all tough now, huh? You a dirty

fighter Sinclair. Ain't nobody gonna mess with your ass no mo'," Malcolm told her.

"Good. And I like it like that," she admitted. It was true. She'd rather have that reputation than that of being an easy mark.

"Hey, I seent your sister back at the hospital this morning"

"What was you doing there? Seeing Mercedes?"

"Yes and no. I went back to get my mama's car. Yo sista was there with your niece again. I think she woke up or something last night"

"Fa real! Oh, wow, I wondered why she didn't come home."

"Dunno, but when I left I didn't see her. Maybe she's on her way."

"So what's what with Cammie? When she getting out?"

"I don't know. I think she just woke up. I heard her praising the Lord and shit. She was sounding like one of them old church ladies."

"Oh my God, you're kidding me."

"Nope, she was real thankful. You should be too."

"Well, if it's true, I am." Just then the pain in Sinclair's arm caused her to seethe through her teeth. "Hey, you know where I can get some vicodin."

"From the pharmacy."

"Stop playin' you know I don't have no money. Been a minute since I worked for Finest. What's up with that anyway?"

"We ain't in the movie business no more. Bigga thangs baby. But I'll see what I can do on the street for some pain meds, okay. You coming by later?"

"Why I gotta come by there? Besides ain't nobody here with the girls."

"You can leave us with Mrs. Newbury," Gina said again being nosy.

Sinclair thought about the pain in her arm. "Okay. Yeah,

I'll be there." She glanced at the clock. "Let me scrounge up some change. I didn't get no bus pass this month. Damn, the first ain't getting here soon enough."

"It's getting here right on time baby. You just need a job that's all."

"I haven't had time to even look and now with my arm all messed up, I can't. Damn, school about ta start in a coupla weeks too. I'm all messed up. I ain't even registered."

"Come stay over for the weekend. We'll go to the school Monday and get you registered.

"Why you trying to get me over there so bad?" Sinclair asked sounding playful, feeling playful.

"My mama is on a three. You know, three on, three off. She won't be home until Monday night. We can . . . um. . . . spend some time together. I need to unwind."

"You so ghetto. Unwinding all up in yo mama's house," Sinclair chuckled. She was game though. She had been burning for Malcolm ever since the day in the shower. She wanted to again feel the way he had made her feel. She wanted him to touch her again like he did that day. He had his fingers all up inside her. He was touching her breasts and sucking on them. *Man that felt good.* Yeah, she wanted it. "So you wanna do it in yo mama's bed?" she whispered, looking at the back of Gina's head, daring it to turn around.

"We can do it in a tree if you want baby. I just wanna do it wit' you."

"You so nasty," Sinclair whispered. She giggled then.

"You sound so sexy. Damn. Yeah Sin, you get some change and get your ass over here before I bust wide open."

"Damn, is it like that?"

"And more. It's gonna be the best you ever felt. I'ma tell you something about a man who needs to nut. . . ."

"What?"

"His dick be hard as stone and when he puts it in a woman she feels like she died and went to heaven."

Hanging up the phone Sinclair quickly clicked off the TV ignoring the girl's moans and protests. "Come on. Y'all going to Mrs. Newbury's place."

"She might be asleep."

"She's old. She ain't asleep. She been up since fo' this morning."

Chapter 16

Unique had been floating on a cloud all night and into the morning. After the doctor confirmed that Cammie was coming out of the coma, she did the jig and headed toward the bus. She was going to go tell the pastor and then go home to change, gather up Gina and Apple and come back to the hospital. When she landed in the Palemos on the early morning bus, she walked past what was once her mother's house. Pausing there she stared at the new foundation. "Yeah, mama, it's time for a change. A change in me and change in my life," she told the air, hoping her mother–wherever she was–could hear. "I'm a new person." Passing there she headed toward the old church.

That was when she saw him; Marquis Sr. He was outside the Digg's old place having a cigarette. After Mrs. Diggs died years ago, her kids sold the place. Unique hadn't paid attention to who bought it because she was too young to care, but now it all came together. Apparently Marquis' family lived there. That was why she passed him every morning on her way to school. That was why he was sitting there in the car. He was related to the tenants of the house. He lived there. If only she had known that then. Maybe she would have told her brother Larry and he'd beat the hell out of him for what he'd done. But then again, Larry had gotten himself shot around that time, so maybe he was into too much mess to care about his baby sister. The more she thought about that time, the harder it was to piece it all together. Her mama was so mad about everything that she had convinced herself that she was mad too. But she wasn't. She'd never been mad at Marquis Sr., not really. At least not for the reasons everyone thought she should be.

She slowed her pace debating if she should call to him.

Her heart decided for her. "Marquis!" she called out.

He looked up from the stoop at her. The beautiful smile crossed his lips. "Hey girl," he said. She slowly approached him. "What you doing here on a fine Sunday morning?"

"I was on my way to the church for early service."

"They don't do no early service no more," he said. "They did a late one last night and then they don't do another one until the afternoon."

"Shoot. I needed to talk to the pastor. My baby girl, Cammie, woke up last night. She came out of her coma. Hallelujah."

"Praise God," he responded. "You in the church? I didn't know that."

"The Lord just came to me last night. I'm saved. I think."

"You think? You 'posed ta know," Marquis Sr. chuckled, before smashing out his cigarette.

"I . . . I do know. I believe there is a God," she stammered. "Anyway, I know I've changed. I prayed last night with all my heart. I prayed and my baby girl woke up. I know it was God."

"Well praise the Lord then," he said, sounding as if he fully grasped what she was saying. Unique had to wonder if he knew what had happened to Cammie.

"You know Jesus?" she asked.

"He been in my heart for a while now. I wouldn't have survived the joint without him. Yeah, I know," he said pointing down at the smashed cigarette butt. "I still got some vices. But that's nothing compared to how far I've come," he admitted.

Unique nodded her head thinking of the possible sins he'd committed on the streets so many years ago. "You know, it's crazy you coming back at this time. I wonder . . ." she paused and shook her head.

"What?"

"I wonder if you're part of my miracle. I mean, I loved my baby Marquis and now here you are—his father—showing up. And now Cammie is waking up. I just feel like something has happened. I'm starting to feel like . . . like a miracle is happening." Unique again shook her head. She was trying to shake the ugly thoughts of that day her mother beat her for falling in love with this man. She tried to shake loose all the thoughts she'd been forced to accept about their encounter. She'd prayed for Marquis's return and she had to believe that this man was part of it.

"Nah, I ain't never been part of nothing like that."

Unique stepped forward slightly, closing the distance between them. It was the second time she wanted to be close to him, to see if she still felt anything.

As a girl she would feel so many things when passing him. She felt excitement, danger and a little magic something. "People change Marquis. I mean who you were then is different than who you are now."

He smiled at her looking her up and down. Then his face took on a serious expression. "I know you didn't change. I mean you have grown up, you know. I've thought about everything and I know I was wrong for what I did to you. I mean, I'm not a fool. That was statutory rape. I know that now. I was wrong for what I did. I knew you was young. I mean, I didn't know you was that young, but I knew you was too young for me to have you like that."

Unique squirmed nervously. She had always wondered

how she would feel at this moment. How she would feel facing the man who had changed her life. How would she feel seeing, again, the man who took her virginity, the man who impregnated her at thirteen? She thought she would hate him for changing her life so badly. He changed everything between her mother and her, her friends and her. Plus he forced her into motherhood before she was ready. He was the reason for all the bad that came from loving a man. She had loved him and only bad had come from it. But suddenly now, feeling God's forgiveness toward her in her heart, she could feel nothing but forgiveness toward Marquis Sr.

"I'm sorry," he said unexpectedly.

"It's okay Marquis. I mean, that was a long time ago and well, without you I would not have had my son."

"But he's gone now . . ."

"The pastor said I'd get him back again," she said, remembering suddenly the other promise from the pastor.

"And how in the hell is that gonna happen? I mean, he's gone!" Marquis said, showing that he too felt some pain. Unique was surprised at his growing emotions.

"Anything is possible if you believe," Unique said reaching out her hands. Marquis looked at them.

"Girl, what you talking about?"

"Take my hands Marquis," she said. He hesitated longer but then obeyed. "Bow ya head."

"What?" he said, as he looked around.

"Come on now. We gon' pray."

He hesitated but then bowed his head. "Okay . . ."

"Lord, give me and Marquis back our son. We believe you can do it. We believe," she said. "In your name all things are possible."

"Amen," Marquis said then.

They both opened their eyes and locked them on each other.

"See. It's just that simple," she smiled.

He grinned broadly. "I hope so."

After a moment or two just standing there silently holding hands, he pulled away first. "So what you do? I mean, you gotta man? You work? What? I mean, I don't even really know you but I feel like we been knowing each other for years."

"Oh, I know. I feel the same way. No," she said then. "I don't have a man."

Before Marquis was murdered, she had begun dating a social worker who was helping her cope with Marquis Jr's anger issues. She had hoped it was going to go somewhere but slowly they had drifted apart over the last few weeks. She hadn't called him and he hadn't called her. She had wanted to call him and see where he was emotionally, but with Cammie in the hospital, she didn't have time. Maybe he really had only wanted to be friends with her for Marquis Jr's sake anyway.

"Fine woman like you ain't got no man?" he asked.

"How long you been out?" she asked, changing the subject.

"I been out a month. I heard I had a son but then when I came looking for you, your house was gone and. . . ."

"Yeah, some nigga blew it up cuz my brother owed some money. . . ."

"I heard about that too. Nigga that blew it up is dead though, so it should be cool fa y'all to move back in when the house get's finished, right?"

"He's dead?" Unique asked. It was the first she'd heard of it. Marquis nodded, patting his pockets as if contemplating another cigarette.

"Nah, we ain't moving back in. Found out it wasn't even my mama's house. It belongs to some white man."

"Damn."

"So my sisters have to stay with me."

"How long Deb got?"

"You know my brother Deb?"

"I hear thangs . . ." Marquis shrugged, sliding the cigarette, unlit, between his lips.

"Then you should know how long he got then," she said before laughing. Just then she felt and heard her stomach rumble. It was loud.

"Damn, girl, when you ate last?"

"Oh, Lord, I don't know when. That hospital food is expensive as hell. It's too late in the month for me to have any money. You know," she said sounding suddenly embarrassed over her financial situation.

"Well I got a few dollars. Let's go to Denny's and eat and talk."

"You serious?"

"Yeah. I can swing a slam jam breakfast." He was teasing now and made her giggle.

"Where's your fancy car?" she asked, taking him back in time to the day they met. He was driving a low riding Impala. She got in and he took her for a ride, took her innocence and then dropped her off at school. Unique tried to block out that part for she knew she had begged for his attention. Every morning she would walk by and stare, smile and in her own innocent way . . . flirt. She asked for the attention of that older boy. She wanted that boy that was too old to be messing with her. She was only thirteen. That was ten years ago.

"How old are you anyway?" she asked.

"I'm thirty," he said.

"How old do you think I am?" she asked.

He chuckled, sounding embarrassed by the question. "You all filled out now. I don't know."

"It don't matter," she said then. "I said I forgave you and I do. Let's let the past go." She reached out her hand for him to take it. He looked at it for a moment before lighting his cigarette and taking a long drag from it. Looking around first, he then took her hand.

They walked toward the Denny's. "I do want you to do me one favor though," Unique began the request.

"Okay . . ."

"I want you to go to church with me tonight," she said. He stopped dead in his tracks. "Please," she added.

He smiled at her then. It was obvious he was attracted to her. Unique was dark skinned but many people said she looked good. She didn't feel she was as pretty as Tanqueray or Sinclair though. Tanqueray was tall and slender with long thick hair. Sinclair had green eyes. But Unique was thick with big round brown eyes, healthy hips and legs. She had full lips and a head full of kinky hair that took a super perm to whip into shape. Her skin was smooth and pretty though. Yeah, she looked okay, now that she thought about it.

"Okay, baby, I'll go," he said. "I owe that much. Besides I feel a sort of connection with you right now. It's like . . ." he took a long drag from his cigarette. He almost looked as if he would break into an R&B jam. ". . . somethin' I ain't never felt before."

"Really? I feel the same way."

He now draped his heavy arm over her shoulder as they strolled like high school kids going steady.

Chapter 17

Sinclair stepped off the bus. Malcolm was waiting. He was dressed in low riding jeans, a white wife beater and a shirt that looked like he was part of a 1960's bowling league. All the guys in the Palemos (the P) were starting to dress like that. Malcolm was always quick to join a fad. He wanted so badly to be in a clique. Sinclair sometimes wondered if he had made the leap. He was looking very different as the summer progressed. He no longer looked like the 'little' boy friend she'd had her whole life. Now Malcolm was starting to look like a man, a thug. He was rugged and even developed a swagger. He was coming into his own.

Sure he was having sex and all that but who knew how long he'd been doing that. Besides, it wasn't as if she cared anything about sex. Well, that wasn't true, not really. Suddenly this summer, it was all she thought about. Maybe it was Marquis's death that brought these feelings to the fore. Maybe it was that loss that had brought about the need to be held, felt and loved. She didn't cry much at the funeral. Now she felt real pent up so maybe that was it . . . or part of it . . . who knew. She just wanted to get laid; that was all she knew, and she wanted Malcolm to be the one to do it. Sure, at first she had gone after Finest. He looked good . . . damn good. He had come on to her a few times, even kissed her with tongue and all, but he turned out to be fuckin' Tanqueray. And just like panties, even between sisters, dick was something ya just didn't share.

Malcolm took her by the hand. It was nice being claimed that way. She enjoyed it. Now that everyone had seen her kick Mercedes ass it was nice to be enjoying the spoils of war. Walking down the sidewalk, she passed the lot where her mother's house was. There was only a slab of empty concrete. "I wonder what they gonna put there," she wondered out loud.

"They haven't worked on it in a long time. Maybe dude ran outta money," Malcolm said, stopping with her to look through the fence that the construction crew had put up around it to keep vandals out. It hadn't helped. Everybody could see the bright red graffiti on the foundation, the markings of the P.

"I miss my mama's house," Sinclair said finally.

Malcolm squeezed her hand tighter. "I know you do."

They reached his mother's house. As soon as they walked in, the scent of beans cooking and warm bread fresh out of the oven hit her nose. She grew wet and ready for all the comforts of home, including Malcolm's soft bed.

"Wanna eat?" Malcolm asked.

She shook her head knowing full well she wanted some of his mother's beans. She was a hell of a cook. *She must have left it for him to eat off of over the days she would be gone and he was warming it up,* she reasoned.

Malcolm smiled pulling her into an embrace. "Or you wanna . . ." he grinned, kissing her quickly before squeezing her butt.

She was getting turned on fast. They sat on the sofa. Malcolm's hands moved quickly, rubbing her thighs and pulling on her titties. Finally exposing one, he sucked on it until it hurt. She wasn't thinking about the pain in her arm anymore. His tongue was down her throat. She could barely breathe. He was kissing her neck, sucking on it, biting. She was going to have a monkey bite mark for sure, but that was a good thing. He even bit her on the tender part of her breasts. He was marking her all up. *This was great,* she thought. *Let them bitches know.*

Unzipping his pants he put her hand down the front of them. His penis was rock hard just as he had said. She felt on it a minute, running her hand along the long shaft, the funny shape of the head. It grew moist. She looked at him, his eyes had been closed, but they opened, meeting hers. Her stomach tightened. His hands wandered up her skirt reaching the top of her panties as he whispered her name in her ear. She could only purr, for her words could not come out of her mouth. Just then, her wetness released, just like her period coming down. *Wait a minute,* she thought.

She pushed out of his embrace, jumped up off the sofa and she rushed to the bathroom.

"Damnit!" she yelped.

"What?" he called from outside the door. He had rushed to follow her.

Sinclair stared at the blood soaked panties. "Shit!" she yelped again. "I just got my period."

"Really?"

Sinclair began rummaging through his mother's cabinets. She wasn't that old, so maybe she still had her monthly. Or maybe she just had the old lady dribbles, either way, something should be in the bathroom, she figured. Finally she found a dusty pad. It looked about a hundred years old, but no matter. She ripped it from the packaging and put it on. Thank goodness she had worn a skirt.

"You coming out?" he called. His tone was different, no longer sexy. He sounded like . . . well . . . like Malcolm.

"Yeah," she said, pouting. Slowly she opened the door and came out. He playfully pushed the side of her head.

"You got just a little too excited," he laughed.

"Whatever, Malcolm. What would you know?"

"I know we gotta wait until you get off the rag. I'm not into all that ketchup on my hotdog . . ."

"Ewww you nasty as hell," she laughed.

"You hungry now?"

"You know I'm hungry. I'm always hungry," she said, all but dragging herself into the kitchen. He turned her to him.

"I love you, Sinclair."

"I know," she pouted.

He kissed her long and deep. "No. I love you as in . . . you ain't just ass to me. I love you."

She stared at him. "Tell me I'm your girl," she whispered.

"You mah girl," he said, smiling broadly at her.

"No other bitches got this," she said, grabbing hold of his rear.

He burst out laughing. "Girl you ain't even got this—yet."

Sinclair wasn't sure what she had taken, but Malcolm had found it in his mother's cabinet. It was for pain. At least that's what the bottle said. So she took the prescribed dosage, but her head was spinning. She wasn't nauseous but didn't dare try to put anything else in her stomach.

They'd been watching a movie, kissing and hugging all day, but now she was feeling kind of messed up. "I gotta go to bed," she said to Malcolm attempting to stand. Everything was spinning now, but at least her arm wasn't hurting, come to think about it, she had no menstrual cramps either. "This works," she said before giggling at the funny thought.

"Sinclair, let me help you," Malcolm said, setting down the popcorn and standing to help her to the room.

"Whatever baby doll," she joked.

Headed to his bedroom she miscalculated the doorway and wham, ran smack dab into it. "Damn," she said, before breaking into uncontrollable giggles again. "That's gonna be a black eye fa sho," she admitted.

"Wow, are you all right?" Malcolm asked looking shocked that she wasn't unconscious. His expression made Sinclair laugh even harder.

Finally she made it to the bed and fell onto it. "Yeah now we're talking," she said, "Man! I'm feeling gooooooood," she said, before passing out.

Chapter 18

"So you know where my bitch is?"

"Yeah. She's right here. She's with some no good nigga named Finest. What the hell kinda name is that?"

"I don't give a damn about his name or his mama that gave it to him. He's got my trick and I want her back. That bitch done cost me a whole lotta money."

"Yeah, I can only imagine because Mr. S. is paying her directly. So looks like you got cut smooth out."

"And you and I both know that ain't right, 'cuz you getting cut out too . . . cousin."

"Yeah, I got your cousin. I'm only your cousin when you want something. That is totally clear to me. Look Omar, I told you from the start that I really didn't want to get involved in your business, but since you want Tanqueray with you and I sure as hell don't want her here with Mr. S., I called, and that's the only reason."

"Whatever. I'm not concerned with your little bougee reasons for turning coat on your boss. Blood is blood and I believe that's why you called. So you know where the bitch is staying?"

"Nah, she just calls and Mr. S. sends me to get her. She's usually at some hotel or on a street corner where every good whore should be. But she's here now with that thug nigga Finest. They've been here all night like it's a damned hotel. I'm sick of them. I'm sick of them both."

"Well, you call me when they leave."

"Works for me, 'cuz I'm about tired of her stank ass fa sho. Layin' up here like she some damn queen or something. She ain't queen of nothing but ho–dom . . ."

"Oh, you got attitude now. What she do to you? She suck yo dick wrong. I know you done got at her, right?"

"She doesn't have anything I want."

"Except your boss," Omar laughed. "You jealous?"

"Omar, do you want the bitch or not? I can call you when I get them in the car. Hell, I can bring them both too you if you'd rather me do that. I'm trying to help yo ass out."

"What about that nigga she wit'? He bad?"

"He thank he bad. He ain't nothing but a thug. I bet if I called the police they'd put him away for life. Don't worry about him. I've seen his type my whole life. He ain't nothing but a wannabe bad."

"Do it then," Omar said. "Bring them both to me and I'll take care of both of 'em."

Cecil didn't feel a thing when he hung up the phone. Well, that wasn't true. He felt cold and evil inside. He felt hostile toward Mr. Sinclair and everyone else in that house that now curried favor for the whore and the Mandingo up in the guest suite fucking for the master's sick pleasure. He had to wonder how much they got for that performance. He'd overheard Cory talking about her little act last night. The one he caught on film. He was comparing it to one of the best porn films he'd seen in a long time.

"Everybody in this damn place is a pervert," Cecil huffed just above a mumble. He was feeling self-righteous now and above reproach. He had half a mind to quit after this. Yeah, he'd let Omar have his bitch back, and then tell Mr. Sinclair to kiss his ass.

Just then he looked around the garage at the nice cars: the

Bentley, Rolls Royce, Mercedes, and Jaguar. He rethought his last decision. "Or maybe I'll have Mr. Sinclair give me something while he's in his grieving state. Yeah. He'll be grieving the loss of his ho and he'll be ready to give me something nice so he can feel better about things. That is how he is," he deduced thinking about how often Mr. Sinclair overcame his depression by throwing parties and giving large presents to the staff.

Chapter 19

Looking out the large window at the morning, Tanqueray stretched in the big bed before glancing over at Finest who was staring at her. "What you looking at?"

"I can't believe I'm up here with you, up in this white man's house in this big-ass bed. What's gonna happen now? We his hoes or something? We supposed to fuck on demand for this cat or what?"

"You so crazy. I told you last night. Mr. Sinclair is really nice. He's got some issues and shit but nothing bad. I mean, nothing worse than my ex . . ." Tanqueray rolled her eyes at the thought of Omar and his freaky ass. "He ain't done nothing to me but treat me well. Hell, five-G's for fucking . . . now you know that ain't bad."

Finest chuckled, "Well you ain't never lied there but . . . still. It's kinda freaky."

Tanqueray turned over and got comfy on her side facing him. "Not as freaky as the way you was checking him out when he was beat'n his meat. You was act'n like it was turning you the fuck on."

"No it wasn't," Finest said almost blushing. It was as if he would not allow his face to give in to his feelings. Under the blankets Tanqueray grabbed at his limp member. He squirmed slightly.

"Yes, you were," she tugged on it. "You were like . . . damn he pulling on the meat kinda tough there, it's like . . . sexy as hell. Oh, daddy, beat that meat," she teased.

He slapped her hand away and rolled on top of her easing himself between her thighs. He entered her slowly. He moved inside her as if they were a comfortable married couple enjoying a good morning hello. She purred and wriggled to a comfortable stroke. "You so pretty," he whispered.

"You supposed to be thug. You up here getting all bitch on me," she teased, stroking his back allowing her legs to lay open wide on the bed.

"Oh, I'll get thug on your ass." He chuckled. "Sometimes . . ." he paused.

"What?" she asked, taking hold of his hips and grinding him into her.

He closed his eyes enjoying the feeling.

She wrapped her long legs around his back before arching against him as hard as she could without increasing the stroke. He sighed and smiled. It was good, she could tell.

"Don't fuck him . . . okay?" he stammered out his request. "Don't fuck nobody else but me, okay? You can dance on his lap, or suck on his dick or let him eat your pussy . . ."

"Finest . . ." she giggled.

"Just don't let him fuck you like this. Okay? Let this be mine, okay?"

She stared at him for a moment. "You love me don't you?"

"I told you that."

"Hmm . . ." she pondered for a moment before suddenly his thrust speed increased. He was ready to cum. She joined him in the mission. They both exploded in the good feeling of the early morning climax. Pulling from her, he laid back on his side of the bed.

"I need something," he admitted. "You?"

"I'm good, I think. I don't know what's up, though," she admitted. "Maybe it's because we been in the bed a long time without anybody coming in to peek, but I don't want nobody catching us getting crunk," she giggled. "Seriously though, I don't feel like I need anything. Not even a cigarette. It's weird."

"You been just getting high off all this good fuckin'. That's your problem."

She climbed on top of him and kissed him. They hadn't kissed in a minute. Really kissed, like boyfriend and girlfriend, kissing with tongue and all that. He held her head while enjoying her mouth. Maybe it was because they had gone to bed sober after enjoying a good meal and a warm Jacuzzi bath that even their morning breath wasn't rank. She could wake up like this every morning. Seriously.

Just then Cory entered the room. Finest pushed her off and pulled up the covers. He was startled more than anything. Tanqueray had gotten used to all the staff seeing her naked . . . well except for Cecil. He'd not seen her naked yet and she wasn't looking forward to his impression of her riding across his face. He'd judge her. She knew that. He'd judge her badly too.

"Mr. Sinclair would love for the two of you to join him for breakfast before you . . . head out," he said as if directly quoting Dustin Sinclair. Even his hand went out as if copying Dustin Sinclair's mannerism.

Tanqueray smiled. "That sounds lovely Cory. Tell him we would very much enjoy that. We're just gonna jump in the shower and then be right down," she said sounding bourgeois.

Finest chuckled under his breath.

"Very good," Cory said, nodding, and then leaving the room. Finest sighed heavily. "This place is weird as fuck."

"You just don't know how rich folks live," she said, kissing him again. Within the moment he was back on her enjoying another quickie before they showered and headed down the staircase to join Mr. Sinclair in the formal dining room.

Cecil said very little as they drove back to the P. He was hatin'. That was all Tanqueray could figure. Being there with Finest made it all clear to her now. Cecil wanted her and now that he saw her with her man, he was hatin'. That was what she deduced in her mind.

She sat all up on Finest too. She was proud that he was her man. He was fine as hell and although she wasn't sure exactly how he made his money, it wasn't as if he was just some po thug. He was a hood figga, with something to show for his hustle. Just like Cecil. Although Finest wasn't driving Mr. Daisy all around town, he worked hard every day too, and best of all, he had her.

"Hey, my man, you smoke?" Finest asked, moving his fingers to his mouth imitating the way he hit his joints. Cecil's eyes locked on hers in the review mirror, but he said nothing. He didn't even shake his head or nod it.

"Yeah ol' Cecil smoke. He ghetto. Tell Finest how you tried to beat my ass the day we met," Tanqueray laughed.

She was feeling good and feeling smart-alecky and loud. Mr. Sinclair had told Cecil to take them whereever they wanted to go so with money burning a hole in their pockets, they made a quick run to a liquor store for a pint of Hennessey—which they were now drinking—and a quick stop in Walnut Creek to score a little blow. Finest knew all the good spots. He was from the Bay Area and knew every nook and crook, especially when it came to getting crunk. Cecil had looked beyond disgusted and said nothing to her while they waited in the car for Finest to take care of his business. Now Finest wanted to pick up some weed. Tanqueray could tell he was going to play this chauffer thing to the hilt.

"So you put your hands on my woman, nigga?" Finest asked him. Finest was being playful. He was happy and well fed and laid. He'd done some new freaky shit that he actually enjoyed. It had been a good day. Before they left, it was clear that Mr. Sinclair was planning another 'party' real soon and Finest was down for it.

Tanqueray was glad. She liked Mr. S. (her new pet name for Dustin Sinclair). Being at his place felt like life outside the ghetto was a reality she could reach for. Maybe Finest felt it too. Sipping champagne in those flute glasses while enjoying those omelets and fancy potatoes—shit yeah—her baby sister Sinclair wasn't the only one who dreamed outside of the ghetto. Baby sister Sinclair had been raised to live outside the ghetto, in Tanqueray's opinion. *White school in the East Bay, always getting rides every-damn-where,* Tanqueray thought now. Maybe because she had a white daddy, their mother felt she could pass her off for white and blend her in with them. Maybe she figured that Sinclair was entitled to a better life. No matter. Either way, in Tanqueray's mind, Sinclair's whole life was built around her getting out of the ghetto. But now things had changed. If Sinclair had those plans, she needed to get over them because *she waddn't gwon nowhere . . .*

"But maybe if I do better with my life I can make a way for her . . . ya know," Tanqueray had rambled on, during breakfast, talking as if she felt good about Sinclair's life. She didn't. She had never felt good about her mother fooling that girl into thinking she had hopes outside of the P.

"Tell me about your little sister," Mr. S. asked.

"Sin?" Finest interjected. Tanqueray gave him the evil eye. He raised his hands in surrender.

"What?" Mr. Sinclair asked noticing the tension.

"Nothing. He just tried to make out with her before. But he

didn't know she was my sister. That's over now . . ." she said nudging him playfully, but with intent.

He raised his hands in surrender again. "She's cute, what can I say?" Finest responded. Mr. S smiled.

They were acting so bougee right then and Tanqueray loved it. Even without the fancy clothes she felt beautiful, rich and above it all but Mr. Sinclair wasn't about to let her leave without something nice. He had all kinds of clothes that fit her and she'd put on something very sporty this morning. She wore a nice baby blue jogging suit and a pair of white heel-out Adidas.

"Her name is Sinclair of all things," Tanqueray explained.

"I find that so interesting," Mr. S. responded.

"I have another sister named Unique, a brother named Debonair and one brother that passed away. His name was Larry."

"And your mother," he asked, sounding seriously interested. He'd even stopped eating to listen to her.

Tanqueray wasn't about to stop eating the good food to talk. She cut at the large slab of ham like it was a T-bone steak.

"Her name was Javina. She was . . ." Tanqueray closed her eyes momentarily enjoying the flavor of the meat as well as the memory of her mother. "She was sooo beautiful. Gosh! She was so wonderful."

"Yes, I'm sure she was," Mr. Sinclair agreed, returning to his meal.

Bringing her mind back to the present, she heard Finest tearing into Cecil.

"You need to quit frontin' mah man. Looks like you gonna be seeing me a lot more often 'cuz your old freaky boss likes the way I lay the pipe with my girl here. It looks like I'm the star of his next little porn movie," Finest said, sucking his teeth before taking another swig from the bottle of Hen. He handed it off to Tanqueray but she was thinking about the pleasant morning and didn't want things to get blurry in her mind.

"He's not a freak, and you will not be back to the house," Cecil finally said.

"Pardon me?" Finest asked, in a tone that was more a statement than a question. Tanqueray too was drawn into the conversation now.

"If anything you two are the freaks, fucking for money and shit. God! You make me sick!" Cecil exploded, turning the corner and pulling over. "Get out."

"Now Cecil, don't lose your job over this," Tanqueray said, growing a little nervous at his impulsive act.

"I'm not losing shit, but my patience. Get the hell outta this car," he said pushing the button that unlocked the door.

Finest didn't move.

Cecil then got out from behind the wheel and yanked open the back door.

That's when Tanqueray noticed he was holding a little .22 that dropped from his sleeve. She grabbed Finest's arm and brought it to his attention.

"I've worked for Mr. Sinclair for ten years. You've only been ho'n for him for a couple of months. And you . . ." he looked at Finest. "You're just a no good black-ass thug from da hood. Y'all both need to just go back to the dirt you came from and leave that man alone."

"I'm not a whore!" Tanqueray yelled leaning into Cecil, but Finest held her back. His face was intense, almost scary. Tanqueray knew that couldn't be good. Finest didn't back down from anything so for him to back down now was worse for Cecil than anybody. That she knew. Finest holding her back just meant that he didn't want her in the way of what could come next.

"Don't do nothing Tang. This nigga wants me to hit him so he can call the police on me. I know how Oreo's work."

"What you know about Oreos? You probably got a white mama," Cecil dug.

"Oh, you color struck, Negro? You got a problem with a light skinned brotha?" Finest said, taunting him back.

Cecil just smacked his lips and with the gun instructed them to get out of the car and move away from it. "Ain't nuthin' about you got me struck, mah man," Cecil said with a sneer. He then climbed back in the car and drove off.

They were a long way from home.

"Shit!" Finest smacked, looking around.

Tanqueray pulled out her cell phone. "I'ma call Mr. Sinclair."

"No, don't. Cecil is already doing that and your call is only gonna make it worse. Trust me."

"But Dustin will believe me."

"You stupid Tang. Dustin is a John. He's an old freaky-ass John who hired a whore—you. And that nigga Cecil was his number one bitch until you came along. He's jealous and wants you gone. I got played for a few grand, believing that he was some kinda . . ." Finest buckled his lip in anger, or extreme disappointment, Tanqueray wasn't sure which. ". . . never mind," he spat. "I don't know what I believed, but it's over now. I got my money and today is over."

"No, it's not over," Tanqueray cried. She was feeling emotional. This wonderful day had gone south real fast and it was Cecil's fault. How could one man take away all her hopes and dreams this way?

Finest pulled out his cell phone and called one of his pawndas named Floyd.

"Hey, yeah, bring my ride. Oh, and y'all know a punk-ass-bitch-nigga named Cecil . . . umhmm. Yeah drives for some old white fuck name Sinclair . . . umhmm."

Tanqueray was upset. She knew what this call meant. Trouble. Trouble for Cecil. Trouble for Mr. Sinclair, and mostly, trouble for her. Finest was angry and going to get revenge on everybody. He was calling in the troops. This was bad.

Tanqueray knew what kind of man Finest was. He was street. She thought she knew what kind of man Cecil was too.

If Finest went up against Cecil maybe he would get his justice for this, but if he went up against Mr. Sinclair it was going to be nothing but bad.

"Yeah, well, Floyd is on his way," Finest said after ending his call. Tanqueray was beside herself.

"So," Finest smacked his lips. "You been ho'n for this dude for a while, huh?"

"What?" Tanqueray asked, feeling confused and sounding the same.

"You playing me too? So that night when you showed up at the hospital all dressed up, you had been with him, huh?"

"You know this!" she said rolling her eyes and folding her arms across her chest. "Look we waddn't even kicking it back then. Don't start!" Tanqueray defended, right before Finest swung on her slapping her hard across the face. He had been humiliated and now she was gonna pay for it. Or so he thought. She slapped him back. "I know you didn't just hit me."

"Bitch!" he yelled pushing her down on the ground. His fist came at her, but stopped just short of making contact.

"I'll kill you nigga if you touch me! Don't nobody touch me!" She screamed. Just then the police rolled up. This was a white neighborhood after all. Besides, surely Cecil had made a call on his way out of the area. Had they started walking

things may have been all right, but no, they had stood around
to argue for a minute—a minute too long. Cecil had counted
on that for sure.

"What's going on here?" the officer asked grabbing Finest
and yanking his hands behind his back. They began to pat
him down. Thank goodness the blow was long gone up his
nose. "Ahh look what we got. A little party grass, huh?" the
white officer said, confiscating the weed. Finest always carried
that much on him. That was not enough to even call a stash
and that's why he had wanted Cecil to take him to get some
more.

Finest said nothing.

"Ma'am, are you alright?" he asked Tanqueray.

Finest looked at her, his lip buckled without opening, however, his eyes threatened her.

"No," she said allowing her anger to come through. "He hit
me," she said, knowing what would happen next.

Sure enough Finest jerked at the officer holding him.
The cuffs went on in one fluid motion as they slammed him
against the car.

"Tang stop this shit right now. Tell them it was just a lover's
quarrel. It was a domestic situation officer. That's my wife . . ."

"You have the right to remain silent," one of the officer's
began.

"Ma'am we can take him away right now. Just say the word."

"Tang!" he yelled.

"Shut the hell up," the officer said, reading him his Miranda
Rights.

Tanqueray sighed heavily. She hated this moment. Looking
around she pondered the worst that could happen to him.
"He's drunk," she said. "He just needs to sober up," she said,
not admitting to the fact that they were both pretty much
faded.

"Okay, buddy. Let's go sober up. You can thank your wife that she's not admitting to anything more."

"Bitch!" he yelled, fighting against the officer's restraint.

"You need a ride, ma'am?" the officer said, no doubt noticing the name brand on her outfit. It was DKNY. *That's nothing to sneeze at,* Tanqueray thought.

"No, I'ma call a friend," she said, pulling out her cell phone to call Mr. Sinclair.

"Don't call him!" screamed Finest, from inside the backseat. "Tanqueray trust me. Don't call him!"

"Shut up Mr . . ." the officer looked at Finest's ID pulled from his wallet, "Mr. Robinson," he read. That was actually the first time Tanqueray had heard Finest's last name.

The one officer not dealing with Finest gave Tanqueray the normal speech about pressing charges and getting a restraining order. While he spoke she noticed a few white faces peeking from behind curtains. She noticed the nice houses and fine trimmed lawns. She realized then how much they didn't fit in here. It wasn't as if no Blacks lived here, but no poor ones did, that was for sure. She realized then how much she wanted to belong here. She wanted to be 'behind' one of those curtains.

The officer waited now while she connected her call. "Hello Dustin. Can you come get me, there's been some trouble," she said.

"Most definitely my dear, Cecil isn't back yet, but I'll call him and send him right where you are, okay?"

"Yeah! Tell him, we're still where he dumped us," she said sounding cold and showing a little anger.

"Pardon?"

"Never mind. Can you come get me? Can you get someone else to come get me? I'll tell you why later," Tanqueray explained, hanging up her cell phone after giving her the location. "My friend is sending a car for me," she said to the officer listening nosily.

Finest shook his head in disgust. She could see him out of the corner of her eye.

The officer smiled then and patted her shoulder.

"That guy there is bad news okay. I'm sure he's got a rap sheet as long as my arm. You go with your friend and stay out of trouble. Okay?" the officer advised before he and his partner climbed back in the squad car and drove off with Finest in the backseat.

All Tanqueray could do was sit on the curb and cry.

The sun was high in the sky but it wasn't hot, not like it could be—not like it was in other places. But then it wasn't as if Tanqueray knew about other places. She'd not been anywhere. To be truthful this was as far in East Bay as she'd ever been. *It is pretty here*, she thought, looking around the area. Omar lives in a nice neighborhood not too far from here.

Soon Cecil would come—with his stank attitude. He was Dustin's only driver. Tanqueray knew that. Dustin would call him and he'd come get her. He'd pick her up obediently despite how much he hated her now. But he'd do what he was told. He wasn't totally crazy. Maybe she'd tell Mr. Sinclair what he'd done. . . . maybe not. Or worse, Floyd would show up first. She'd have to explain how she let Finest go to jail. "Ugh," she groaned, thinking about the repercussions of all that. *He'll be out tomorrow. It ain't no thang*, she decided.

Just then she saw a sight that stopped her heart. It wan't Cecil, or Floyd, but a familiar car slowly approaching, "Oh, shit," she exclaimed. It was Omar, her ex . . . or whatever he was. She jumped to her feet and started walking. Maybe he hadn't seen her. Maybe it was an accident that he was here—a coincidence.

But no, he started moving a little faster. She sped up her pace as well. She was dressed too damned cute to run. Sure she had on a jogging suit, but her shoes were not running shoes but 'cutesy' shoes. Normally Tanqueray was always ready for fight or flight. She'd let her guard down— with Finest she'd let her guard down and now things were going bad. *Where the hell was Cecil?* she asked herself, attempting to pick up the pace.

"Get in the car woman," Omar said, flashing his gold tooth at her. It was a new addition to his already jacked up smile.

She hadn't seen him in over two months, not since she'd broken into his condo and stolen money and clothing from him at gun point. *But he owed her that stuff. That was her stuff!*

"No, Omar! I got somebody coming for me. You besta drive on," Tanqueray explained, not stopping for a minute.

"You mean Cecil? My cuzin Cecil," he said.

Tanqueray froze. She knew instantly, she'd been played, and lost.

"Get in the car," he said, pointing a gun at her. He wasn't trying to hide his like Cecil was. He was just right out in the open with his shit.

How many times today would she be threatened at gun point; and they weren't even in the ghetto.

"No. I'm not gonna get in that car."

"Don't make me shoot you here in front of all these white folks," he threatened.

"You might have too."

He climbed out of the car, looking around nervously before jerking her arm. She struggled dropping her phone. He didn't wait for her to pick it up, but snatched the door open and pushed her inside just as she noticed Finest's Escalade coming their way.

It was Floyd but there was nothing he could do but wonder

why she was leaving with another man, and then wonder where Finest was. For sure those questions went through his mind because as they drove past him, he had those questions all over his face.

Chapter 20

Unique sang her heart out at the service. All the old songs came back to her. She clapped and felt the spirit filling her to the brim. She wondered every once in a while why her mother had never introduced her to such happiness.

Marquis Sr. had spent the entire day with her. They talked about so many things. They caught up and filled gaps. It was bittersweet. How she would have loved for Marquis Jr. to meet his father. How it may have helped him with his anger issues. Marquis Sr. had done many bad things but he had repented and was now rehabilitated. He was a new man. Unique could tell. How she wished he had come back just a month earlier. Perhaps overlooking the past was not healthy but then again, what did she know about being healthy. Okay, so she read some magazines like *Oprah* and stuff, but really, she never felt any of that advice was meant for her. She could only draw on her heart. Marquis Sr. had taken from her what was innocent at the core, but on the surface was no better than what he had given. They were even, the two of them. No matter what people or society said, they were equal in sin and forgiveness and now they shared a loss.

Marquis Sr. didn't sing but he seemed to enjoy listening to her. Unique had a beautiful voice—always did. Many said she sounded like Whitney Houston—*before Bobby*. She used to dream of a singing career, but then she had too many babies.

But that afternoon, she sang as if she had not a care in the world. Sinclair was home with the kids so surely all was well. For once she felt safe and secure. Cammie was still progressing nicely to a full recovery. She was going to let her sleep the rest of today and see her in the morning. She told the doctor to tell her she loved her, and she meant it.

"I thought about you a lot while I was locked down," Marquis Sr. said, as they walked toward the bus stop.

Unique smiled. "You did?"

"You so pretty," he said, touching her face softly.

Unique felt the heat rising up under her cheeks.

Suddenly he took in a chest full of air as if bucking up before asking her the question, "Hey, you think a woman like you would wanna spend some time with a man like me?" he asked.

Unique stopped walking. Their pace had landed them not far from where her mother's house once stood. She smiled at him. His once dark, menacing eyes had taken on a new softness during the day. "What you mean spend time?" she smiled.

"I'ma be honest. I haven't been with nobody since I got out. So basically you was the last woman I was with."

"You lyin'," Unique said. Her good sense told her it was a lie but her heart wanted to believe.

"Swear," he said, biting his bottom lip and touching his chest with two fingers as if he were a boy scout.

"We just went to church Marquis so don't be lyin'," she said, giggling flirtatiously. All day with a man felt good to Unique. She wanted to be loved. She needed it. In her heart she felt it was what she was on earth for. Without it she wanted to die. Maybe Marquis Sr. was the reason for her void. He had been the first man she really loved, after all. Maybe he was the reason she had been with so many bad men; she was trying to make them meet his standard—the one she hadn't even set.

She could almost hear her mother's voice belittling her for being pregnant by Marquis Sr. Her mother was so abusive. So many people felt Javina Nation was so wonderful, but not Unique. She hated her. There she said it, albeit in her mind, she'd admitted how she felt about her mother.

They held hands and walked back toward the house where Marquis Sr. was staying. It was his mama's house. Together they went inside. "Mama!" he called.

"I'm here Markey," she yelled back. Unique smiled at the name she called him. She too would use that name from now on.

"Come out. I want you to meet somebody," he called back.

The woman came to the living room. She looked Unique over but didn't smile. "Hello."

"This here is Unique Nation. She had my boy, the one that got killed."

The woman's face dropped. "My grandson. You was his mama, huh?"

"Yes, ma'am."

"We gon' do some talking in my room," Markey said then, pulling Unique past the woman without much more conversation.

The woman watched as Unique followed the big man through the hall to the back room where he stayed.

Unique wanted to talk to the woman more, but Marquis had other plans for them at the moment. Talking wasn't one of them.

"I wanted to visit with your mom some," she said, watching him as he closed the door. The room was small. They were small just like she remembered the rooms in her mother's old house to be. He had a small, neat bed. His clothes were all put up and there wasn't much on the dresser. She had heard about ex-cons and their fetish for neatness. She figured he was still going through some adjustments to being on the outside.

He began to undress.

Unique sat on his bed watching him. His body was taunt and muscular from the years of working out on the prison yard. He had many tattoos that covered his torso, neck, and arms.

"You loud?" he asked her. "'Cuz you can't be loud," he said after dropping his pants to the floor.

Unique tried to remember the size of his manhood. But all she could remember was the pain. He had raped her, but still she was here. *Is there something wrong with my brain*, she wondered. *Why am I telling myself it was something different than what it was? It was different. My mama said rape. I say it was love.*

He touched her and unconsciously she jumped. Too much thinking had made her nervous. "I thought you wanted to do this?" he asked.

"I . . . I do," she whispered. "I'm just scared, I guess. I mean . . ."

"It been a long time for you or something? I mean, with you being a church girl and all."

"No." She chuckled, realizing what he thought about her. Nobody had ever mistaken her for a church girl. "Nah, um . . . it ain't been that long," she confessed.

"Oh, and here I was thinking you was all innocent."

"I got fo' kids. Well, I mean . . ." she grew instantly sad," . . . three."

He squatted down to face her. "You gon' have to let Li'l Markey go," he said, touching her face. A tear ran down her cheek. He caught it with his finger. "You sho is pretty. I do remember that. I remember thinking when I used to see you on yo way ta school: Markey, she sho is pretty," he said, laying her back on the bed. She lay still while he unbuttoned her jeans and wriggled them from her. She pulled her top over her head and unhooked her bra. He touched her breast. "You held up good girl. Fa fo kids," he said, before licking her nipple and then sucking at her breast.

She could feel his erection forming against her thigh. Unique had been with many men over her life but for some reason being with Marquis— this return to where it all began—was just a little scary.

He moved up on her.

She could tell he was removing his shorts.

He pressed against her entrance.

Yes he was endowed. Now she remembered the pain as he tore against her innocence. Even now she bit her lip as he pushed his thirteen inches inside her. She wanted to cry out but didn't dare. She was frozen stiff as he rode her for what seemed longer than normal, twisting this way and that, as if trying to find a comfortable fit and stroke for his big dick.

She tried to feel good. She wanted to enjoy it. She wanted to love him.

"You too tight. Open ya legs more," he said. "Put your legs around my back," he requested.

She obeyed. Now with the deepened penetration it was nearly impossible to keep silent. It must have felt better to him, as he was getting a little rough.

Deep and fast was his stroke now. He was humming in his pleasure. She whimpered. He shushed her. She pushed at his chest until finally he held her arms up over her head. On and on it went with no end in sight. He would not cum no matter how much she begged him too.

"Relax," he finally said to her. She tried, but there was no comfort to be found in this act. Hot tears streamed down her face. Finally he went deep and slow, swaying his hips back and forth. She could feel his thrust nearly to her spine. Then suddenly, quick, quick, slow. Grunt. Grunt. A couple more humps and he was done.

He lay on top of her for a moment longer before pulling out. She felt wet as a stream down below. It was as if he'd cum a river.

"Maybe next time it will be better," he said. "Sometimes it's not that good on the first time," he said, pulling on his shorts. Unique lay there with the tears pouring from her eyes. She wasn't sure how she felt. Just then there was a knock at the door.

"Markey, y'all gonna eat something?"

"Yeah, mama, we gon' come out and eat," he called back. "Come on, girl, get up and get dressed."

Unique was sore and unable to move quickly, but she did the best she could. Still she had said nothing. She didn't know what to say.

The big black bear of a man smiled at her. "You sure are pretty," he said again.

Chapter 21

Sinclair thought about the girls for a moment as she lay next to Malcolm. Surely Unique had come home by now and picked them up. Frankly, at the moment, Sinclair didn't care if Unique was mad at her for leaving them with Mrs. Newbury or not. "They ain't my kids," she mumbled.

"Hmm?" Malcolm asked, opening his eyes slowly. It was way past noon but they had been lazy, which wasn't hard to be after smoking a little weed. Malcolm had told her that it would help with the pain of her cramps. She didn't believe him at first but after a Supercharge, she was convinced. Sitting on the bed, Malcolm put the blunt in his mouth backward and told Sinclair to put her mouth over it. He then exhaled, the Supercharge was potent and she was high as a kite within a few minutes. Turning the blunt around, he finished it off, sharing only a few more hits with her. Soon they were making out again.

"I wanna see your dick," she had finally said giggling crazy from the high. He laughed too and pulled it out for her to play with. She stroked it and tugged on it before allowing him to straddle her, laying it in between her small breasts. What a turn on that was, as she squeezed her breast around it while he moved it back and forth. She was naked down to her panties now. Having found a box of pads in Malcolm's mother's room she was feeling okay now about Mrs. Rosie's visit.

Laying on her, he let his stiff member fall between her tits and humped her in emulation of the sex act they were avoiding. Still it felt good to her just having him laying on her sucking on her titties and kissing her.

"Nothing," she answered, bringing her mind back to the now. They were still mostly naked laying there. She reached between his legs and tugged on him again.

This time he grabbed her hand. "Look, this ain't workin'. I need something," he said.

"Not on my period. Not for my first time, Malcolm. I don't want it like that." she explained.

He nodded. "I understand, but check this out. You could do something for me," he said. "And I promise as soon as your period is over I'll do it back," he said.

"What?" she asked.

He rose up on one elbow and leaned in to whisper in her ear. "Gimmie some head," he requested.

She jerked back. "What? Uh, uh, Malcolm . . . no," she protested.

"Come on, now, Sin. Quit playin'. Either that or let me do you in the ass . . ."

"What? You straight up freaky Malcolm!" Sinclair yelped. Just the thought of him doing her in the ass made her weak in the knees.

He didn't budge or back away as if joking. He was serious. He wanted some head.

She'd heard Tanqueray talking about sucking on dicks. She didn't make it sound all that bad. "I don't know how," she admitted.

"I know that. You don't know anything," he teased, reaching over pulling another blunt from the dresser top. He lit it. "We smoke this and then you smoke me," he said, hitting it and then handing it over to her.

She took a long drag from it, fanning the smoke upward into her nostrils as she had seen him do earlier. Soon the high came after a few more hits and again, Malcolm started looking real good to her as he again fondled her body, squeezing her butt and probing her butthole with the tip of his finger. He had her hot. Dipping below the blankets as if diving under water she fished around for his stiff rod, taking it in her mouth.

Throwing the covers off them, he grabbed the back of her head pushing it forward as he cocked up his leg and forcefully thrust into her mouth.

She gagged, closing her eyes tight, yet holding onto his penis while mouthing the stroke.

Malcolm purred and cooed and panted, moving with her oral stroke, until finally he came.

She pulled off just as the hot semen entered her mouth. Quickly she pulled the sheet up and spit into it. "Shit, Malcolm, that was nasty," she balked.

"That was good . . . hell . . . what you talking about. Baby you a pro at that shit," he said, smoothing back his nappy wild hair. "Whoa . . . that was the shit right there," he chortled before pulling her face to his and kissing her. "I needed that shit," he told her, not noticing the scowl she wore. He re-lit the blunt they had started and together they finished it.

Soon she felt better about the whole thing and even a little like doing it again. But she didn't.

Chapter 22

Dustin Sinclair pondered Tanqueray's change of heart. When she called she sounded desperate. She sounded wanting and needing. He'd never heard her sound that way before. It was strange too, as when she left he felt as though she should not. He wanted her to stay. He wanted them both to stay. Not for sex but more because he needed to tell her the truth about things and he knew she was na need her man friend for support once she heard the truth, the truth about Javina Nation, her mother, and him.

He was going to tell her how Javina Nation had been his lover from the past. He was going to tell Tanqueray that her mother was the reason he could not make love to her—well not the way a man like Finest could. He was going to tell her the relationship he had to her sister Sinclair. Yes, he was going to tell her that he was Sinclair's father. Sure it hadn't been proven with DNA, but that was purely academic. He knew he was her father. He'd not even seen the girl but knew he had to be her father. "Her name is Sinclair for crying out loud," he reasoned aloud while pacing his room wondering what was going on and why she wasn't there.

What had gone wrong? He'd called Cecil to pick her up despite the fact that she had asked him not too. But after about twenty minutes, Cecil called back and said she had changed her mind about coming back to the house once he got there to pick her up. Cecil said that she had decided to go off with her boyfriend. But on the phone, Dustin could sense that Tanqueray wasn't with Finest anymore. She hadn't asked him to pick them both up, she had asked only for herself. She sounded as if she was alone. *And what was that comment about being dumped off?*

"Cecil," he said over the intercom.

"Yes," Cecil answered sounding tired.

"I'm sorry if you were resting. Were you resting?"

"Uh . . . no sir, just down here cleaning out the car."

"So you say she just changed her mind?"

"Yes, sir."

"Where was she when she did that? It didn't sound like she was near home. Why did she say you dumped them off?"

"Don't know, sir."

"It's just so peculiar. I've called her phone several times and it just goes to the machine," he went on. "I'm puzzled. Was she upset when you dropped them off? Were she and Finest fighting?"

Cecil was silent.

"I can go get her, sir. I can go see if she'll come this time."

"Maybe I should ride along and . . ."

"No!" he snapped.

"No? Why?" Dustin asked.

Cecil hesitated.

He hesitated a little too long for Dustin's taste.

"Sir, why are you bothering with her? I mean there are many other hookers out there you can have at the snap of your finger and . . ."

"She's not a hooker!" Dustin blurted. "And why suddenly, is this any of your concern?"

Cecil again was silent.

"Is that what you think? Is that what you think she's here visiting with me for? She's not a hooker, Cecil. She's a very special person to me! I've told you that. I've told you that she's special to me!"

"I'm sorry, Sir. I know you've tried to explain it but I just don't get it. She's just a regular tramp to me—just like the rest."

Dustin's head hurt now. His blood pressure was going up. Why did people always judge so harshly the women he loved? He remembered his wife when she found out about Javina. He remembered the horrible things she said about her. "Get the car ready. I'm going to go get her myself."

"I'll go, Sir. I'll go . . ."

"No. I'm not an invalid. I'll go! This is my damn life and I can do what I want, when I want. Something does not smell right about this. I don't understand why you would be lying to me but I feel as though you are."

"I'm . . . I'm not."

"Well, good because if you were, there would be consequences Cecil!" Dustin Sinclair pushed the off button to the intercom with intent. His heart was pounding. His doctor had told him about getting stressed out. Being rich had its repercussions. He was stressed out and in poor health. Tanqueray had been his joy, in just these few months he actually felt as if he was on the upswing.

"Sir, let Cecil go retrieve Ms. Tanqueray," Cory said, having overheard the exchange.

Dustin turned to him slightly. He was still highly agitated.

"Very well," he agreed, pushing the button again. "Cecil, go pick her up," he ordered. "Go to where you picked up Finest and see if she's there. Go wherever you have to go until you find her!"

Chapter 23

Unique crept into the apartment. She hoped everyone would be preoccupied and not have any questions for her about where she had been. Maybe they would just assume she was with Cammie. Surely they had no idea she'd been with Marquis all this time. Surely they wouldn't be able to tell she'd been laid up with a man—again. Maybe it was guilt she was feeling. Who knew?

At first the thought of sleeping with Marquis was a good idea, or maybe just a knee jerk sensation to his powerful presence and the words the preacher had said. Or maybe he had just been caught up in what she wanted to believe about magical things and miracles, but once she got into the mess, his hunger for her felt wrong. Never had anyone been so hungry for her before. It was just like it was when she was a girl. He was hungry for her in an unnatural way. He clung to her. He mastered her. It took everything to get out of his bed. After the first time, they got dressed and went into the kitchen to eat even though she was far from hungry. What she needed was a long soak in a hot tub. But at least she got to talk to his mother and hear her thoughts on the grandson that she'd only seen a couple of times from afar.

"I thought he might have been my Markey's boy, because he looked so much like him. I used to see him playing in the streets you know and I wanted to ask him a couple of times who his mama was but . . . I didn't," she said, sounding shy.

Unique felt warm and happy talking to her. Markey's mother was a sweet woman and she made Unique hate even more what she had missed out on. She had missed out on what her own mother, Javina, had taken for granted. After enjoying the food, Unique told Markey that she was ready to head back to the hospital to see Cammie. Marquis was fine with that and went with her.

Cammie was sleeping soundly and had done well all day. There really wasn't much she could do there at this hour, so Marquis insisted they go back to his mother's. Unique did as there was no way he was coming out to her house. She was trying to stay firm and determined not to repeat her past mistakes. She was determined not to let him get too comfortable in her home. It was all garbled thinking now, but in her mind she had to start setting some boundaries. *Why you so weak, Unique?* she asked herself constantly.

When they got back, his mother had gone out, so again, Marquis took her to his bed. This time the love making was fierce and intense. He twisted her this way and that, taking her thug style—on the floor, against the wall, doggy style over a chair. He was relentless, all the while telling her how pretty she was. She came this time, more than once. She hollered out his name and called out to God above. Never before had anyone brought out so much from inside. Even when he went down on her he was rough and hungry, sucking hard on her tender lower lips while pushing her knees far apart and dipping his tongue deep inside her, turning her over, rimming her anus until she purred from an anal orgasm as well.

Unique rubbed her brow at the memory now, feeling the tingle between her thighs. Yes, after a while she enjoyed it. And now she was afraid she would start to crave it again.

Girl, why you so weak for the dick, she asked herself again. *And of all people, Marquis's daddy. I'ma have to pray on this.*

"I'ma go see pastor Williams tomorrow and ask him what he thinks about all this. I ain't ashamed to tell him nothing. I mean, I kinda feel like, this is like . . . like . . . right," she said, glancing at her reflection in the glass door of the microwave. Her face looked different, less strained. She wasn't sure if she looked happy but then she had to admit she'd never really seen happiness on her face. Maybe she was happy. Maybe she was content. She didn't know. All she knew was this—she was surely confused.

Her phone rang.

"Hi baby," it was Marquis.

"Hi," she whispered.

"Why you talking soft. You gotta man at home?" he asked.

She chuckled. "No. I think my kids are asleep. It's quiet here. I just walked in, and I haven't checked to see if they are here or with my baby sister somewhere. It's late so they should be here," Unique said looking around noticing the unfinished bowls of cereal on the floor in front of the TV.

"Took you a long time to get there. You didn't stop nowhere, did you?"

"No," she answered.

"Good. Wouldn't want nobody to try to get at you or nothing."

"You so crazy . . ."

"You fine as hell and . . . well, damn, my nose is wide open. Got me all jealous and shit. You gon' let me come over there?"

"I told you no."

"Yeah, okay, I understand. But I wanna see you tomorrow, okay?"

"I may have to go down to the work center. I don't know. I haven't been there in a while and they gon' start bugging me about closing my case and shit if I don't comply with what they ask."

"I hate welfare. You want to get off? I got money. I'll take you off."

Unique thought about what he was saying what he could possibly mean. What kind of money could an ex con have except dirty money? She wasn't stupid. "It's okay. I been on it for so long it's okay. I know how to work it," she said.

"I'ma take you off. My baby mama don't belong on no welfare. I'ma see to that."

"I . . ." she paused. Her first thought was that she was no longer his baby mama. But the words could not come out. Again she thought about the pastors words 'You'll get Marquis back.' And she had. She had Big Marquis seemingly eating out of the palm of her hands in only one day. Maybe she misunderstood and thought he meant something else when in fact maybe the pastor meant that God had sent her Marquis Sr. The thought made her smile and suddenly made her heart grow light. Again she looked at her reflection. Yes maybe this odd look was happiness. "You really wanna come over here?"

"I thought you said . . ."

"I know, but I've been thinking, and maybe this is right. Maybe being with you is right."

"I been trying to tell you that," he said.

She could almost sense his broad smile through the phone.

Just then the door opened and the girls came rushing in, happy to see their mama.

"Where is Sin?" she asked.

"She left yesterday. Where you been?" Gina asked.

"I been," she paused. "At church praying. Guess what? Cammie woke up!"

"She did! I wanna see her!" Apple and Gina both chimed in.

"Markey," she said, turning back to the phone. "Tell you what. . . . I'ma call you when my girls go to sleep okay?"

"Okay, baby. I understand. We gotta keep this on the down low from the kids for a minute. I'm diggin' it. I totally get 'down low', besides, they didn't seem all that comfortable wit' me when I was there before," he told her.

"Yeah, that's all it is. They just need a little time."

"I want you Unique," he said then. "You take all the time you need. I want you."

She was stunned, "You do?"

"Yeah. I do. So handle ya business and then call me back."

After hanging up Unique took a deep breath. She was feeling a little overwhelmed.

"Mrs. Newbury said if you were here for you to go talk to her."

Now it was to come. She was gonna get the fussing out from Mrs. Newbury again. Unique took a deep breath. Together with the girls they headed down the hall to her door.

Mrs. Newbury was waiting up in her rocker. When Unique and the girls walked in she grinned widely. "How is the baby?" she asked.

"Unique smiled. "She's awake. I'm so happy. She came out of the coma and she's awake. I went to church and prayed and my baby woke up," Unique said, telling her the truth . . . at least most of it.

"You seeing Marquis daddy, Unique?" she asked bluntly.

Unique's smile left and she swallowed the lump that came into her throat. Her head dipped in a shame-filled nod.

"It's okay. You grown. I was just wondering because the girls said they saw him again yesterday."

"Mrs. Newbury, I'm grown as you say and—"

Mrs. Newbury held up her hand. "You asked me to watch the girls and I said okay. I don't have no worries about watching these girls. I don't have no grandchildren so it's just beautiful having them here," she went on.

The girls had climbed up on her plush sofa, occupying themselves with the number books they had apparently been looking at before they heard the elevator and went to check to see if Unique had made it in.

"You don't have to watch them if it's too much trouble. I didn't know my sister had brought them here and—"

"I said I don't mind. Just tell me what you're doing and I'll watch them. But Unique, I just want to say to you that God don't make mistakes. When He took Li'l Marquis, there was a reason and you can't change that reason by bringing Big Marquis into your life. It's like you're disagreeing with God's plans and he don't like that."

Unique took a defensive stance with her hand on her hip. "Where you get that from? I went to the pastor and he told me different. He said I'd get Marquis back and I think he meant Big Marquis. I think this is right, Mrs. Newbury. So don't judge me."

Mrs. Newbury held up her hand. "Unique, I'm not judgin' you. I been in your shoes before chile. I've lost a child before and I thought I could redo what God had allowed . . . ya can't. All I got was heartache tryin'."

"You think I'm trying to bring my child back?"

"Yes. I do. I think you're trying to redo what has been undone."

Unique laughed. "No I'm not." She glanced at the girls and for once they truly were not in her conversation. "I'm not trying to make another Marquis with that man. He *is*

Marquis," Unique chuckled. Mrs. Newbury was way off, in her opinion. "He's the Marquis the pastor was talking about."

Mrs. Newbury was shaking her head.

Unique was glad this wasn't a brow beating for staying out over night, but still this was a conversation she was finished having. Nobody was going to tell her who to sleep with and who not. Those days were long over . . . fa sho. "Come on, girls," she said. If Unique had been confused about Markey, she wasn't anymore. He would be in her life. He would be coming to the apartment. This conversation with Mrs. Newbury cinched that.

"Now Unique don't get mad," Mrs. Newbury said wrestling herself up from her chair.

Unique held out her hand. "I'm not mad Mrs. Newbury, you're just wrong about Markey."

"Unique, just listen to me . . . please. Pray on it harder. You ain't hearing the right answer. Something in my spirit telling me you ain't hearing God right."

"You talking like a witch Mrs. Newbury. Besides, I don't even know how you know about Markey—" she looked down at Gina and Apple. "Y'all tell Mrs. Newbury thangs about Marquis's daddy?"

They shook their heads to the negative and then to the positive. "We told her he was here yesta-day, that's all," Gina finally confessed.

Mrs. Newbury shook her head slowly and sadly. "They didn't have to tell me more than that. I know 'cuz it come to me in a dream," she said, pausing to take a deep breath. "You wonder why I'm so attached to you? It's because it's my callin'. I'm your guardian angel, Unique and you ought to be listening to me."

"Oh, yeah, I'm taking my girls home now." Unique was growing agitated now as she rushed the girls from her apartment.

"Please Unique . . . hear me. Don't let him in your life," she said, before Unique closed the door separating them.

"Whew! I'm not gonna let you guys go over there anymore. She's crazy as hell!" Unique laughed.

"Mama, where you been?"

"I told you and tomorrow we all gonna go see, Cammie," she said sounding bubbly and happy.

The girls cheered and rushed to their beds in order to get an early start.

As soon as Unique heard the giggles quiet down she called Markey.

He was there within minutes, as if waiting around the corner for her call.

Chapter 24

Tanqueray coughed and choked on her own blood after the third punch to the face. She'd fought Omar back at the start. They'd gone round and round that living room all day, until he hit her with that chair. Then he sat on her, slugging her again and again in the face.

"Omar please," she begged holding up her hand to stop the abuse.

"Oh, now you beggin'," he said. "Bitch. You done broke stuff up in my place and now you gonna beg. I got company coming and you done tow up shit," he said slapping her again before pulling her up by her hair, forcing her to her feet, and slinging her over onto the sofa.

She covered her face. She knew he probably figured by now she'd be a wet pool of tears but for Tanqueray the tears just would not come. Maybe had she cried he would have stopped. Maybe that was what he wanted, to make her cry, but crying just wasn't part of her makeup, it just wasn't her. She thought about Unique and how easily she could be brought to tears. All mama had to do was raise her voice a little bit and Unique would become a puddle of sobs. *But not me*, Tanqueray thought now, while watching Omar move around the apartment, as if thinking of something else to do to her. All Tanqueray felt was smoldering rage.

He picked up his cell phone and made a call. Turning to

her he smiled now. "Like I said, we 'bout ta have a party," he promised.

She was shaking her head unconsciously knowing what he meant by that. He had men coming over. He was gonna let them pull a train on her. She was no fool. Omar got off on shit like that. He was gonna get paid tonight off an investment of her gold—the gold between her legs.

"Get up!" he yelled.

"No!" she argued, only to have him grab her arm again. This time she kicked him and bit his hand.

He yelled out and ran over to his bar. Reaching over, he retrieved a gun.

"Shit, Omar!" she flinched, covering her face thinking for sure he was going to shoot her.

"Now get up and get in that room. Put on one of those sexy nighties on the bed. Shantel left some nice ones."

"Where did she go?" Tanqueray asked.

"I don't know. I sent her out to a party and never seen her again. I thank she dead . . ." he said, sounding blasé and careless.

She glanced at the clock. She'd been there for hours and still had not been rescued. But then again, who knew where she was. Cecil maybe? All this had to be Cecil's doing. Mr. Sinclair would never have let this happen to her.

No. She shook the momentary thought from her head. No, he would never let this happen. He loved her.

"Get undressed," Omar said, biting his bottom lip as if eager to see her body after all this time, as if he missed her.

She slowly pulled off the sweat jacket and tossed it over onto a chair. He'd already had her out of her shoes as soon as she got there. She guessed he figured she wouldn't leave without her shoes. Little did he know she would leave without panties if she could just get out. Sliding into the skimpy nightie, she sat on the bed to wait for the first John to arrive.

Omar was trying his best to make her a whore. One way or another, he was determined to make her what she, in her heart, felt she was not.

"So you been laid up in the lap of luxury these days, huh?" he taunted. "Yeah, I heard about you stealing my best John from me. Well it's all good. I got plenty where he came from," Omar chortled.

After about fifteen minutes of his verbal abuse, she heard the front door open. Omar had told whoever on the phone, to just come in and apparently he did. Omar went out to the living room and greeted him. "God," she grumbled as the short fat ugly as hell white man entered the bedroom, grinning like a Cheshire cat. She could see he was hungry for black meat and just knew he was going to have a feast tonight. She was bloody and bruised. *How could he want this? How sick could a man be?* She pondered.

Omar still had the gun but wanted to hide it. *Yeah,* she thought, *there's nothing like doing your nasty business while your hurt'n and under duress.*

The white man unbuckled his pants quickly, his little Peter springing into action. He shimmied up to her as if she were a latrine.

"Open wide, baby," he purred.

Tanqueray was past humored by this whole thing. She opened her mouth allowing the man entrance and then clamped down—teeth first.

The man howled and screamed pushing against her forehead.

She let him go just as she felt the butt of the gun upside her head.

Chapter 25

Cecil drove around for about an hour before stopping at a café. He called Omar. No answer. "Are you done yet?" he said to the voice mail. "You didn't tell me you were gonna keep her all damn night. I need to get her back to Mr. Sinclair. He keeps calling me. I'ma lose my job! Call me back."

He hung up the cell phone and glanced around the café looking and feeling guilty. Sure, nobody knew him here. He wasn't even in his own neighborhood. He'd driven out closer to Omar's place just in case he was finished with the tramp, so he could pick her up. He wasn't sure how he was going to convince her not to spill the beans on things once he took her back to Sinclair. But surely Omar was gonna work his magic on her. He was gonna convince her to take what he gave her and shut the hell up about it. Besides, she deserved whatever she got. She was nothing but a whore. She was a whore—just like his mama was.

Cecil immediately shot the thoughts of his mother from his mind.

Omar made him sick but he was blood. His whole life made him sick but yet he had to keep living.

The waitress came over to his table. "What will you have?" she asked.

"Just some coffee," he answered, looking her over from head to toe. She was cute and all that, but he wasn't really interested in Black women. He wasn't really interested in anything having to do with the Black condition. It wasn't that he didn't feel he was black; it was just that from what he'd seen here in the Bay Area, there were a lot of haves and have nots. Sure he'd enjoyed Sinclair's Black cast offs but they were just for the flesh. He didn't really "like" them.

Cecil looked out the window onto the street. He'd watched the day closing in on him. What would he do if he had to change his life right now? Where would he go? Again he shook his head. He didn't even have a life, well, not one he could really relate too. He remembered his childhood. His mind drifted to playing in the Oakland streets with Omar and his other cousins. His mind drifted to the cars that would pull up in front of his house and the men inside them. One of them was his father. He was the worst of them, in his mind. Cecil's father was a man everyone called Switch. He was a bastard of the highest order. He was a pimp, a pusher, a booster, and a thief. He preyed on the downtrodden and vulnerable around him. Cecil remembered once trying to love him. He remembered trying to get into what his mother apparently felt for this . . . this human. But he felt nothing.

Once the man touched his head, patting it in the way a man would pat a dog. He said, "So you're my son. Yeah, I guess I can see it," and then he gave him a dollar.

Cecil shook that day from his mind. As well as the many other days he lived in the ghetto before his mother, a whore, did the one thing he'd always thank her for. When he was sixteen years old, his mother got him a job working for Dustin Sinclair. That was over ten years ago. Now there was a good chance that because of another whore his life would change again.

The waitress came with his coffee. He sipped it slowly. Cecil's mind wandered. Soon an hour had passed and then two. By then he'd ordered some food and ate mindlessly, listening to the clock on the wall. It seemed to tick loudly, overshadowing the murmured voices that filled the café. The day passed slowly and then darkness fell. Mr. Sinclair had called more than a dozen times but he'd refused to pick up after the initial few lies. It was then Cecil realized he was numb. Inside he was sickeningly numb. What if Omar had killed that girl? What would become of his life if Omar killed Tanqueray? He called Omar again. There was no answer.

Chapter 26

Sinclair tossed and turned. The pain was nearly unbearable. Maybe her arm was infected. She was scared to look under the bandage. It hadn't been changed in two days now. What with Unique not coming home and Tang—

Where had Unique been and where was Tang anyway? Sinclair thought, dragging up from the muggy room. It was balmy from the little girl funk that filled the air. Gina and Apple were hard sleepers, squirming and coughing and passing gas. They had apparently come in after she had knocked out. *Damn they gonna kill me,* Sinclair growled.

After spending Sunday in bed with Malcolm, Sinclair decided she didn't want to stay overnight again. He was too horny for her. She told him she didn't want to suck him off again—no matter how much weed he was trying to get her to smoke. Things had changed between them and she wasn't sure she liked it. She liked the weed smoking for sure, but all that sex— well—it just wasn't for her. It had turned out to be a major disappointment. Getting all juiced up was fun and the feeling was good but what came next wasn't. She didn't like how she felt after Malcolm got what he wanted. She didn't like all his nasty sounding moans and grunts. He was nasty and she was hard pressed to figure out what the big deal was. Unique had spent her life chasing the dick. At least Tanqueray was getting paid for doing what she did. Now she was on to something there. The next time any man made her suck on his dick, including Malcolm, he was going to have to pay her!

When she got home last night, nobody was there. Unique had left a note that she had gone to the hospital again and had taken the girls. There was no mean message about finding them at Mrs. Newbury, so that was cool. Tang . . . nothing. Nobody ever knew where she was. But that was okay, she didn't 'need' anybody to know. Tang didn't "need" anybody.

"I'ma be like that. I can do my own shit. I can register myself for school," she mumbled, dragging herself to the kitchen for something cool to drink.

While chugging down the green Kool-Aid from the pitcher, she pondered her pain relief. "Oh, yeah, Unique always got a headache. Maybe she got a little sum sum in the bathroom," Sinclair said, heading in without wondering why the light was on. She pushed open the door.

"Hey!" the large bear pissing like a facet yelled out.

Sinclair screamed and slammed the door closed. "Sorry! Sorry!" she called out.

Within seconds Unique came from the bedroom.

"Who is that?" Sinclair asked nearly shaking from the startle.

"Be quiet," Unique shushed her. "It's Markey," she said using the name his mother called him.

"Markey who?" Sinclair asked. "Marquis's daddy?" she asked now, with her voice at a high pitch.

Unique nodded.

"Ah, nah. Unique. Don't do this. You promised you wouldn't have no more men up over your kids. Damn! And now you got an ex-con up in his muthafu—"

"Sinclair stop it! Don't judge," Unique pleaded.

The toilet flushed and the water shut off before Marquis appeared in the doorway. Sinclair got an eye full of his demonic looking tats covering his muscular chest—skulls and vampires dripping blood. "Damn," she groaned, looking at Unique again as if she were out of her mind for having a man like that there.

"We working through some things Sinclair. I need him here," she explained. "We just lost our son . . ."

"This ain't about Marquis. You need a dick that's all. You sick," Sinclair said slamming past her into the living room. She knew now about the dick and to her this was stupid and weak. She looked around for some shoes to slip on her feet. "I'm outty," she growled.

"Where you going in the middle of the night, girl. You can't go out!" Markey told her.

"Oh, no," Sinclair held out her hand. "Remember you're . . . you were . . . Marquis's daddy but you sho as hell ain't mine! Don't even try to tell me shit!" she barked. "And it ain't night no more if you knew how to tell time. Oh, but wait," she cocked her head to the side. "Time should be something you have very little concept of," she smarted off.

About then Apple came from the room. Upon seeing Markey she screamed and ran back in the room.

"See Neek! You got cha girls all scared and shit. What is wrong with you?" Sinclair asked pointing toward their room.

"Don't judge me, Sin. You're not my keeper. You just a chile," Unique answered, heading toward the girl's room to calm Apple down.

"I'm a grown-ass woman. I know what's what! I know why he's here." Sinclair scolded now, looking him up and down. It was more than obvious what was going on. The house was fully quiet when she snuck him in and apparently she assumed everyone was tucked in tight. Perhaps they were, but it was morning now—early as hell—but morning.

Sinclair could tell Unique had been laid up under the big black bear for probably most of the night. She strained to look at him. She was too upset right now to even care if he looked good or not. *Who cared anyway, it was wrong that he was here,* she reasoned internally. Storming out of the apartment, she thought about her next move. Her hair was a mess and she had on the same clothes she'd worn the day before. *But who cared right?* She headed for the staircase. There was no sense waking up the entire building with that loud-ass elevator.

Thank goodness for people with jobs though, because without them the buses wouldn't be thinking about running this early. *Fa Sho.* Digging deep in her pocket she found the few dollars she snagged from Malcolm's dresser. She was so broke it wasn't funny. All the money she'd been stashing away had gone to the funeral, "And that nigga didn't put a dime toward that piece of business," she fussed on in an undertone thinking more about Markey.

Her face must have scowled because a man on the bus on his way to work smiled at her. She rolled her eyes and looked out the window. Normally she was dealing with the bus driver flirting with her but at this time of morning it was just regular folks riding. She realized it didn't matter who it was though, even these innocent folks were on her nerves. Her arm hurt, her sister was in the apartment with some new pervert and folks were trying to be pleasant. "I'm not feeling that," she mumbled under her breath. At the next stop a boy around her age got on and sat next to her. He was a Mexican mix, but clearly a school boy or hard worker as he bore no tats, no mouth jewelry and no wife beater. Nothing. He probably was already taking care of a big family. There were many like that around here. They had moved over from the valley and worked at good jobs sending money home to their big-ass families in

Southern Cali near the border of Mexico. They worked hard at staying out of the cops' radar. Many of them had past gang affiliation in Southern California before their families got them up here in the Bay for safe keeping. But this boy looked pretty clean, clean enough to make her wish she had taken a shower that morning.

He noticed her smoothing back her hair and nodded at her, smiling.

She smiled back with her lips tight together. She didn't want to share no morning breath or nothing like that.

"What happened to your arm?" he asked. His accent was strong.

"Oh, I um . . ."she was trying to think fast. He probably could relate to a street fight but why tell him. "I got cut trying to cook," she lied.

He chuckled. "Wow, I guess that takes care of me asking you to come over my house for dinner. Shit man, you'd be having everybody bleeding," he joked.

Sinclair chuckled. "Nah, I'm okay. It was just this one time."

"Lemmie see," he asked reaching for the bandaged area.

"You a doctor? Noo," she said pulling back. "It hurts like crazy, and I don't have nothing for pain."

He looked around. "You don't? You got some money?" he asked under his breath.

She found herself looking around too. "Like how much?"

"Just a few dollars. I got Vicodin. I sell it like a dollar a pill."

"Really. You got some on you?" she said whispering now.

About that time both their heads ducked below the view of the driver as he reached down into the backpack between his legs. She peeked in. Deep in the crevasse of the zipper part, he had a stash from heaven.

"Man, I only got like two or three bucks. The first is tomorrow and I can probably get a few dollars from my sister."

Sinclair hated saying that. But it was true. She'd become a member of the system. Maybe she always was, but Debonair, her brother, hadn't made it feel so obvious. Unique wore her poverty like a badge sometimes.

"I do credit," he grinned.

Sinclair had to smile back on that one. "Can I have like ten?"

"Girl, you gots real pain . . ." he said, reaching over and pulling the cord. She looked around. They were nowhere near the Palemos. He stood and with his head swung it his way for her to follow him. She thought about the extra two bucks getting off the bus early was gonna cost her. But the pain was leading her in his direction. She got off with him.

He had someone waiting for him. The guy was apparently a coworker or whatever. They both greeted each other in Spanish.

"This is . . ." he turned to her.

"Sinclair," she answered.

"She and I got a transaction to do but then, maybe we can drop her off where she was going."

"Where you going pretty girl," the older dude said eyeing her up and down. It wasn't in a nasty way, though. It was just one that said, "damn, you'd probably look pretty good if you had a bath."

She could dig that and just smiled. "The P."

"Well, we don't usually go that way but sure, get in," he said, aiming his head swing toward the back seat. Both she and the boy from the bus got in the back seat since another Mexican dude was in the passenger seat. After about a block, the boy counted out ten pills.

"I don't have ten dollars right now. I told you that so. . . ."

"Your boyfriend got ten dollar?"

"I don't have a boyfriend," she admitted reluctantly. Malcolm hadn't yet come around all the way correct so nah he wasn't her man yet. And with all that dick sucking and fake fuckin he probably wasn't gonna be. They were better friends anyway, she thought allowing the melancholy thought to cross her mind.

"Hey, Robert . . ." the driver called, snickering wickedly while looking in the rearview mirror. The passenger laughed too.

"Nah, she's from the P. Them dudes over there like to fight over their stuff too much," Robert said. The boy's name was apparently Robert.

"Their stuff? I'm not nobody's stuff," she fussed.

"I didn't mean it like that," Robert said, trying to clean it up now.

"Clean it up, Robert," the passenger cackled.

"Look, I just want ten bucks," Robert said then.

"You know where I stay?"

"No, I don't."

"I stay in W.E., the stop before you got on," she told him.

"Cool," he said pouring the pills in her open palm. "Then you're good for it. Folks in our hood, they come good when they owe."

She smiled.

"Don't take them all at once."

"How you hurt your arm?" the driver asked.

"She was cookin' eh," Robert answered. The laughter broke out again.

"Damn!" the men in the front said between bouts of laughter.

After the laughter died, Robert and Sinclair settled into a

little bit of conversation. He was nice, and about to graduate from school—just like her. Well, just like she hoped to if things would ever get straightened out with this school mess.

"Yeah, I gotta change schools now," she told him.

"Damn, what a mad summer," he told her.

"You ain't neva lied," she agreed, rethinking the brief run down she'd given him of all the madness she'd been through. Her brother going to the pen, her mother's house blowing up, her niece getting molested, her nephew dying to revenge her honor and now, after all was said and done, she was going to have to change schools.

The driver reached the border between the P and where they were going. There were so many defining lines in gangland that people who lived there just knew them and respected them. These guys knew when they reached the P just by landmarks and they had no interest in entering today. "What's your number," Robert asked before she climbed out.

"555-8945," she said, rattling off Unique's house number. She started to give him a fake number but why should she start trouble with the Mexicans if she didn't have to. Folks get crazy over their drugs and she just wasn't about to get in that kind of mess. It wasn't as if she was a crack head and needed a lot, she just needed a little sum sum for her arm. That's all. She needed it just until her medical came through. That's all.

She still didn't have a cell phone so she was going to have to walk the few blocks to the tract where Malcolm lived. It wasn't too bad of a walk. She ducked quickly into an early morning donut shop and swallowed two of the pills at the water fountain near the rest rooms. The pills hit quickly and she was high as a kite before she even got a block. She hadn't eaten and wasn't even thinking about the immediate effect.

These vicodin pills were stronger than the ones she had gotten from the doctor at ER and they were better than whatever she had taken out of Malcolm's mama's cabinet.

Sinclair was stumbling but she couldn't tell. She saw crooked as straight, until she hit the sidewalk in front of Chu's little mini market.

Chapter 27

Unique was furious. She could barely think. How dare Sinclair put her on blast like that.

"Y'all be fight'n' like that often?" Markey asked while sipping from the cup of coffee she had made.

Unique noticed Apple eyeing him up and down. "He's Marquis's daddy, Apple. He go by Markey. Don't he look like your brother?"

"No," Apple answered quickly. Gina confirmed with a quick shake of the head.

"Well, he does," Unique said calmly grinning at the girls. Just their faces took her mind off Sinclair. She loved her kids. She really did. Glancing back at Markey she realized how deep her feelings for him had gone too. Over the years he had stayed in that special secret place in her heart. This was like a dream having him here. It really was. It was a dream that nobody else could possibly understand. "Hey, y'all wanna go see Cammie again today? She is probably gonna be awake and I know she would want to see y'all." Unique requested suddenly bubbling over.

Gina and Apple, caught off guard by their mother's unusual excitement, squealed with delight.

"Then we gon' stop in at the church and see if the Pastor is holding a weekday prayer meetin' or something."

"I think he does," Markey added.

Apple clapped her hands but Gina just stared in confusion. She had no idea what a prayer meeting was and clearly wasn't sure if she wanted to find out.

About that time the phone rang.

"Hello?" Unique answered with the smile still on her lips.

"Hey, this is Finest. Is Tang there?"

"It's early Finest," she reprimanded.

"Um, I didn't ask what time it was. I asked about Tang. We got separated yesterday and now she's missing."

"Missing?"

"Yeah, as in, I think she got snatched yesterday or worse. We was bamboozled and I think she got ambushed. I just got outta jail but I'm out looking for her now. I wanted to try you first before I went out and raised hell all over da Bay."

"Finest, you know Tanqueray, she's always into stuff. She's probably just holed up over at her friend Kashawna's place."

"Nah, I done already woke her up. I done even called that old white dude she be kicking it wit' and he ain't seen her either so it's 'bout to be on. Somebody about to get hurt up in his mutha fuck," he growled.

Unique tried to hide her true concern. She tried to tell herself that maybe this was just a lover's spat. After all, she had no idea Tanqueray had even forgiven Finest for his mess. How was she to know they were sweethearts now? Last she heard Finest was on a short shit-list. "Why do you think she's in trouble like that?"

"My pawdna said he saw her getting into a car with some nigga that he didn't get a good look at."

"Well, there ya go," Unique tried to explain tactfully without just coming right out and sayin', *Well, you know my sista is a ho. She could have gotten in the car with anybody!*

"Nah, it ain't like that. My pawdna said didn't look like she wanted to go. Besides, Tang wouldn't be caught gett'n in the car with a nigga if she knew my boy was on his way."

"Hmm, I . . ." Unique paused to think clearly. "I just don't know."

"When's the last time you seen her?"

"Friday," Unique admitted. "She was asleep on the sofa when I left for the hospital."

"What's up, baby?" Markey asked now, clearly noticing her discomfort.

She held up her hand and shook her head. "Look, Finest. You call me if you hear from her and I'll call you if she calls home, a'ight?"

"Yeah," he said hanging up.

"What's up?" Markey asked again.

"Oh, it's just Tanqueray. She's hiding out I guess. Her man can't find her."

"Damn you and your sisters be having some drama," Markey chuckled, heading to the kitchen.

She followed him in there to start breakfast.

"What choo got planned?"

"Well, I just promised the girls we'd go see Cammie."

"Well, all right then," he said, agreeing to go with a smile.

Chapter 28

It was Monday morning. Cecil walked into Dustin Sinclair's house as if nothing was going on. He had not slept well hoping and planning how he would pull off this charade. It wasn't a true act. He didn't know where Tanqueray was. It wasn't as if he'd gone by Omar's to check. And it wasn't as if Omar had answered the phone to confirm her being there. The only thing he prayed now was that Mr. Sinclair didn't dot his eyes in Omar's direction.

Cory and the other staff members looked tense, yet Cecil tried to hang onto his casual appearance.

"Where have you been?" Dustin said busting from the library as if sensing his presence. "I've called you all night!"

"I'm sorry. After I got that detour from that Tanqueray situation I figured you wouldn't need me so I . . . I, uh, went to visit a friend," he said, trying to make it appear as though that was something he did often.

"A friend?" Dustin asked, showing true curiosity and puzzlement. Cecil immediately felt defensive. Yes, he had friends. It wasn't as if he didn't. At the moment he couldn't think of any but he knew he had some. Besides what else could he say? I spent the night calling my cousin who was probably busy murdering your whore.

"Yes, I met a nice woman last month. She called me right after you did and well," he covered his mouth covertly and snickered. "I got a little distracted. I'm sorry," he added. Dustin didn't seem amused in the slightest. This was serious. He sucked in a chest full of air. "I'm sorry about the car," he continued hoping to refocus his concern to where it should be pointed. The car was valuable and that was where his concern should have been in Cecil's opinion.

"I'm not really concerned about the car, Cecil. I'm concerned about Tanqueray. I thought you had an understanding of how important she is to me."

"Of course I do. She's like a new toy, and now you can't find it," Cecil said allowing some of what he felt come out.

Cory had entered the room and cleared his throat, interrupting the tense moment that was growing. "What is it Cory?" Dustin asked.

With that distraction, Cecil quickly walked away, heading toward the garage where he normally spent most of his day. He quickly called Omar again. There was no answer. Guilt was going to eat him alive today.

Waiting for a moment or two, Cecil realized that Dustin wasn't going to come out to the garage where he was. He reached for the rag that he normally used to wipe off the cars. His hands were shaking. Yeah, today guilt was going to kill him.

Chapter 29

The day was drifting by as Sinclair fell into and out of the high left over from the first dosage of the pills. After falling down from the first couple she made sure to get some food in her stomach before taking another. She'd finally gotten to Malcolm's mama's house in one piece if she didn't count the knot on her head. She had spent about an hour or so on the street just wandering. "They were kinda strong," she told Malcolm who looked one of the pills over as if that helped to figure out what they were.

"Where you get 'em?" he asked.

She shook her head. "Can't tell. You'll get all pissed and crazy," she said. "He's my new boyfriend so I mean, don't want you beefing with him," she teased.

"You ain't got no new boyfriend," Malcolm said laughing loudly.

"Ain't got no old one either," she smarted off. She was feeling better now. The second dose of the pill didn't hit as hard. She'd eaten a big bowl of beans and some cornbread. She was feeling playful and happy again and best of all, pain free.

"You got me," he said, sounding serious. "Why did you leave any way. Fa real? Don't give me that crap about Unique and the girls and all that. Tell me why did you leave?" Malcolm asked.

"I don't know," she lied, shrugging and looking off.

Malcolm examined the knot closer, touching it slightly causing her to seethe and move her head back quickly from his hand.

"Don't be hurtin' me. I'll have to get . . . um . . ." she tried to think of the Mexican boy's name. "My boyfriend on ya," she teased.

"Stop saying that Sin," Malcolm said now, draping his heavy leg over hers. They were sitting on his bed as was their common place when hanging out. Since grade school, they'd been friends and besides her growing curiosity over having sex with him, they'd always be friends. Sinclair knew that. She was going to fix what had been broken between them during this summer. It was only this way because of her so she was going to fix it. Maybe she'd help him get back with Mercedes. . . .

"You don't have another man but me, and I don't want you talkin' to no gang banger either."

"Mexican gang banger at that," she corrected.

"What the hell! You got these from some Mexican?" Now he tried to grab the rest of the pills form her.

She pulled them back tucking them deep in her pocket while he wrestled her playfully, careful not to hit her arm.

"I told you that and I still owe him money so stop it. I owe him ten dollars. I may have to sell my booty for ten dollars. So don't make me lose em. The least I can do is to enjoy them," she said laughing heartily.

"You ain't selling no booty . . . not mah booty," he said, pulling on her shirt.

He was flirting now. She could tell. She liked it when he gave her attention. She just wasn't really ready for sex today. Malcolm was looking good though. Each day he was looking more and more like the boy she wanted to have by her side. His muscles were tight, his chest getting defined. He was coming into his manhood. But having him all over her was just not what she wanted. Despite that, she hoped she looked good to him too. He seemed to like how she looked but then again, he had chosen Mercedes. Mercedes had big tits and wide hips. She was thick and had a pretty smile. She liked sex, of that Sinclair was sure. Mercedes was a girl who liked a lot of things. "Am I pretty, Malcolm?" she asked out of impulse.

He laughed. "Oh, shit you getting all white girl on me again," he said, pulling away from her and climbing off the bed.

She regretted the questions immediately. "No I'm not. I . . ." she began but then changed her mind about saying the rest. She felt dumb. "When we gonna go do something fun?"

"We do fun stuff. This is fun," he said, looking around his cluttered room. Movies and music were everywhere.

"This ain't fun. We used to hang out."

"When was that? In one of your Barbie dreams? You know good and well we never 'hung' out. You were too busy with your little school and white friends."

"No I wasn't."

"Yes, you were. Until your mama's house went up, you were not thinking about me," Malcolm sounded put out.

Sinclair never realized how much he resented her going to a school outside the hood. She only went because her mother wanted the best for her. She wasn't trying to live above those around her. Okay, so that was a lie. She was and she knew she was, but she was going to be leaving this hood. Next year she would be going to college. She had to think as she would be living. She had to put her mind into the life she was going to be living. The worst that could happen was to move out of the ghetto but not be able to get it out of her. She'd seen that before and it was ugly. She'd heard Black folks in important positions using Ebonics. Just the thought made her cringe.

Besides, all those plans were gone now, right? She was just going to have to live here. Do what everyone else here did. Maybe she'd have a baby like Mercedes . . .

"What if I told you I wanted to have your baby Malcolm," she blurted out.

He looked at her. "I'd say you were crazy. You have to . . . make a baby . . . before you can . . . have one . . . and um . . ." He shrugged. "Ain't happ'n," he teased. "Apparently."

"What?" she said up straight. He burst into laughter.

"You the one with a new man! You should know what I mean. You the one givin' away mah booty."

"He ain't my man. He's just my drug dealer," she said, rising up to her knees on the bed.

Bending over her now he stared deep into her eyes, "Right. 'Cause who's yo man?" he asked.

She grinned broadly. The tingling feeling came quickly and she knew she was getting turned on again. Malcolm always made her stomach and thighs feel like that when he acted this way. He was sexy as hell. As much as she had convinced herself she didn't like sex, she was again, feeling the pull of her nature.

"You," she purred before busting into a giggle. "And don't you think differently or I'll pull out ya nipple ring," she teased reaching up and squeezing his nipple under his thin cotton wife beater.

He yelped playfully and covered his chest before grabbing a hand full of her hair and pulling her into a big kiss.

Sinclair closed her eyes and enjoyed every minute of it, tongue and all. After pulling away from the kiss she reached into the pocket of her jeans, pulling out another little white pill. She slid it between her lips.

"Your arm hurting?"

"Nah. I just like how these make me feel," she giggled before kissing Malcolm again. This time she allowed his hands to wander into her blouse. His fondling her breasts was the last thing she remembered before giving into the feeling of the drug creeping into her brain and taking over. In her mind she saw Robert; she saw little Marquis, big Marquis and her sister Tanqueray. She saw her mother's house going up. Before long she was into Malcolm's jeans searching madly for his erection so she would suck on it like a bottle full of life sustaining milk.

"Let me have it Sinclair. Give me your pussy," he begged between pants and grunts, until finally he came in her mouth. This time she didn't spit.

Chapter 30

"So you don't remember what the nigga looked like?" Finest asked Floyd.

"Nah, man, I told you that. He was ugly as hell though, had some played out blond shit on his head for hair. He was like some fucked up looking Cisco on steroids. I know baby didn't look comfortable. She didn't look like she wanted to go wit' the dude."

Finest tried to think. "Who woulda took my baby girl from that area that would have even known she was there?"

"Maybe it was her other man," Floyd suggested.

Finest growled audibly. "She ain't got no other man," he snapped.

"I'm talking about that dude she was livin' wit', the dude who owned that condo and shit. You remember him. I mean, he lived kinda far from that area, but he coulda been passin' through or maybe she called him."

"She didn't call him," Finest insisted. "He wouldn't even have thought about her being there. Nah, that's farfetched. Cecil had something to with that shit. I feel it in my gut man."

"You remember what that dude looks like?" Floyd said, staying on the subject of Omar.

"I ain't never seen him."

"Well, maybe it was him that got her."

"I need to find Cecil," Finest said, ignoring his implications.

"Well, then what does Cecil look like?"

"Tall, black, ugly . . ."

Floyd laughed. "Sound like every nigga out there."

"Yeah."

"Well, is Cecil blond?"

Finest laughed "No fool. Let's ride out there though and see if there's anything we can find out. Maybe ask some of them white folks some questions."

"Don't get yourself put back in jail."

"I ain't going to nobody's jail."

Fighting the start of midday traffic, he and Floyd made their way to Walnut Creek where Cecil had dropped them off. It was way out of the way, but Finest hoped he'd find some kind of clue or hint as to where she might be. Looking around, Finest found her phone laying there in the gutter. He picked it up. "It ain't like her not to have her phone."

"I told you man, she was struggling," Floyd said now.

Finest frowned. "You did not say she was struggglin'. Man, tell me exactly what you saw. First you said she was getting in the car. Then you said she didn't look like she wanted to get in the car, now you saying she was fightin' to stay outta the car . . ." He held up her phone. "And dropped her phone."

Just then Finest's phone rang. It was Mr. Sinclair.

"Yeah?"

"Finest, have you heard from Tanqueray yet?"

"Yet? You still ain't heard nothin'?"

"Well, at first I didn't want to accept it, but now I must. Cecil returned home today after being inexplicably missing last night. I don't believe what he told me about his whereabouts. And. . . ." Dustin paused. "I believe Cecil may be behind her disappearance."

"Cecil!" Finest was on full alert now. "I had a feeling. But my friend said she got in the car with somebody else.

Somebody that didn't sound like Cecil, somebody that isn't even connected with Cecil so, I'm confused."

"Well, Cecil said she was with you. He said he dropped you two off back in the hood," Dustin Sinclair said, sounding proper but making his point clear. "When I called him to pick Tanqueray up after she called me, he claimed she had changed her mind and decided to stay with you."

"She waddn't with me and we didn't get back to the . . . hood. I got my ass picked up in Walnut Creek. I was in jail I told you that. That happened in Walnut Creek. Cecil dropped us off well the hell outta our neighborhood and just like took off. If she called you she was still in Walnut Creek."

"What on earth were you doing out there?"

"Never mind that, point is, somebody snatched her there. I believe that and I believe Cecil knows who did it."

"Well, I do too. Unfortunately, I went out to confront him. He's gone again, and he's not answering his phone."

"Where does Cecil stay?"

"He lives here—"

"He don't have no family or nothing?"

"Well, yes, he's got a mother and that cousin Omar and . . ."

"Omar is his cousin?" Finest asked, looking over at Floyd who was nodding as if it all made sense to him.

"Maybe they're together. I mean it was through Omar I met Tanqueray and—"

"I bet they are and I bet they have Tang. I'm on my way over there."

"I told you it was Omar!" Floyd said having overheard Finest's end of the call.

Finest looked at him. Floyd shrugged stupidly. Finest shook his head. Floyd was good riding shot gun and even better on a caper, but when it came to everyday shit, he was past annoying!

Chapter 31

Tanqueray slowly came to consciousness. She could feel heaviness over one of her eyes and the other was totally closed. Her ribs ached as well. Omar had really done a number on her. She'd seen many movies where someone was hit with a pistol but had no idea it would hurt that much, maybe because on TV they only got hit once or twice. Omar had done batting practice on her head and face. After that white dude got done screaming, Omar all but killed her. She could tell one of her teeth was loosened now. "Fuck," she groaned, slowly coming too. She was tied to the chair still wearing that short-ass night gown. It was all ripped up now. Her arms were behind her back and her ankles were tied around the legs of the chair. All she could think about was how she had spared Omar this humiliation the last time they were in each other's presence. She should have slapped the shit outta him with his own gun and maybe even put the fireplace poker up his ass, but no, she just held him there and got what was hers. All she did was cuff him to that heffa Chantal. Now what did he want? There was nothing about her that belonged to him. Why was he doing this?

So much regret was going through her mind right now.

If she hadn't sent Finest to jail . . .

Well, he was in jail and she was here captive to this pervert. *That's just how it is Tang,* she reasoned.

About that time, Omar came from the bedroom. He was wearing his leopard print thong and a matching robe. He looked all coked out and no doubt was. The gun lay on the table now. It had blood on it—her blood.

She closed her eyes at the memory. Actually she only felt the first couple of blows anyway. She was out not too long after that. He was a prick and as soon as she could she was going to kill his ass. That is if he didn't kill her first. And for what? Some blow and a few thousand dollars and some clothes? The question in her mind made her head go back as she tried to see him through her swollen eyes. "Why?" she managed to ask.

He looked at her. It was almost as if he hadn't thought she was alive. He seemed surprised.

"What?" he asked focusing on her.

"Why you do this?" she asked. He walked up to her and squatted down to her level.

"Because. You took my money. You came up in my house and humiliated me. Because you been stealing what belongs to me by seeing my clients on the side . . . well client. That's theft. You . . ." he pointed at her. ". . . you thought you could get away with that shit. Well, you can't Tanqueray. You ain't good enough. You ain't big enough. You just a hood rat! A chickenhead skank. You ain't even worth livin'."

His words were bitter tasting in her mouth so much so they formed a ball of spit that she had to expel and she did—right in his damn face. He raised his hand to slap her but hesitated. It was as if he wasn't able to find a clear shot that wasn't already bloody.

"You," he chuckled wickedly. "You sure you ain't gotta dick." He shook his head while wiping off the spit from his cheek. She wasn't sure if he was just furious or a little impressed.

"He's gonna find me," she said of both Finest and Mr.

Sinclair. The men she loved. Yes, she loved Finest and Lord knows she had fallen in love with Dustin Sinclair. He had offered her a taste of freedom she could never repay him for. Whatever he wanted from her was his—

"Ain't nobody gonna find your black nasty ass. Cecil gonna make sure of that. He's gonna tell your John that you dead." Omar said interrupting her reverie.

"He won't believe that. He won't—"

"He'll have to because it'll be true. I'm just waiting until dark," Omar said before moving away from her to his bar. He poured himself a stiff drink.

Tanqueray heard the words, but refused to believe them. There was no way her life was going to end today. Not this way. No way. And if it was to end Omar was going down too. Tanqueray thought about her life up 'till now. It hadn't amounted to much and right now she wasn't about to start promising shit that she wasn't going to do. But she did promise one thing: If she got out of this, she wasn't ever going to be a ho. She was going to stop chasing the paper, at least for a while. The thought of her weak promise made her smile. "Lord, I ain't no good," she breathed in an undertone. "But you know I don't deserve to die like this . . . not at his hands."

"Wanna drink?" Omar asked standing before her again with a tumbler full of dark liquor. "You always like to drink." She said nothing. He poured the drink over her head. The pain surged through her. She screamed in the agony of the burn, jerking at the ropes.

"You fuckin' bastard," she growled. "Bastard, I'ma cut your balls off before you kill me. And if not, I'll have to come back to do it. But I swear you gonna get yours," she promised through gritted teeth.

Omar laughed and sauntered back to the bar. About that time his phone rang.

"Yeah," he said. "Yeah, she's still here! I been busy," Omar said rolling his eyes. "Yeah, I did. I beat her ass, what choo thank? Tonight . . ." Omar laughed. "Yeah, I did. I'ma prove it." He hung up and then took her picture with the phone.

She could see him sending the picture to the caller. She thought about her own cell phone. She'd dropped it when Omar forced her in the car. Not that she could call anyone right now, or get a call. His phone rang again. He answered it and laughed. "Well you are involved cousin. But no worries, she aint gonna tell nobody what you did. Please Cecil, stop being a pussy okay? If you gonna play in the dirt you gonna get a little dirty okay?"

Cecil. *Damn, straight he was involved and he was going to pay for his betrayal too,* Tanqueray thought now.

Chapter 32

Cecil was beyond upset now. He sat back on his sofa. He loved having his own place. Even Mr. Sinclair didn't know about it. It was private and secure. If he wanted a woman to spend some time with him, he'd bring her here. If he wanted to just think, he'd come here. But suddenly this place had become more than a sanctuary; it had become a hide out.

Omar had beaten Tanqueray to a pulp. "Idiot!" Cecil yelled looking at the picture mail again on his phone. He hit the button deleting it from his phone. "What am I gonna do?"

He thought about calling Finest and sending him to Omar's place. "Surely that fool will kill my cousin. I can't do that! Can I?" He thought about calling Mr. Sinclair.

"There is no way in hell, I'm calling him," Cecil said, noticing again, how many times, his boss had called him. He was surprised the car hadn't been reported stolen. It just confirmed again, how much Dustin Sinclair trusted him. He just up and split and Mr. Sinclair had let it happen. He was acting like a spoiled child—Sinclair's child. Maybe that was how Dustin Sinclair saw him?

Well, he won't see me that way anymore, Cecil thought now.

"Why did I get so upset over that little bit of money," he asked himself, thinking about the changes Dustin Sinclair was making to his will, the changes that would provide monetarily for Tanqueray and her sisters. "Arrg," he cried out.

Yes, Cecil had let jealousy ruin everything.

"Maybe I could just act like I don't know anything," he said, pondering again, a call to Mr. Sinclair. "I would just go back and act like I looked for that tramp all night long. I could act like I got so upset that I just went lookin'. " He shook his head. "That's not gonna work. I'ma have to help Omar get rid of her before I do that. I'm going to have to make sure nobody finds Ms. Tanqueray."

Cecil took a deep breath knowing that by the end of this day he would be an accomplice to murder. *What is he gonna have me do? Am I gonna have to help him?*

Cecil thought again about growing up with Omar. He was always in some kind of trouble. He was always needing money or wanting some help with some half baked scheme to get rich quick. Cecil was relieved when he got a chance to move away from him. And then he got hooked back up with him. "Ugh!" Cecil groaned, thinking about the scheme that brought them together as partners, the money, the women, all of it. And now, how far would it go. "How far will this go before it's over. Wars were started over whores like her." Cecil mumbled, thinking about the beautiful, yet foul, Tanqueray Nation. Who else wanted her as much as Dustin Sinclair?

Chapter 33

The city is a wonderful place to live. It's a great place to work. However, around this time of day, living, working, and driving are a bad combination. At least this was what Finest and Floyd found out.

Bumper to bumper traffic had them pinned in for what seemed to be hours. Fender benders, stalled cars, and just plain stupid-ass drivers had them sitting in a freeway gridlock, going nowhere fast.

"Fuck!" Finest finally exploded, slamming the steering wheel like a madman. Floyd just watched in silence.

"Chill, man. You 'bout to lose your mind!"

"You just don't get it do you Floyd. You just don't fuck'n get it!"

"I guess not because I ain't never seen you act this way ova no bitch before."

Finest stared at Floyd debating if he was going to open the door and toss him into traffic. He was just that frustrated. Instead, he took a deep breath and grinded his molars a second or two before speaking. "She is more than that."

"Oh, I know," Floyd quickly agreed, sounding bubbly and stupid.

"No, you don't, so just shut it up. I don't want to talk to you about it. I don't—" Finest fumed a second longer. "I don't want to talk to you about it."

"Oh, I know," Floyd said again, turning toward the window.

Chapter 34

Tanqueray didn't know what to think about the situation she was in. Waiting for darkness? This was crazy. Omar continued to drink like a damn fish out of water. Soon he'd be drunker than drunk. She'd have to wait for that before trying anything. She wasn't about to just sit here and let this fool take her life without a fight. Soon Omar would let his guard down.

She wriggled at the ropes where they were still damp from the alcohol he'd poured on them. She halfway thought she felt them a little looser than before. She wasn't sure though, and didn't want to wriggle around too much in case his drunk ass noticed. Just then she saw him run a line up his nose. Apparently he was planning a real party; had coke lined up all over the damn place for his guests. *But after biting that dude's dick earlier, waddn't nobody else coming over this joint, ever again,* she thought to herself. That kind of news travels fast. About that time he glanced over at her. He had that look. "Shit," she groaned.

He picked up the gun and sauntered over to her. Pointed it at her forehead and he pulled out his dick and parted her lips with it. "You bite me, I'll blow your mutha fuckin' head off," he threatened.

She wanted to bite that shit off as he rammed it into her mouth as if they were in the bed fucking like true hot lovers. She was gagging and he didn't care. And yeah she had a loose tooth for sure because his pushing in her mouth knocked it out. *One, two, three, grunt.* Yep, it had come out, because she was sure she swallowed it now along with his nasty cum. *Damn, Omar was nasty.*

He gave her head a hard push with the barrel of the gun before shoving his shit back in his thong, sauntering back over to the bar and making himself another drink. Omar held the gun loosely while swallowing his drink now. As the glass came down from his mouth he staggered a little. That's when he looked at her. "It's almost time Tang," he said. "I hate summer. Takes so fuckin' long for the sun to go down."

"Yeah, the devil don't like no light," she said.

He glared at her. "What choo know about the devil?" he asked her. "Oh, yeah, I forgot, you his daughter."

"Omar, if I'm the devil's daughter then you should be real scared 'cause you about to go home with me to meet my daddy," Tanqueray answered coolly. Her heart was cold and she felt fearless. It was a strange phenomenon that occurred in her when she knew she had to be brave. It happened when she knew there was only one of two options to take—fight or flight.

That comment didn't sit well with him at all. He staggered over to her. He just stood there as if thinking of something else nasty to do to her. He looked down at her and took in a deep breath. "You was gonna be one of my best hoes Tang. What went wrong between us, baby?"

"Well, for one, I'm not a whore," she answered.

"That's what they all say," he said, snickering. Suddenly as if noticing the damage he'd done to her face he lightly touched her temporal area.

She didn't even flinch. She'd not felt pain for a while now. She was past numb.

"Look at your pretty face. It's all messed up. Now what? Now what will you do with your sorry life?" he asked.

"More than you could ever do with yours," she answered.

Out of reflex he hit her hard, knocking her over, taking the chair down.

An angel must have stepped in. He must have been tired of watching all this, because the way the chair fell, the back of it cut the rope. At first she didn't believe it. But the moment Omar lunged at her she knew it had to be true and her only chance to get away.

Freeing her hand she swung as hard as she could, catching Omar off guard and knocking him backward. He dropped the gun. *Aw, lawd it was within reach.* She scooted herself toward it just as Omar scrambled to his feet and dove for it.

Both of them had their hands on it.

Tanqueray cried out in her fervor and desperation.

Omar grunted, puffed, and struggled to get the gun from her. He wrestled with her with the chair between them still tied to her at the ankles.

Finally she felt the trigger and pulled it. The gun fired. Omar fell backward. She dropped the gun and quickly untied her feet not caring if he was dead or not. She heard him groan. She reached out and grabbed the gun again as she got to her feet.

He was laid over his white sofa, blood running from under his hand which was on his shoulder. His eyes widened and mouth dropped open but he shut smooth up, when she pointed the gun at his heart and cocked it.

"Kill me bitch. Kill me!" he screamed.

She swallowed hard. "I'm Javina Nation's daughter. I ain't got no devil in me!" she growled, aiming instead at his leg, firing the gun into his knee cap.

He screamed, grabbing at his leg, shaking and trembling in pain.

Tanqueray didn't care. She fired again into the other one.

Again he screamed and grabbed at the pain.

She then spat on him again. "Now what you gonna do with your sorry life without no damn legs," she asked, before charging for the back door without waiting for an answer. She wasn't crazy. If folks saw her coming out the front door as messed up as she was it could only spell some jail time for her. It didn't matter who was right or wrong in a neighborhood like this. Glancing into the laundry area that was by the back door, she noticed one of Omar's sweat suits. She snatched the pants and slipped her feet into a pair of his flip flops. They were too big for her but she didn't care. Out the back door she went and on through the gate to the alleyway where the trash sat out for pick up. The balmy air hit her, the sting from the bay waters caused her face to tingle now, but she was free. As she struggled to put some distance between herself and that condo, she didn't look back.

Chapter 35

Finest and Floyd fought traffic, it was just a little less insane now after two hours. Midday had drifted quickly into early rush hour but they were still ahead of that mess by a little bit. Trying to make it from East Bay down to South Bay at any time of day was tricky. It wasn't like on their side of the water. It was simple over there, every town was connected by Highway One. Over here it seemed you were constantly off and on, jumping on this bridge and that. Finest couldn't wait to get back to the P. Hell, even the West End sounded good right about now.

"What we gon' do when we get there?" Floyd asked. He'd been quieter since Finest's explosion earlier. He must have sensed how close he was to walking on the freeway.

"If Tang is there, I'ma see what's going on. If she wants to be there, then whatever. You know," Finest squirmed uncomfortably with the thought of Tanqueray choosing some punk-ass pimp over her. Yeah, Omar was a pimp. Not too long after he and Tanqueray met, Finest had done some checking with Dub Dub, the local "go to drug man." He'd inquired about Tanqueray right after their first encounter just to see who that chick was that had his nose open so wide. He never let on that was why, but that was why. No woman on earth had ever affected him the way Tanqueray had.

Finest remembered that day. He and Floyd were on a delivery

to Omar's place. As a matter of fact, Sinclair was riding shot gun. They had just met too. He had no idea that little cutie was Tang's sister. Sinclair was mixed, just like him. She had green eyes and all that, just like him, so how would he figure that she and Tang were sisters, huh? Anyway, he had her sit in the car while he went in to do business with Omar. Everybody was crunk and she was floating on a contact so he just had her wait and maybe sleep, like that fool So and So in the back seat. Oh, man, So and So was high as a mutha fuck and OD'd in the back seat. He almost died right there in the backseat. *That would have been a mess for sure*, Finest thought back.

Anyway, he and Floyd were doing some runnin' for Dub Dub. They were running a little blow to the rich side of town. This delivery had gotten all messed up because Dub Dub couldn't move the blow or didn't want too, so he had said to take it back—no questions. They did. They got to Omar's condo looking for some dude named Omar, but it was Tanqueray that answered the door. Finest was sprung from moment one! They shared the blow and fucked like rabbits right then and there. He didn't care that she was probably married to the dude whose dope it was or whatever. She was fine and looked fresh and rich. She said her name was Suga, had it tatted on her inner thigh. Yeah he saw that up close and personal, along with that gold hair down there on her snatch. She was down for whatever and he had whatever for her ass too.

"Damn," he groaned, feeling his hard on rising. He missed his wifey, Tanqueray, now. He could only think about how it felt inside Tanqueray. "Damn," he groaned again, shaking his head in growing agitation. Something didn't feel right about this. There was no way she was okay. He felt it now in his bones. Tanqueray was in trouble.

"We gon' find her," Floyd said, attempting to comfort him.

Chapter 36

"God, Omar. Look at you!" Cecil gasped as soon as he entered the condo.

He had a key, but rarely if ever used it. It wasn't as if he really wanted people to know he was related to Omar. Mr. Sinclair had found out, unfortunately. But that was okay in the end because Omar had what Mr. Sinclair wanted: whores. That's what they all were ya know, just whores. Why any man thought anything different about them was amazing. They had sex for money. They were whores. Mr. Sinclair liked to think he made a difference to them by not touching them—just paying them to be naked or take baths or sit around naked, talking. Still they were whores. No matter how to cut it, all black women who were willing to spend that kind of time with an old white man for money, well, what else were they? His mother had been one of those women. She met him one summer while working in his store and next thing ya know, she was having her son working for him. She'd done something with him. She'd shown him her titties or her snatch or her . . .

Cecil's mind was spinning so fast with thoughts about Mr. Sinclair and his mother that he nearly forgot the urgency of Omar's situation.

But at least Cecil wasn't fooled by what appeared to be. He wasn't naive like his mother was. She thought white was right and money meant power and ability to change the world.

White didn't mean shit and money was for the taking. Cecil had plans to take it all. Just a few more years and Dustin Sinclair would be out of the picture, okay maybe quite a few years, but it didn't matter. He was set up for life for sure and in the end he was going to get a bundle in that will. Mr. Sinclair didn't have any kids, so why not? Everything was a done deal until Tanqueray came along.

There was some haunting going on around that girl, Tanqueray Nation. She had Mr. Sinclair's nose wide open. So much so that he was changing his will and shit. He was talking something crazy about this old black ho he used to love! And now he was going to leave Tanqueray all this money because she reminded him of her? That is crazy. Cecil had heard him on the phone talking to his attorney while driving him to one of his stores one day. He didn't get it all, but either way, he'd heard that much! And then when he got that news about that trust fund or whatever, he about flipped. But check this out! Tanqueray wasn't going to get that money! There was no way in hell Cecil would let that happen. But after seeing that picture that Omar sent and now seeing Omar all bloody—

"Shit! This is getting complicated," he exclaimed running over to this cousin and looking him over. He didn't want to touch him. There was too much blood. Who knows what kinda whatever Omar could have fooling with these nasty bitches.

"Help me," Omar groaned. "Bitch shot me. Three fuckin' times. I knew I shoulda killed her quick."

"You're a fool Omar. Why did you have a loaded gun here? I need to get you to a hospital."

"No! They call the cops when it's a gunshot wound . . ."

"So, we'll say it was an accident that we were cleaning the weapon and—"

"You punk-ass crazy nigga! What weapon? Cleaning it for what? Duck hunting? Shit! The bitch done took the gun and she's gone now. We can't say anything to the cops about anything," he groaned. "We gotta find that bitch. We gotta find Tanqueray and shut her up for good."

"Well it's obvious she didn't go to the police or they would have been here by now," he said hoisting Omar up from the sofa.

"Where we going?"

"My place. Nobody will think to look there," he said.

"Nobody is looking for me," Omar assured.

"I wouldn't be so sure about that," Cecil said looking around the living room—the knocked over chair, the rope, the cocaine. He could only imagine the atrocities Omar had committed on that woman. He had a payback coming. It was one for the books! Apparently Omar had no idea who he was dealing with.

"We gotta get these bullets outta my legs," Omar groaned. "The one in my shoulder went through but the ones in my legs—" he bit his lip and panted in pain when he shifted his weight onto Cecil's shoulder. "They are still in there. God!" he cried out.

Chapter 37

"It's Tang. You gotta help me. Omar kidnapped me and beat my ass good. I'm hurt real bad," Tanqueray whispered.

"What the hell! Tang where are you," Unique gasped getting everyone's attention especially Markey's. They had just returned from visiting with Cammie. Markey had treated the girls to ice cream. They were laughing and talking like a family in the living room. They'd even coaxed him into playing a video game with them. Unique missed her Marquis. He used to always be in front of the TV playing those games.

"I'm . . ." Tanqueray looked around. "Shit! I don't know where I am . . ."

Unique could hear voices. There was a sound of people giving directions. She wasn't alone but apparently she wasn't where she could get help. "Tang!" Unique yelled. "Get to a hospital. Can you get to a hospital? Can you get on a bus or something?"

"Girl, I'm at the Marina or near it. Don't ask me how the fuck I got here, 'cause I couldn't tell ya. I been running for hours. I finally found some folks to give me a ride," she said.

Again Unique heard the voices.

"But you gotta come get me . . ."

"Girl, I ain't got no car. I—" Unique began, only to have Markey touch her arm and nod.

"Okay. Okay. We on our way," she said then, realizing that

Markey had the car situation covered. "Just give me a minute or two."

"Hurry girl I'm hurt like a muthafuck and tryin' ta keep the cops from taking me in. They keep looking at me and shit," Tanqueray said, "I look like I'm homeless and shit," she chuckled weakly before hanging up.

Markey reached for the phone and dialed a number. "Buck—yeah, I need y'all ta come get me. Yeah, at my babyma-ma's house. We got a pick up," he said, sounding authoritat-ive. He hung up and smiled that pretty smile of his.

Suddenly Unique didn't care who he had called. She had been trying to not think about Markey's affiliation. Today, she was just glad he had the hook-up.

"Come on, girls you gotta go to Mrs. Newbury's apartment."

"What about the ice cream?" Gina whined.

"Oh, we gon' eat some ice cream, I promise you that. And, these days Mama keeps her word!" Unique assured, ushering them to the door.

Mrs. Newbury was sitting on ready as if expecting Unique to come by. She opened the door wide upon her hard knocking.

"Good evening Mrs. Newbury. God Bless."

"God Bless," she said back, looking down at the girls.

"My sister done called me and Lord knows she's in trouble. Me and my . . ." she looked at Markey. "Me and him," she said, pointing over her shoulder at Markey, "We gotta go help," she said.

"No need to explain chile. Go get your sista. These girls are always welcome here."

"Thank you," Unique said, rushing the girls in and hurrying to the elevator with Markey behind her.

Markey's partners were local to the W.E. and within a moment or two they pulled up in a black Impala. It was low riding just like the old days but it was clean. She got in.

"Where we headed boss," the driver said.

"The Marina," Markey said.

"Cool," was all the driver replied before they sped off.

Chapter 38

Tanqueray handed the phone back to the woman who had given her the opportunity to call. She was a hooker, but one that was apparently doing well. She was clean and dressed well. Her shoes were high but comfortable looking and her makeup was applied perfectly. Her nails were, well, Tanqueray didn't even want to compare her own to that.

"Girl, what kinda pimp beats up his money like this?" she had asked Tanqueray again, examining Tanqueray's face and body bruises closer up. She'd come up on her while Tanqueray dozed in the grass. It was getting to be dinner time, but eating was far from possible right now.

"I ain't his money," Tanqueray had responded.

"Yeah, whatever girl. I know what you feel," she went on to say, clearly not believing Tanqueray one bit.

Tanqueray had gotten as far as she could in them damn flip flops. They were big and crazy looking. But after shooting Omar, she wanted to get as far away as she could and fast. There was no telling where he had put her nice shoes; the ones Mr. Sinclair had given her. There was no telling where her new sweat suit was either. Here she was, looking raggedy again. She could have called Dustin with her only use of a phone, but she was tired of him seeing her this way. She always seemed to be in a jam, always messed up. If she'd given herself a minute she'd have gotten a little depressed, but what good would that do?

She'd ditched the gun. She sure as hell didn't want to get caught with that and sure as hell didn't want another gun to end up at Unique's place. The last one had spelled disaster for their whole family. Of course Omar didn't get the fault for owning the gun that killed Curtis, Unique's ex, the one li'l Marquis shot at the hospital that night. That gun came up clean as a whistle under the spotlight. She thought about poor little Marquis. He really thought he was going to be a hero when he shot the man that was molesting his little sister Cammie.

Tanqueray smacked her lips at the memory of that night. She knew in her heart there wasn't anything going to become of this incident either, except the wrong person paying the price. Omar again would get off the hook for owning a murder weapon. If anything she was going to go to jail for shooting him and probably killing him. Surely he'd bled to death by now. Maybe she had it coming. Maybe it was time for Karma. Who the hell knew?

"Either way it ain't right. Not this time," she had told the bus driver who had let her get on free. He went past the hospital and she had told him she was hurt. She'd ridden with him before and they had a good rapport. Despite the folks fussing about her free ride, she rode.

She got off at the hospital stop but after he pulled off she realized that she didn't want to go in. There was no way she wanted to go through all that paperwork. She'd pondered it when she got on the bus, but by the time she got there, changed her mind. Besides, she didn't have any ID on her. After all was said and done, she'd have been the one who would have landed in jail for sure. She'd borrowed a phone from a man waiting in front of the hospital and called Finest but he didn't answer. *Probably still in jail*, she reasoned. She didn't want to call Mr. Sinclair. She didn't have the heart or the energy to tell him about Cecil. Maybe he knew already. Maybe Cecil and Omar were right and he just saw her as his whore.

Never that! she mentally fussed.

"Well, girl, I'ma leave now. Looks like you gotta ride coming and well—I gotta get back to my kids," the well-dressed hooker said having apparently ended her "shift." Or maybe she was just on a break. It wasn't all that late. Actually she didn't know what time it was. She was sure it was still the same day though. She was sure that just that morning she'd started out her day in heaven only to end up in hell by dusk. She was sure of that.

What a life, Tanqueray thought. Her mind went back to the hooker. Just watching her took her mind off her own troubles for a moment. "Po' thang. Sexing for money then turning around and handing over your money to some jive turkey come the end of a hard working day. Ugh, and now she had to go home to some 'kids' that think she's the best thing since gravy," Tanqueray mumbled, shaking her head as if the woman truly had a worse life than she had. "That'll never be me," she said aloud, as the ladies of the night, including the one she had befriended, caught the next bus to pull up. They'd be back; this was no doubt just a dinner break. Tanqueray figured it had to be around dinner time. The day had flown by.

Tanqueray felt like shit. The pain was hitting her now. The adrenaline of making her getaway had passed. She flopped down in the grass. Everything on her body hurt. Things that hurt could no longer be rightfully identified. She just knew she hurt and she was sure she should probably see a doctor. She laid back and closed her eyes, feeling safe. There was no way Omar would find her here. Even if he managed to get someone to take his ass to the hospital he'd still be there explaining who busted those caps in his knees.

"Yeah," Tanqueray groaned. "Explain that shit," she panted through painful laughter. She needed something for the pain now. She needed somebody to make her feel better. She thought about death for a second, right before drifting off to sleep.

Chapter 39

"What we gon' do when we get there?" Floyd asked again shifting nervously in his seat. He was quite a fidget before a drive by and even worse before a face to face confrontation.

"We gon' kill a nigga that's what," Finest said, pulling off the freeway and easing through the suburban streets where he remembered Omar living. The day Finest met Tanqueray at that condo, Dub had told him to return the drugs to Omar. He told him that Omar was bad news and tough business. Dub wasn't about to go up against a pimp like Omar, not as sweet in the jeans as Dub was. But Finest? Damn that, Omar didn't scare him at all. He was going to break his neck if Tang was hurt. He loved her and he believed in his heart that she loved him. What they had was powerful in his mind.

Sure Tang may truly be a ho, and Finest had his doubts that she wasn't, despite her protesting it all the damn time, but still, if she was a ho, she was his ho, his boo, his wifey. She was the bitch he loved. He was sprung off her from day one and it hadn't faded a bit. He'd even stopped fuckin' other bitches for her. There was no way he'd tell anybody that. He did have a rep to keep up with, but it was true. He'd not laid it on any other bitch but Tang since shortly after they met. "And if that Omar done fucked her . . ." Finest shook his head and gritted his teeth. "I'ma fuck him in the ass with my baseball bat. Feel me?" Finest promised, speaking his thoughts out loud.

Floyd just nodded.

"Then I'ma cut his dick off and make him eat it," Finest added to the visual.

"Ouch, man . . ." Floyd took in the air through his teeth. "That's gonna be a lot of blood."

Finest rolled his eyes and sucked the diamond in his tooth. "Floyd you always worried about shit like that. I guess 'cause your mama's a nurse you got them kinda details in your brain. You crazy fa sho," Finest laughed. Floyd was not only his cousin, but a loyal pawdna fa sho. They'd done plenty of dirt together over the last few years but hadn't done any dirt that a nigga didn't deserve done to him. That was how Finest figured it.

Sure they'd probably do time together one day too, but like he just implied, it would be for a good reason. Like when they took out Gold Mouth for blowing up Javina Nation's house. He deserved that shit. nigga knew that wasn't part of the deal.

Finest and Floyd pulled up in front of the condo and parked. Finest stepped out of the car. He was trying to look inconspicuous. He'd just gotten out of jail that morning. He didn't want to catch another case carrying a gun into a white neighborhood so he had to play it straight. Floyd was sagging though, so he was sure the scary folks were peepin' out their windows at them.

Reaching the door, Finest tried it, as if maybe by chance it was open. Of course it wasn't, so he headed around the back. Tanqueray had told him once how she had broken in from the back door so he thought he'd try it too.

The back door was locked too so he busted out the window. "Fuck an alarm," he said, anticipating a lot of noise but there was nothing. He assumed it was probably silent and hurriedly opened the door by reaching through.

"Come on, man!" Floyd rushed him anxiously.

The door opened and they rushed inside with guns drawn. Floyd was packing too. They were both going to kill the Negro on sight. Scanning the living room, they didn't see anybody. The room was dark, not pitch black, but still they needed some light. Finest found a switch and turned on the light. Immediately he noticed the chair and the ropes. He saw the blood on the carpet. His heart started pounding.

"Shit!" he cried out. His eyes were burning. He was furious.

"Looks like the nigga's on the move!" Floyd deduced.

"Yeah, but where?" Finest pondered. He looked around for clues. Just then he spied a cell phone. He picked it up to check the numbers, text messages, anything, and that's when he saw the picture of Tanqueray all beat up in the chair. Again he cried out, cursing bitterly. He then tried to hold it together as he went through the phone for more clues.

He saw it then, Cecil's name. "Cecil! Sinclair was right!"

"You think that white man behind all this?" Floyd asked. Finest had told Floyd about Mr. Sinclair and Tanqueray. He left out the part about what he had done while he was there because that wasn't important—not really—but he'd told Floyd about Tanqueray's *friend*, the old white man.

"Nah. I thank that punk ass Cecil is behind this alone. It's too sloppy and ghetto. If Mr. Sinclair was behind it, it'd be clean and untraceable—you can believe dat," Finest said. "Man got too much money to be fount out this easily. I think he is looking for Tang too."

"Why he didn't know Cecil is dirty?"

"Phst, Cecil been his boy for a long time. It's hard to face facts I guess, but this one," Finest began and then glanced at the picture mail Omar had sent to Cecil of Tanqueray. "This one he won't be able to deny,"

"Where he stay? Cecil?"

"I don't know. But I'ma fine out cuz that's something I think Mr. Sinclair would know, and like it or not, he gonna have to tell me," he said, dialing Mr. Sinclair's number. There was no answer.

Chapter 40

This was more drama than Mr. Sinclair had seen in many years. He was used to hostile takeovers and other corporate matters, not this street action. He had taken off looking for Cecil. He had to accept that Cecil had actually and in all reality crossed the line and returned to the life he'd been removed from so many years ago. He'd stolen the Bentley and probably aided Omar in committing some kind of heinous crime against Tanqueray. With that he called inOnStar to locate the vehicle. If nothing else he'd find the car. Maybe in doing that he'd find Cecil and maybe Omar too. What he'd do when he found them both he wasn't sure, but he was ready for anything . . . almost. He wasn't ready to find Tanqueray hurt.

"Why would you do this?" Dustin Sinclair mumbled under his breath turning the corners, exiting and entering freeways that would lead him to Cecil and the car. He told OnStar not to dispatch the police that it was indeed a private matter. He'd attend to it himself.

For the most part Cecil stayed at the main house. Cecil had basically everything he wanted ever since he started driving for Mr. Sinclair at eighteen. But Mr. Sinclair wasn't naïve. When Cecil reached his manhood he was ready to get his own place. Dustin Sinclair knew this. Despite Cecil's efforts to be secretive, he found out where the place was. He'd never had a reason to visit it, but it was nice knowing that he could locate it if he had to and tonight, he had to. Just a few minutes ago, OnStar told him that's where he'd find his car.

Taken from the streets, Cecil had been Dustin Sinclair's protégé. He'd taken Cecil under his wings, teaching him the business and how to become wealthy. Unfortunately, Cecil didn't like to work that hard and was content to be a driver. *If it doesn't fit don't force it,* Dustin Sinclair decided about trying to fit Cecil into corporate America. He allowed Cecil to live the life he was comfortable with. It made his mother happy. At one time, making Cecil's mother happy was an endeavor of Dustin Sinclair's, but only momentarily. Not too long after that he met Javina Nation and his whole life changed forever.

It was his own penchant for young black women that brought Dustin to this night. He knew this, but life's circle could be both kind and cruel. This he knew. This was also true of Cecil's life. Here he was attempting to live a life outside of his upbringing, yet falling so easily back on his street smarts and inner curses. Cecil's father was a notorious bad-actor they called Switch. Apparently Switch was everything from pimp to pedophile and it wasn't until he'd run into the wrong end of a blade did the name Switch really take on a double meaning. Cecil's mother wanted to keep Cecil from that element and possibly the same end, begging him to give Cecil a job and take him in. It was the least he could do even after their affair ended.

As much as he wanted to believe he'd served to change Cecil's life, he had come to believe that all he'd done was make things worse. The more money Cecil made and the easier life he gave him, the easier it seemed to have been for him to slip back to where he began. Maybe it was for bragging rights that he reconnected with Omar. "Maybe," Dustin said aloud with a sigh of guilt following his words, "Maybe it was my fault. Maybe it's in his blood . . ."

So many things were innate. He thought about Tanqueray, Javina Nation's daughter. Javina never claimed to be a whore either. That thought tickled him. It made him laugh thinking of how often Tanqueray made the same claim.

"And maybe you're not," he said, pulling into the parking lot of Cecil's building. "And maybe Cecil is innocent of all that's happened to you this night," Dustin said, sounding almost as if praying for that to be true. "Even if you are a whore Tanqueray, it doesn't matter. It will never matter to me. But if Cecil is in on this . . ." he allowed the thought to drift.

Dustin pulled up in front of Cecil's apartment complex to wait. He'd brought no gun or any form of protection. He had no fear of Cecil. He knew what jealousy could make a man do, but in this case, he didn't fear that Cecil would act desperately. *Who was Cecil jealous of? Tanqueray? Why?*

Maybe he was fooling himself, but Dustin Sinclair wanted to believe that he could talk some sense into Cecil, that he could get Cecil to tell him where his cousin Omar had taken Tanqueray. Finest seemed to think they were together and that was what had him thinking the same, but what if Finest was wrong? Finest was crazed when he called. He was talking out of his mind with rage. He threatened to kill Cecil. Maybe that was the biggest reason Dustin Sinclair left his house that night. To find Cecil, to find Tanqueray. He wanted to end this madness. Omar can go to hell. Omar wasn't one of Dustin Sinclair's concerns really. If anything he was the cause of everything–maybe.

Dustin Sinclair was full of guilt right now. He wanted to cast blame off of himself, off of Cecil and onto someone like Omar. The car wasn't anywhere to be seen. Apparently it had been at this location and now was gone. But he wasn't going to go chasing it all over the city. He would wait right here for Cecil to return. Surely he would return soon.

Many of the cars that drove by were filled with young black men. The music pouring from their cars was loud and filled with hip-hop lyrics. But Dustin Sinclair had Cecil on his mind. He wasn't sure what he would say or do if Cecil pulled up in his Bentley, but for sure, if nothing else, he needed to hear it from Cecil that he was not involved in Tanqueray's disappearance. He needed to hear that he hadn't betrayed him that way. He'd pull in alone and tell Dustin the truth about how he tried to keep Omar from hurting Tanqueray . . .

"Yes. That's what he'll say," Dustin Sinclair convinced himself.

Before long his Bentley pulled in, with Cecil and another man inside. The man was slouched down in the seat. They pulled into the parking lot around back. Dustin's heart sank. He knew the other man had to be Omar. But there was no sign of Tanqueray with them.

Dustin climbed out of the car and eased to the side of the building so he could see without being seen. Yes, it was Omar. Cecil was helping him walk. What had happened? Dustin didn't know or care, all he figured was that if Omar was this badly hurt, chances were that Tanqueray was in worse shape. Without thinking, he pulled out his cell phone and retrieved Finest's number from when Finest had called him earlier.

Chapter 41

Unique nearly leapt from the car at the sight of Tanqueray laying there in the grass looking half dead. "Tang!" she screamed loudly running up to her and dropping down to her side.

Tanqueray stirred, looking around disoriented. "Wow," she said, smiling broadly. "You came." She seemed dazed as she looked around at Markey and the driver who now stood over her as well. "And brought the fuckin' cavalry and shit," she chuckled, groaning at the pain that was in her side, grabbing at it.

Markey bent down now and lifted her to her feet.

"Who did this?" Unique asked.

"I told you. Omar," she answered, flatly and matter of fact.

"Who is Omar? Yo man?" Markey asked as she limped to the car being supported by Unique and Markey's driver. The rest had stiffened her joints.

"Shit, nah! Mah man wouldn't think about touching me. He . . ." she paused. "He loves me," she said, before suddenly her lip trembled.

Unique didn't know what to think seeing Tanqueray suddenly grow emotional. Maybe she was in more pain then she originally thought. Unique couldn't tell but she did know that Tanqueray needed medical attention and fast.

"How long have you been like this Tang?"

"All day. That nigga had me penned up all damn day. He was waiting for dark to kill me."

"My God," Unique sighed, sliding into the backseat next to her.

"Take me by there," Markey insisted.

"No! The hospital first," Unique blurted.

"I shot him! We can't go by there. No way," Tanqueray exclaimed sounding scared and unreasonable.

Unique was panicking more and more with each passing second, "Oh my God Tang. Did you kill him?"

"Nah, I didn't, but I wanted to. I wanted to real bad," she explained. "I left that fucker bleedin' on the couch. I hope he bled to death."

"Where's your man?" Markey asked.

"I don't know. We had a falling out and so, you know . . . whatever, whatever," she explained. "He's probably still locked up."

"He's not locked up. He called looking for you already," Unique confirmed.

"You need to call him," Markey said. "We need to get this shit straightened out with that fool who hurt you." Markey was one for retaliation, of that Unique could see. He had vengeance in his eyes.

"Nah, I just think I need a doctor," Tanqueray said sounding weaker than before. Suddenly she heaved and blood came from her mouth.

Unique screamed. "Shit!"

Tanqueray moaned. "Yeah. I guess I'm hurt bad Neek," she said sounding cool yet, with fear edging her words. She held her hand at her chin to catch the blood flow.

"Hurry, Markey!" Unique screamed. "Please take her to the hospital."

Markey turned to see what was what in the back seat. "Shit!

Hold on baby girl. You a soldier fa real. We gon' get you some help!" he said before patting the shoulder of the driver urging him to go faster.

Chapter 42

Omar was rambling, but it was understandable after what he'd been through. Cecil ran to the window to close the blinds but that's when he saw it and his heart about stopped. "Shit!" he yelped.

"What? Why you screaming like a bitch?" Omar asked, sounding groggy.

"My boss is here," Cecil gasped, seeing Dustin Sinclair's car.

"I thought you said he didn't know where you stayed."

"Apparently he knows everything. Who the hell knows how long he's been out there." Cecil was panicked and crazed with fear. Without thinking he picked up his .22 and headed out the door. Half way down the steps he met Dustin on his way up.

"Cecil what are you doing? Where is Tanqueray?"

Cecil looked around hoping no one would see. It was Monday night. *Everyone was just getting their week started, right? Nobody was into craziness, right? That was reserved for the weekend, right?* "You shouldn't have come here. This was a mistake."

"Yes, and let's fix it."

"No! You're coming here was a mistake," he said holding out the gun, pointing it at him.

Dustin blinked slowly. "Cecil stop it. Don't make this worse."

"I'm not. You are. Now come inside. Hurry up before somebody sees you—"

"Cecil I called—"

"I don't care! You'll call them back—whoever it was—and tell them you changed your mind on whatever it was you told them. Get inside, Mr. Sinclair!"

Dustin sighed heavily and obeyed him. Cecil knew he must have looked crazed as his eyes were wide and he'd broken a sweat. This was all just too real now. Cecil knew now there was really no turning back. For a split second he wanted to point the gun on himself and get out of this mess, but he was a coward. Of this, he was now certain.

"Jesus," Dustin gasped upon seeing Omar laid out on the sofa with his knees wrapped in bloody rags.

"Tanqueray shot him," Cecil explained.

"And what did he do to her?" Dustin asked.

"I killed that bitch. I killed her," Omar growled.

"Jesus, God . . . no," Dustin gasped, dropping to the chair and holding his chest.

Chapter 43

"Well, for one you're pregnant," the doctor said, sounding blunt and less than caring.

Unique gasped grabbing Tanqueray's shoulders.

"I'm what?" Tanqueray tried to yell. The bandages around her middle were constricting. Yes, Omar had broken one of her ribs. The cuts on her face were held together with butterfly bandages. The one over her eye was deep enough to scar for sure.

"You want to tell me who raped you. It's clear you were raped," the doctor said. He'd examined her thoroughly and could tell she'd had sex recently—rough sex. But then again, that was Finest's style. Omar hadn't been the one between her legs but she'd already put Finest through enough. She wasn't even going to mention his name.

"His name is Omar. He's my ex-boyfriend. We broke up and he didn't like it I guess," Tanqueray lied. "So he beat me up and raped me. He tortured me and tried to kill me."

"Is he the father of the baby?" the doctor asked. She frowned up at the thought of Omar having planted seed in her body. Only once in the last three months had he actually penetrated her. It was the day they broke up. Perhaps had she had a regular period since then, she would have been able to say for sure, but actually her monthly visits had been extra light and kind of crazy lately. She figured it was because of her change of sexual habits as well as her increased recreational drug use.

Yeah, Finest had been a definite change of both habits. Finest had been working her body over good for the last few months and so she figured he'd changed her cycle. *But pregnant?* Had Finest made her pregnant? She thought about Finest's pretty eyes and hair. She thought about how she felt about him. Sometimes she loved him. Sometimes she hated his very existence. Right now? She didn't know which feeling was stronger.

"Hell, nah, he ain't my baby daddy," Tanqueray lied again. Truly she had no way of knowing. But in her heart there was no way she was going to have Omar's baby. It was just that simple. So why even put Omar in the mix.

The doctor looked confused for a moment and then his face straightened out. He'd heard worse stories. Tanqueray was sure of that.

"Is the baby okay? I mean, with her ribs. Can a baby survive that?" Unique inquired.

"She's still pregnant. That's all I can say," the doctor answered bluntly. "You need to get to a clinic and start your prenatal visits. Baby's can survive a lot but they aren't invincible. If you don't want to continue this pregnancy you need to get busy dealing with that."

"I don't have medical. I don't got a job," Tanqueray explained.

"With this paper," he said, handing her a Pregnancy Verification Form, "You can get what you need medically from the County." He sounded short and curt.

She rolled her eyes reading his mind, "I don't want no welfare if that's what you mean. I don't need the County's damn checks and food stamps and all that. My man takes care of me!" She got loud.

Unique touched her shoulder sensing that she was getting wound up.

"He'd be here right now if he wasn't out tryin'a find that

nigga that did this to me!" Tanqueray yelled. Her emotions were soaring now. "He loves me!" she cried now. Hot tears began rolling down her cheeks. It was the first time in forever since she actually remembered putting on an ugly cry like this. But the moment deserved it. Even if it didn't, she couldn't hold it in any longer.

Chapter 44

"You're at the hospital?" Finest said, his face breaking into a wide grin. They were only blocks from Cecil's pad but killing both them niggas could wait! Mr. Sinclair had called him to tell him he had spotted Cecil and Omar. He told him the address. Finest was surprised he'd sold his boy Cecil out like that. He must really care for Tang, was all Finest could figure. He wasn't jealous. Tang needed a daddy type person, even if he was more of a sugar daddy type person.

Besides, Mr. Sinclair was probably there trying to 'talk' to them. White folks cracked him up. His mother was that way. He remembered when he got his tats she was so upset and tried to 'talk' to him about it. She did the same when he got his diamond inlay. *White folks always wanna "talk" to a nigga,* he mentally mused.

"Oh, Frank, we need to "talk" about this," she said calling him by his birth name—Frank.

He hated that name and it didn't fit him—not like Finest did. Especially since he knew he was the finest hood figga out here walking. Couldn't anybody touch his shit! Couldn't anybody even smell it!

"Yeah, baby. You need to come see about cha' girl. I got something to tell you anyway," Tanqueray said. She sounded tired and out of breath. Finest could tell she was not at her best. She sounded hurt.

"What? Tell me now. What did that nigga do. I'm right by his place I'm about to putta cap in his—"

"I'm with chile," Tanqueray said sounding motherly suddenly.

Finest's stomach tightened and his heart leapt.

"What you say?"

"I said, I'm pregnant fool! Knocked up! And I'm all hurt and shit too. Come see about me!" she barked, sounding like the Tanqueray he really knew!

"I'm on mah way, bitch! Don't be raising your voice at me. You ain't my mama," he added before ginning. "You my baby mama," he said in a low voice before he chuckled again.

Floyd caught that last comment and his eyes nearly bugged out of his head.

Chapter 45

Kidnapping Dustin Sinclair hadn't been in Cecil's plans but it had happened. Cecil couldn't face him. He was filled with so many mixed feelings and thoughts. The hours passed quickly as he pondered what he would do next. Would he let Mr. Sinclair go with a promise to forgive and forget? Would he kill him and bury him somewhere no one would ever find him? He was freaking out. Omar wanted to extort money of course. Money was all he ever thought about, even in desperate times. But Cecil, right now, seeing the man he'd grown to love like a father bent over in that chair, tied up and battered, he just wanted to turn back time.

As soon as Omar could get off that sofa, he slapped Dustin around a little bit. Dustin was already weak from the news that Tanqueray was dead and didn't put up much of a fight, especially tied up the way he was. Omar threatened him with death if he even thought about going to the police. "Who'd you call!" he screamed.

"I called my assistant," Dustin finally admitted. "I'm sure Cory has called the police. I told him I'd call him back and I haven't. It's been too long. I'm sure he's gone to the police."

Cecil wasn't sure what to believe but it sounded like the truth. Surely Dustin wasn't G enough to lie at the risk of more beatings from Omar or worse, a bullet that wasn't meant to kill. Omar wasn't one to be merciful. Cecil could tell by the pictures of Tanqueray. He had tortured that girl and still had plans to kill her slowly, of that Cecil was sure.

Life was never going to be the same after this, no matter how it came out. Omar was stupid enough to think it was going to come out good.

"We gonna get on a plane to Jamaica, man!" Omar blurted realizing the goldmine they had in Dustin Sinclair. It was as if he sat there thinking about this stupid shit. "This fool gonna buy our tickets and even if we have to put his ass on the plane with us, we gonna be up and gone, real soon. I don't know about your ass, but he's my ticket outta this shit."

"Would'na been no shit if you knew how to get outta the ghetto and stay out. But no, you too busy fooling with them hood rats and shit," Cecil said, sounding surprisingly calm.

Omar twisted the toothpick in his mouth, his eyes blazing with emotion and face dripping with sweat. He pointed at his bandaged leg, "Hell, without them hood rats my ass woulda been dead—shit." He was referencing the woman who had removed the bullets from his knees and tended to his shoulder wound.

And what a nightmare that was to live through . . .

They'd made it to the house where Omar's 'friend' lived. It was way out in Sebastopol. She was waiting and had her sons help Omar inside. It was clear she did many illegal things in her home as there was weed growing like tomato plants outside in her yard and other signs of illegal drug creation.

But was she a doctor?

She didn't look like one.

"Used to be an ER nurse in Vietnam," the woman said. "But you know the white man don't want you making a livin' once you get back. Ain't no love fa da vets," she said, glaring at Dustin Sinclair as if her plight were his fault.

They'd had to bring him along considering he showed up at the door before they could get out of there. Why had they come back to his place in the first place? Why didn't they just go straight to this woman's house? Had they done that Dustin would be home in his big bed now, safe and sound. Maybe he would have just put this entire night out of his head. Maybe Tanqueray—wherever she was—would have called him and they would be together right now. Taking pictures of each other's asses or whatever the hell they did when they were up in his room. Cecil sighed now at the memory of how the evening had gone. Why had he even gone to Omar's condo in the first place? What did he owe Tanqueray anyway? Was it guilt that took him there? What was he going to do once he got there? Was he going to save Tanqueray? Why didn't he just let Omar do what he wanted to her? She'd be dead and this would all be over. Why did he even get involved? He could have played it off as if he was none the wiser to this whole thing. Why did he let his own greed get him in this mess?

Cecil wasn't a criminal. He just wasn't. Well, not until today.

His mind drifted to the screaming.

Omar screamed like a little girl when that woman started working on his leg. She'd only given him a mild sedative as if that was going to be enough to hold him. She claimed she didn't have time for a full knock out procedure. She said he was a 'fit in' and that she had other clients coming for business.

"You gonna have to shut that up," she had instructed, pausing for a moment to regroup. It was clear her nerves were bad. Maybe it had been due to too many years spent in the ER. She looked around for something, finally grabbing a rag. "Bite this," she said stuffing it between his teeth. Again she cut at the open wound.

Cecil's knees weakened and he turned away.

Omar's eyes closed tight as his muffled screams hid his agony.

"Okay! That was easy," she said, holding up the bloody bullet. "Record time too. I was always fast at this shit," she bragged.

Omar's eyes fluttered for a second before he momentarily lost consciousness.

Quickly she wrapped up his leg. "Hey! You need to wake the hell up," she said slapping his face. "This ain't no hospital! This is triage! Plus I got one more bullet to find!"

Omar's eyes shot open.

She pulled the rag from his mouth. "Open up," she instructed. Omar obeyed. She dropped in a small white pill. "I don't have that many so I save it for when you really need it. Like now." She grinned. "Here," she said handing him a bottle of Jack Daniels after taking a swig herself.

He quickly guzzled from the bottle. Cecil watched his Adam's apple bobbing with each hardy swallow.

She retrieved the bottle noticing how much was gone. "Whew, nigga got a long throat," the woman chuckled again looking at Cecil as if expecting a light hearted comment to come. She went at the other leg, again retrieving a bullet. When she was finished, she held out her hand for payment.

Omar pointed to Mr. Sinclair.

She smiled and quickly sauntered over to him.

All this time Mr. Sinclair hadn't said a word. He'd only watched in silence.

"Wait," Cecil interjected knowing Mr. Sinclair never carried cash on him. "I got it," he said. "How much?"

"Five hunnad," she said without hesitation, spinning on her heels and changing direction.

"Fine," Cecil said, rolling off the bills. Mr. Sinclair paid him well and so he was used to carrying lots of money on him. Maybe it was his vanity but in this case he was glad. It had paid off to be so vain. No telling what she would have done had there been no immediate cash. Mr. Sinclair sighed. Cecil heard him, and maybe that was when he started regretting this whole thing.

Looking at his watch, almost out of reflex, Cecil realized it had been hours since this nightmare began. Surely everyone—and his mother—were looking for them. But then again, nobody had come to the apartment which was rather puzzling considering Dustin had said he'd called someone. Cecil wondered now why Cory had not acted on the alert, if indeed he'd truly been alerted.

"We can't get outta the country. We can't even get outta town! Cops are looking for this man!" Cecil attempted to explain now. "You are a fool Omar! You don't even know who this man is." Cecil shook his head.

"He's a rich white man," Omar said, snarling at the words. He was sweating again. He'd not really stopped since leaving the woman's house. His leg was tender looking and red. It didn't look anywhere near able to heal. It looked infected. Cecil was fairly sure it was infected. Using his sleeve he wiped his own head as if he too was sweating as much as Omar.

"Damn, it's hot in here!" Omar yelled out.

"Be quiet! Why you gotta get all loud. Shit!" Cecil spat. He was losing it too. It was true. It was way hotter there in that apartment now, much hotter than it would have been in his room at Mr. Sinclair's mansion. He was tempted to go back there. It was big enough to hide out. They could easily keep Mary and old Cory quiet. Mary was illegally in this country and Cory—with his scary faggot-ass, he was far from a threat. Cecil hated Cory. Cory was racist. He hated black people and felt they were smaller than him. That's what Cecil believed.

"Hell, who does he think he is. He ain't nobody but a butler," Cecil mumbled. "Hey," Cecil said then. "You need to call Cory and tell him you're all right. You need to tell him that you found some nice Black ho to spend the night with. Matter of fact . . . yeah. You need to tell them you're with Tanqueray." The plan was coming together as he was speaking. "You need to tell him to call off the cops . . . yeah. Why didn't I think of that earlier! Tell him you're with me and this has all been just one crazy night that was misunderstood." Cecil handed Mr. Sinclair the phone. "Call him."

"He won't believe me. You know that Cecil." Dustin spoke quietly. It was clear he was not feeling well.

"Then tell him you were so upset because she didn't come back that you left town. Tell him something," Cecil growled. He was losing it.

Omar was sweating bullets and his .22 still had one left. He would shoot one of these men in this room before this night was over if something didn't change right at this very second. Dustin seemed to sense his growing frustration and picked up the phone. Cecil dialed the house.

"Cory? No, noooo I'm fine. Yes. I'm with . . ." he looked up at Cecil. "I'm with Tanqueray. Yes. We are at a lovely little spot. Cecil? No, he's not done anything wrong. No. We had a slight falling out but I found him and we talked. No, there is no need for the authorities. Yes, Mary is a Worry Wart. You're right though, I should have called earlier. I'll be in by morning." Slowly Dustin handed Cecil back the phone after saying good-bye. "There," he told Cecil, who sighed in relief.

"Okay, so now we're gonna leave. We're gonna go to the airport and get outta here," Cecil explained as if now Omar's plan made more sense.

Dustin glanced over at Omar. "He's not going anywhere.

Look at him. He's not well Cecil. He needs a real doctor," he explained.

"He's gonna be fine!" Cecil demanded. Out of reflex he pointed the gun at Dustin.

As if suddenly tired of this whole thing Dustin's chest puffed out, "What's that for? Are you going to kill me?"

"Maybe," Cecil bluffed.

"Cecil, let's talk. Let's understand why this happened."

"Let's shut the fuck up-shit!" Omar blurted out again. "This happened because of you."

Cecil looked back at Omar. Yes he was sick. He was very sick. Bullet wounds to the knees were seldom deadly true enough, but an infection was and Cecil had witnessed a surgical procedure from hell just a couple of hours ago. There was no telling what she cleaned those tools with.

"Omar, we need to get you to the hospital. We need to say you got shot another way and—"

"No! I'ma be fine," he groaned.

"No, you're not," Cecil flopped down on the sofa's edge. We have to find a way to get outta here."

Just then Cecil's phone rang. It was from Omar's phone. He looked at the number and then groaned. "It's your phone," he said.

"Mah phone! Shit!"

Chapter 46

"Your sister needs you. My mama said she was up in the hospital," Malcolm yelled pushing Sinclair awake.

"What?" Sinclair sat up.

"Omar beat her up."

"What the hell was she doing with him? I thought she was kickin' it with Finest," she said, rubbing her eyes. She'd been asleep for a while. She looked around for her shoes. No matter what, her sisters were the most important people on earth to her and now Tang was hurt. She needed to get to her. "Where is she now?"

"She's home, at Unique's place," Malcolm told her.

"Oh, she's home? She ain't hurt then. I thought she was in the hospital or something."

"She was. They let her out. You know how it is when you ain't got no money. You can't stay," Malcolm said. "Did you know your sister was pregnant?" Malcolm said apparently relating more of what his mother had divulged. Forget HIPPA where round da way folks were concerned. Sinclair, only for a moment wondered what else he knew about her family.

Sinclair's eyes widened. "Pregnant? Who Unique?"

"No, Tang," he said.

"Tang! By who?" Sinclair blurted, moving a little faster now to get ready. This truly was serious. Tanqueray had been beat up and she was pregnant. Shit, this was too much drama to be going on at one time. "Who's the daddy?" she asked again without thinking.

Malcolm raised his voice a little bit. "Who else she been fuckin' wit'!"

"I don't know, shit. I'm just sayin'. I don't know all ya sex crazy folk's business!" she said, following Malcolm out to his mother's car. It was past late. Apparently Malcolm had gone to pick her up and she was now home in bed. *So much gets past your mother, Malcolm, she works just too many hours to be trying to run a household,* Sinclair reasoned in her mind.

"Alls I know is it besta be Finest's baby or he'll kill her. He's killed more than one person before," Malcolm told her.

"Well, he ain't gonna kill my sister, not without claiming his own ticket to hell. I promise you that," Sinclair said, climbing in the passenger seat. Malcolm drove her to Unique's place.

Sinclair still didn't fully grasp the situation—that is until she arrived and saw Tanqueray all bandaged up. She was laid up on the sofa with a throw over her legs even though it was far from cold. She looked like a Mack Truck had gone over her a few times.

"Oh my God!" Sinclair yelped rushing to her side. "Omar did this? Oh mah God," Sinclair repeated, looking around and only seeing Markey looking back at her. Finest and him seemed to be cavorting in the kitchen.

"Why are you here?" she asked, Markey.

"I'm the one that found her at the Marina," Markey answered.

"Where were you?" she asked Finest, who smacked his lips, blowing her off with a fan of his hand.

Tanqueray looked bad. Her pretty face was covered with cuts and bandages. She hadn't said a word. Clearly she was waiting to see what Finest was going to do or say about not being there for her.

"So is Omar in jail or what?" Sinclair asked. Her innocence again came through as all around just seemed to ignore the question.

Even Gina and Apple were quiet as if they'd been hearing what they should not about Omar's upcoming fate. Sinclair could tell jail was not in the stars for Omar. She gulped air. "What cha'll plannin'?" she asked Malcolm who said nothing. "You knew about this Malcolm?"

"Get me some water Sin?" Tanqueray asked, as if wanting her to move off the sofa so Finest could sit in her place—which he did.

"Hey, girl," Finest said before breaking into a smile and putting his hand on her stomach. "So you really got my shawty in there, huh?"

"I guess," Tanqueray said. "I ain't never been pregnant before so . . ."

"At least that explains why you been acting like such a bitch lately. I'ma forgive you for letting me go to jail too," Finest said.

Tanqueray smiled weakly and laid her head lightly against his. Sinclair stood watching the tender moment for just a second before realizing the setting, the moment—the reality. Another baby was to come into the world. It would be poor, black and disadvantaged, born to an unfit mother and a good for nothing father. The thought made her let out a copious sigh.

Unique noticed. "Stop being a hater," she snapped.

Sinclair glanced at her out of the corner of her eye. "I ain't hatin' I'm just . . ." she caught her words. "You'd never understand."

"I understand. It's you that just don't get it. Love is a godly thing. No matter where you find it. Tanqueray found love and the devil tried to take it away. You will never understand because you don't pray for such understanding."

Sinclair looked deep in Unique's eyes. *Was she blind? Did she not see all these men in here planning to go after Omar and kill him? Did she not see that there was nothing "good" about this situation at all and that a baby was just another complication, considering that it was probably Omar's baby? Why was everyone being so obtuse? What was godly about this situation? Nothing!*

"What happened to your arm?" Markey asked. It seemed as though he'd asked her that before.

"I got hurt," she answered reluctantly before taking Tanqueray her glass of water, breaking up the tender moment between her and Finest.

Tanqueray looked up at her taking the glass of water. Her face asked the same question.

"I got in a fight," Sinclair answered.

"Who you fightin' Shawty?" Finest asked.

"Bitch named Mercedes," Sinclair answered. All of the men's heads went back in mutual understanding, except Malcolm's, of course. "Malcolm's girlfriend," she added on a sarcastic note.

Finest looked over at him and shook his head. "Wow Malcolm didn't know you was going out like that." he laughed getting up and rejoining the men in the kitchen.

Unique had pulled out some beers now and Malcolm cracked one open. "Mercedes is a sho nuff ho!"

While the men jeered Malcolm, Sinclair moved closer to Tanqueray. She was having a hard time picturing Tanqueray as a mother. It just couldn't sink in. Maybe it was because she was sitting up here all whooped up as a result of her life running the streets. Sinclair imagined the apartment permanently filled with all kinds of folks—Finest, Markey,

Unique and her kids, Tanqueray and a new baby. She even imagined Malcolm coming by more often for his sexual needs. She shook her head at the visual. There was no way she was going to live this way. Something had to give. Some money was going to have to drop from the sky or some damn where pretty quick here, because this wasn't going to happen. Maybe she could find out who owned Mama's house and beg him to let her live there once she turned eighteen.

Or . . .

After a summer of training in "ghetto life" she was ready to start her own "street business." Everybody was making that chedda and now it was going to have to be her time. She had to get out of here.

Summer was over and things were going to change up here pretty quick. She was going to turn eighteen on New Years and even though she'd still be in high school finishing up her senior year, she was going to have to make some big moves. She was goinig to have to bounce up out of this going nowhere-ville she was in.

Again her thoughts came back to her as she realized she and Tanqueray were in a mindless stare down. She half way wondered if Tanqueray's thoughts were worth the penny she was about offer her. "Penny for your thoughts," she said, repeating something her mother used to say to her often when finding her deep in a daydream.

Chapter 47

Okay, so now what?" Finest asked.

"Now you know they are together. If Cecil had answered the phone that would have told me they weren't," Markey said. "Cecil woulda answered the phone and been acting like he didn't know nothing from nothing. But he is with the nigga so he didn't even pick up. Now call that Mr. Sinclair cat back. If he don't answer that means we got trouble . . . means he's got trouble. I don't know the man but your girl seems to care about him. I mean, he is her little sugar daddy and all that."

"Right. Right," Finest agreed.

Tanqueray was asleep now. She looked like an angel laying there on that sofa. He wanted to lay down with her, but Markey and his boy looked like they were ready for business and business only. Finest knew that he had to get his mind right. He needed to get his mind back on the war they were in. They were in a war between the *them* and the *us*. Today the mission was Omar and Cecil. It was a seek and destroy mission. Mr. Sinclair hadn't called for hours and that wasn't like him. The last call was to report that he was at Cecil's place. All Finest could imagine was that Sinclair had done what he'd told him not to do, which was to go up there or let Cecil see him. "Fool probably got in the mix in a bad way if he tried to talk to Cecil as if Cees was gonna pay him any attention. I hope they didn't kill him."

"They didn't kill him. He's their ticket out if they got any brains," Markey assured him after they all ventured outside.

"Then why don't we wait," Finest offered, again hoping to edge out of a confrontation. He had Tanqueray back. He was through with this for a minute. He'd kill Omar another time.

Markey shook his head as if reading his unspoken thoughts. "Your girl and yo little baby gonna be right here. But that fool that almost took all that away from you? You gonna let that ride? No, he got tah go," Markey said. "Besides, I owe this family somethin'."

"What?" Malcolm asked.

"I owe them justice. I owe recompense for my past acts," Markey said sounding deep and full of philosophy.

"What did you do?" Malcolm asked.

"I accidentally killed their brother Larry," Markey confessed aloud for the first time in many years.

"Damn!"

After a moment of thinking things through, the men pondered on a way to find out where Cecil and Omar could be hiding out.

"If Mr. Sinclair is with them and he's got his phone, his folks can use the GPS to find him," Malcolm said popping up with the answer.

"Leave it to the school boy," Markey teased. "Now how we gonna find that out?"

"We need Tang to call somebody. She's tight with that staff over there. She needs to call somebody and see what's going on. If Mr. Sinclair is safe he'll tell us what we need to know. If not, they sure as hell will help us find old dude because he's their paycheck. Besides, they all like Tang over there."

"Word," Markey's boy agreed.

"Then let's go wake up sleeping beauty and get busy."

Chapter 48

"I can't believe y'all didn't tell me Mr. Sinclair was missing!" Tanqueray gasped. She was clearly upset.

The men gathered around the sofa as Finest tried to calm her down. "Just call Cory or whoever the hell else over there and see if he's home. He may be home. It's not like he could have called you," Finest said reminding her of her separation from her phone. He'd not told her he had it—it had slipped his mind. But nonetheless, it hadn't rung so no matter, right?

Tanqueray took the house phone receiver and dialed the number. Cory answered.

"Hello Cory. This is Tanqueray."

"Hello there, Ms. Tanqueray. It's very early in the morning," Cory said sounding calm. Tanqueray's heart filled. All was okay.

"I know. But can I speak to Dustin."

"Dustin? He's not with you?"

"No. I've been . . . I've been in the hospital."

"What?" Cory's voice peaked unexpectedly. "Where is Dustin then? He said he was with you . . . hours ago."

"I had hoped he was home."

"No. He went looking for Cecil and said he'd found you instead. It was a strange call. He kept saying call them off. I didn't understand it but you know how he is . . . so playful."

"No game Cory. He could be in danger. How can I find

him? What kinda technology y'all got over there to use to find him?"

"Good Lord! Mary!" he called out. Cory was losing it. "Mary, good Lord, Dustin is missing."

"Good heavens," she yelled in the background.

Tanqueray rubbed her head waiting for the two senior citizens to get a grip and come back to the phone.

"We have GPS and Onstar for his car. We can locate his car," Mary told her. "That's how he found Cecil. I'm sure of it. He'd said he'd found Cecil and the car so he had to have used the service. He said that, right Cory?"

"Yes."

"Okay, cool. Then we need to find Cecil again, okay? Call whoever you need to call and get a location and then call me back," Tanqueray insisted.

"Yes, Tanqueray and then you'll get him?"

"Yes, ma'am. We gon' go get him. Don't call the police whatever you do. Do not call the police."

"I promise. We won't. Thank God for you Tanqueray."

"Just listen to me carefully now . . ."

"Yes—"

"No matter what, do not call the police," she repeated, sounding more than ominous.

Chapter 49

Cecil was packing. They had decided to head to the Bahamas. It was going to be the two of them and Mr. Sinclair for security. Thank God Omar wasn't talking crazy about killing him or anything like that. Omar was dozing in and out. The extreme pain had subsided, but only after a quick run to purchase some blow for him. Cecil was amazed at how easy that purchase had gone. It was like a knee jerk reaction that he knew where to go and what to do. He had dressed in a casual looking jogging suit, nothing too expensive, and hit the "block." Within moments he was approached and made the purchase. He was back within twenty minutes since traffic was nearly invisible.

"Cecil. Let me go. I'll give you the money for your trip and let you and Omar leave without any interference."

Cecil stopped for a moment, contemplating his words. Just then Omar moaned in fit-filled sleep. Cecil shook his head. "No. I couldn't live looking over my shoulder for life."

"If Omar killed Tanqueray you will be living that way."

"He didn't kill her," Cecil whispered. "She's the one who shot him. If anything, she's back in the hood where she belongs, back with her kind, licking her wounds. While me . . . look at me, I'm running for my life. He'd not picked up the gun again noting that Dustin Sinclair had stopped attempting to get free from the binds that tied him to the dining chair.

"You're not being fair."

"Fair? What is fair? I lived my life trying to do better. Trying to rise above and for what? I worked like a slave for you—like a son. I was like a son to you," Cecil paused growing emotional. " . . . and for what? For you to give all your money to a whore you don't even know."

"I know her mother. I knew her . . ." Dustin paused. " . . . mother. She was not a whore. We were to be married. I loved her Cecil. She had a child for me and—"

"Tanqueray is your daughter? You had sex with her. You had sex with your daughter!" Cecil's face twisted up in disdain. He went back to packing, grabbing enough shirts and slacks to share with Omar.

"No. Tanqueray is not my daughter and yes, I've perhaps crossed the line even still because Tanqueray is that woman's daughter. But no, Tanqueray has a little sister named after me. Sinclair. That's my daughter."

Cecil stared. His arms dropped, releasing the clothes onto the floor.

"I was putting the money in trust for my daughter. I don't know what you heard but that's what I was doing. I would have never left you out. Not you, or Cory or Mary. I have enough for everyone I love Cecil," Dustin explained. "But . . . I have a child and you just don't know what that means to me. I've always known but . . . until I met Tanqueray, I just . . . I just can't explain it."

"Dustin, I . . ." Cecil began only to be interrupted by the door bursting open and the four masked men, dressed in black and wearing gloves, charging in.

"Get him," the big man said, pointing at Dustin who was quickly snatched from the chair by two of the smaller hooded men. They quickly rushed Mr. Sinclair outside. The big man pointing the gun then motioned for the other man to close the door, which he did.

Cecil's mind scattered. It was coming up on three A.M. Where were his neighbors? They always seemed so concerned before. They always seemed to notice when he came in late or left early. Surely they'd heard this commotion. Surely they'd sensed his danger. Where were his neighbors when he needed them to be nosy? His mind came back to the moment.

The second man had pulled out a gun as the bigger man walked over to Omar. He kicked him in his side waking him up in a start.

"What the fuck!" Omar gasped, raising his hands high as if blocking an oncoming punch.

"You look like Cisco on crack," the big man said, laughing wickedly.

"What the . . . who are you?"

"We're the angels of the dark. We avenge the hood. We take back what's ours," the big man said.

"We have nothing of yours," Cecil protested. He wanted them to go away. The irony of being jacked in the middle of a kidnapping attempt was just too coincidental. Plus they had snatched their victim. Something was foul here.

"You did . . ." the big man said, before quickly backhanding him across the face. He fell to the floor. The other hooded man laughed wickedly. "But we took it back."

"You mean that whore Tanqueray?" Omar growled before the big man hovered over him. Omar flinched now, with his hands going back up to block his face.

"Look at you. Even if I wanted to shoot you in the back of the head you can't even get on your knees," he said pointing at Omar's bandages.

"Then how we gonna do this boss?" the smaller man asked.

The big man handed off his weapon and pulled the duct tape from the pocket of his black jogging suit.

Omar's eyes widened as he grimaced in pain finally releasing a high shrill scream behind the duct tape when it covered his mouth. But the big bear of a man paid it no mind while rolling him over on the sofa to where he was half on and half off.

The big man ripped Omar's loose fitting jersey shorts over his hips. Omar's head swung back and forth.

Cecil could not believe what he was about to witness as the big man pulled from his shorts a stiff erection. Before he could blink the big man began to sex Omar in the ass as if he was the love of his life. Full to the shaft he had entered his rectum, twisting this way and that.

Finest too couldn't help but just stare; he'd seen nothing like it before. "Shit," he mumbled.

The room was silent except for Omar's muffled whimpers and the big man's passionate, pleasure-filled grunts. It was like a train wreck. No one could turn away.

"You gonna do him next?" the other dude asked Finest.

"Hell, nah. I don't roll like that," Finest admitted proudly.

Finally with a couple of good humps the big man apparently came. Omar's eyes glassed over, and then closed. He was weak and in addition to the pain in his knees he was just about done for the night, Cecil could tell. The big man pulled up his sweats over his used manhood and motioned for his partner to hand off the gun back to him. He turned and smiled at Cecil letting him know he was next in line. Cecil could say nothing as his mouth was quickly duct taped by the big man. He just shook his head wildly. This nightmare was just beginning. As much as Cecil thought it was going to be over in just a few hours, as much as he had imagined the warmth of the balmy Bahamas sun on his back and the pretty, tanned white women at his beck and call, he knew there would be none of that in his future.

The smaller man quickly took over where Markey had left off. He entered Omar's rear end hungrily. It was clear anal sex was his preference, whether female or male, it didn't matter to him. He had a 'style', that was clear. He slapped his palm against Omar's thigh as if riding a bucking horse. Yes he was enjoying himself even more than the big man seemed to.

"Oh, yeah," he purred, screwing Omar who now cried like the bitch he was. Markey laughed at the sexing style of his partner. Cecil fought the tears from coming. He knew he could not give into the fear he now felt growing in his heart.

"You nasty," he laughed as his partner gave Omar a spank on the rump in jest.

"Ride 'em cowboy," the partner joked.

"Y'all 'bout to turn my stomach," Finest said, gulping air as if the sight truly did upset him. This was all too much, even from where Cecil sat now. He too would have preferred just being shot in the head and being done with it than the torture that was ensuing.

Markey smiled at Finest wickedly. Cecil could have sworn he saw him wink covertly.

"We gon' be done soon. We just making it look like what it is, you know, a lover's quarrel," Markey explained. "Gather up all the phones and other shit that might be important around here," he ordered Floyd who quickly obeyed.

Chapter 50

Heading over to Cecil, Markey put the gun to his forehead as Tanqueray had said Omar had done to her. After they got off the phone with Cory, Markey had Tanqueray relate what Omar had done to her in detail. He'd added in the sodomy from his own imagination.

"Come here and take this tape off his mouth," Markey ordered Finest who quickly obeyed. He used his free hand to tug on his manhood until it began to stiffen a little. He then shoved it roughly into Cecil's mouth slitting the sides of it. The blood trickled down. Cecil's eyes closed tight.

Firmly tapping the gun against his forehead he said, "You bite me I'll blow your brains all over this living room." He began to get his stroke on until he came in Cecil's mouth.

Finest swallowed hard having apparently again witnessed something he'd never seen.

Just then Floyd stepped forward. He'd done his one task and was ready now to get in on the action. He stepped up with his dick hanging out. Markey stepped aside, but continued to hold the gun until Floyd took it from him. Floyd wasn't a big man in the dick department, but his little peter had sprung into action at this opportunity. This whole thing had clearly been turning him on.

Finest stepped back out of the way.

"Oh, shit," Floyd said, swilling his hips as Cecil sucked him like a baby bottle. Cecil's eyes were wide now, with both fear and the unknown.

Finest could only see Floyd from behind, but he was really getting into it. "Holy shit, suck my dick Cecil. Harder, harder!" Floyd growled. "Oh, nigga, suck it like you mean that shit!" Floyd cried out in pleasure. "Ain't no bitch ever worked my shit like this!"

Markey was laughing.

Finest then realized that the other dude was still fucking Omar. It was a crazy scene. It was one he'd never been a part of. His mind was spinning until suddenly the gun pointed at Cecil's head went off. His head whipped back in that direction.

"Shit! I didn't mean ta do dat!" Floyd yelped, jumping back. His dick was limp now as he had just cum. His orgasm was apparently so intense that his hands tightened on the trigger and he shot Cecil between the eyes.

What was left of Cecil's head fell back. At that, Omar's eyes opened and the other man pulled out roughly. Markey quickly grabbed Omar off the sofa and dragged him over to the lap of Cecil while pushing Floyd out of the way.

"What you fidd'n ta do man?" Finest asked when Markey pulled Cecil's dick from his pants. "Open ya mouth," he said to Omar after he ripped off the duct tape. Omar said nothing and did nothing more than obey, taking Cecil's limp dick in his mouth.

Finest jumped slightly when the partner pulled out the gun with the silencer and pushed it quickly against Omar's head. The gun went off, sending the bullet through Omar's temporal area.

"Let's go," he then said coolly.

"Yep. This looks like a faggot fight to me," Markey said,

looking back over his work as they reached the doorway. Floyd was silent. Finest knew what he was thinking . . . *Let's get outta here before they start shitting everywhere.*

Chapter 51

When the men reached the Escalade, Malcolm was panic stricken. Mr. Sinclair was pale and clammy looking.

"What's going on?"

"I think he's dyin'!"

Floyd, out of instinct, reached over and checked his pulse. Yes, he definitely took after his mother in the healthcare arena. "This man is going into cardiac arrest. We need to get him to the hospital."

"This couldn'a been betta timing," Markey said, smiling all the while.

He truly had a wicked mind Finest realized.

Chapter 52

Mr. Sinclair was doing better after his mild heart attack. That night's events had been just too much for him. The report that his trusted assistant Cecil Johnson was found dead in an ugly compromising position with his incestuous lover Omar Johnson was more than he could handle. The police questioned him in the hospital as soon as his vitals were stable. They also questioned Cory and Mary along with the other staff members. Only Cory conceded in telling the police what he suspected concerning Cecil's sordid secret sexual life. He claimed he'd overheard lurid conversations between Cecil and Omar during work hours. He said they'd been fighting lately so this incident did not surprise him. "Cecil has been gathering information about the Bahamas recently . . ." Cory went on.

Dustin Sinclair had no comments one way or the other. He was tired and stressed over his business and had finally been beaten by the economic swing. That had to be why he had suffered the heart attack. About the young man Frank, who had brought him in, he was a new assistant. They had been going over some new projects until well into the night. The news of Cecil's death had been a shock.

"Cecil was like a son to me and I'm devastated. I hope this investigation is brief," was all he committed to the police. His having left Cecil such a substantial amount of money in trust cleared him of any suspicion in connection with his death.

Cecil's mother was reportedly the hardest hit by all of this as she swore on God's hand that her son was no homosexual.

She came to see Dustin only once but was not allowed in the room. Her anger was evident as she pointed blame in Dustin Sinclair's direction. She threw one accusation after the next in his direction, however, no one regarded the woman after finding a large sum of money deposited into her account—transferred from her son the night he died. It was clear Cecil was conspiring something. He was plotting something that never transpired or, maybe it had, and that's what ended his life.

Two guns lay on the floor of the apartment, with only their prints. Obvious sexual activity, and a half packed suitcase, ended the badly wrapped case of the two ghetto boys found dead outside of their hood. A screaming Black mother pointing fingers at a rich White benefactor, bellowing out unsubstantiated claims of foul play on his part, was not enough to raise an eyebrow on the police.

Chapter 53

Finally out of the hospital, Tanqueray and Finest were invited over to visit Dustin Sinclair, along with Unique and Sinclair. Tanqueray was excited to bring her family in on her newfound treasure, that being, Dustin Sinclair. Dustin seemed even more excited to meet them, especially Sinclair. *Maybe it was because they had the same name,* that's all Tanqueray could figure. She'd put her mind on many fantastical things over the last month. She'd worked hard to block out reality. Finest and Markey came in the next evening without a word to say about what had happened when they went to see Omar. She wasn't about to ask, and neither was Unique. Sinclair of course, was all about the questions but they shut her down without much trouble. That girl was going to have to learn the ways of the street. One would have thought the trouble she had with that Gold Mouth hood back when summer first started would have stopped her ass from asking so many nosy questions.

Tanqueray had put two and two together on that situation also. She had to accept that even though Finest wasn't as hard core as Markey was, Finest had a dark side, one she didn't want to cross. She'd never really fooled with a thug before, and wasn't sure if this was going to be her ticket out of her current situation. But for now, Finest was the man she felt something for, so she was just going to go with it. Hopefully he wasn't going to end up in the pen or anything like that because there was no way in hell she was going to run up and down the road to see him. That she knew. What she was really hoping for was that Mr. Sinclair might want her. Deep inside she felt something for him beyond just an easy dollar bill.

While he was in the hospital, she checked on him every day. She dressed really nice and acted like she had something when she would go see him. The nurses treated her with respect too, as if she was something. It felt good. He was always happy to see her. When he got out, he called her to come over, but Finest had started getting a little jealous so she squashed it until today when he invited everybody over.

Now, as Dustin watched Sinclair swimming in the pool, Tanqueray didn't even feel jealous as if he was watching her with sexual eyes. He wasn't. She could tell. He was genuinely taken with her—almost as the way . . . almost the way a father would be. Yeah, that was it. Now that she thought about it, he had acted really paternal with Sinclair. Offering her everything a child would want. It was cute in a way. Sinclair being like a daughter to him and she being like a wifey—yeah Tanqueray had the entire fantasy in her mind for a second. She'd move in and bring Sinclair along for safe keeping and they would live happy ever after.

Oh, yeah . . .

The baby. Well, it had been a nice thought.

It was a funny thought too, because now that Tanqueray noticed it, Sinclair seemed like a fish in a familiar stream there in that house. Tanqueray did feel a little twinge of jealousy in that regard. Sinclair had such an ease with this kind of life. It was as if Sinclair was truly born to it. *And me? Maybe I was just born to the West End,* Tanqueray thought, before her mind came back to Finest who slid up next to her running his hands over her belly. He was doing that a lot lately.

He was so in love with that baby. All he wanted to do was kiss on her belly and eat out her pussy. It was as if he just couldn't wait to kiss that baby. She laughed thinking about how mushy he had gotten in bed. None of that rough stuff anymore; he was downright tender now. But she had to admit, it was real good. Being pregnant made it real hot and juicy down there and she loved the sex even more—if that was possible. She had to admit that as much as she wanted to be with Dustin Sinclair, nothing beat Finest between the sheets. She'd be hard pressed to make a decision if faced with one.

Sliding her hand around the back of his head, she now kissed him tenderly, but with a promise attached to it that later he'd have to get busy digging for some gold if he wanted more than a peck on the cheek. He caught on and discreetly squeezed her tender titty. Oh, yeah, they were getting bigger too and they both were digging that. Tanqueray would have to say she was happy right now in body and mind.

Her injuries were healing well, but still she wasn't up and at 'em like she used to be. "I guess we both need to go sit on an island and recover," she told Dustin watching him moving slower than she'd ever seen him move when he came from pool side to join them on the patio. He must have tired of watching Sinclair swimming back and forth in that long pool.

He was dressed in sharp panama white from head to toe. Owning a line of designer boutiques all around the world, he knew how to dress and always did a great job of it. He truly was a man after her own heart. Since learning about the baby, he'd done nothing but shower her with expensive maternity clothes. More than she could even wear in the time she'd be pregnant. But she did wear at least two outfits a day. She knew she was looking damn good too.

Mary had fixed a wonderful snack for them. She also seemed

to be fascinated with Sinclair who now came with Apple, dripping from the water, toward the tray of food. They were both intercepted by Cory who handed them both towels. Like a model on a catwalk Sinclair accepted the towel gracefully as if she expected it, without so much as a break in her stride. Yes, she was wearing rich well and it looked good on her— even at seventeen, Tanqueray noticed. She wanted this for her sister. Deep inside she wanted Sinclair to have it all.

Apple quickly climbed up in the seat next to Mr. Sinclair as if he was grandpa for sure. "You're an old White man. But you're a nice old White man," Apple said, taking a large bite from the strawberry he had on his plate, after dipping it in the thick cream.

He smiled broadly.

Tanqueray just shook her head in embarrassment at her ghetto family.

Unique, as soon as she realized there was a music room, all but locked herself in there with Gina while they both sang their hearts out recording their voices. It had been a dream of Unique's to be a recording star and now she was living it. She had a voice that sounded a lot like Whitney Houston's and she should have been famous by now. But damn! There weren't just too many Bobby's in her life. Today was her moment to shine and Gina's too. Gina had a bit of a voice on her too.

Just then a tall, handsome, well-tanned young man came from the house onto the patio. Tanqueray had never seen him before. He looked around twenty or so. He was dressed in sharp Euro cut summer slacks and a cool looking polo shirt that fit his muscular frame well.

"Damn," came from both Tanqueray and Sinclair before they caught themselves. Only Tanqueray got a nudge from

Finest, Sinclair was free to gawk. She even sat her lemonade down to make sure she didn't miss any sides of him as he handed Mr. Sinclair a note and whispered something in his ear. He was discreet, which was a great trait, Tanqueray observed.

He then turned and smiled at them—Sinclair first.

"Oh, yeah, he's fine," Tanqueray said to Sinclair who just blushed.

"This is Antonio, my new driver," Dustin introduced. There was a little sadness in his voice but it quickly subsided.

Cecil's apparent suicide had come as a shock to everyone. According to the final report, Cecil had been in an incestuous gay relationship with Omar. When the truth threatened to come out, it was too much to deal with and he took his life after shooting Omar in the head during a sex act. No one talked about Omar's tie with Tanqueray and why should they? Her injuries came from a fall she'd taken while rushing to catch the bus . . . right?

Antonio reached out and shook everyone's hand and Tanqueray could have sworn he lingered with Sinclair, pulling back slowly and sensuously. It turned Tanqueray on just watching the exchange. Maybe there was something to this voyeurism thing. She was suddenly kind of hot!

"Join us Antonio," Dustin offered, pointing to the seat next to Sinclair. He must have noticed it too.

"Oh, no," he said shyly. "I have to tend to the car," he said.

"Oh, lawd, he's got an accent too?" Tanqueray blurted.

Everyone chuckled, even Antonio who shyly and nervously nodded his excuse and backed away from the group.

"Oh, where did you find him?" Tanqueray asked.

Dustin laughed. "In Paris," he answered. "He'll be your ride home when you're ready, but you can stay all night if you like. I have plenty of room here," he offered looking straight at Sinclair.

She squirmed a little.

"Nah, pawdna, we prolly need ta make it back to the hood," Finest said stretching as if he and Dustin were old buddies.

"Um, he's yummy. Maybe we should stay," Tanqueray said, licking her lips in Antonio's direction. "I wouldn't mind making a movie with him," she teased flirtatiously. She knew Dustin liked that kind of humor. It had been a long time since they'd had any fun together. She missed his tenderness and adoration. Dustin laughed.

Again Finest nudged her while pointing at Apple and Sinclair. "Cut it out."

"Boy don't nobody care about me and what I say," she fussed.

"No, Aunt Tang 'cause you're right. Tonio is yummy. Like a strawberry," Apple said taking another big bite. Everyone laughed.

About that time, Unique came from the house with Gina. "What's so funny?"

"Tonio the Strawberry," Apple answered not looking up from the food on Mr. Sinclair's plate. Again everyone laughed.

Chapter 54

The night was warm for the Bay. It was balmy and calm. Maybe the worst was over but then again, maybe it was just the calm before the storm. It was in the air either way. *Change gon' come.* Summer was coming to an end and what a crazy mad summer it had been.

Unique sat on the stoop thinking about the events over the last few weeks. Cammie had awakened from her coma and would be coming home soon. Sinclair finally got enrolled in school. She wasn't going to the fancy white one she was used to. She was going to one in the P. As much as Unique had tried to get her to register for one closer to the apartment, she decided to go with Malcolm to the high school he attended. No matter, she was still close to home, even if it was the new home in the W.E. She was still seventeen and that's just the way it was going to be. Unique had added her to her welfare grant finally, and therefore needed to be more aware of her comings and goings. She was closely monitoring her actions and relationship with Malcolm. Of course Sinclair had denied they was anything going on, but Unique knew better than that.

After that fight she and Sinclair had about Markey, Sinclair had kept her stank attitude. It *probably was because she was fuckin' now and felt she was woman enough to get in my face,* Unique thought to herself, assuming she knew what was going on between Sinclair and Malcolm. *Folks always think they're grown once they started fuckin'. She'll be coming up pregnant soon if she ain't careful.*

Unique groaned thinking of Tanqueray and her pregnancy. "And that baby is gonna be messed up," she mumbled under her breath. *All the shit Tang has done. That baby ain't gon' be no good. All she been doing since getting back on her feet is, smoking and drinking.* Unique went on, thinking about Tanqueray and her continued love of partying. Now that she and Finest were really a couple, they partied all the damn time. Finest had yet to stop celebrating the safe return of his sweetheart and the announcement of a baby on the way. They had been together every night up in that room in her apartment.

"You'd think nobody else had babies," Unique groaned loudly, rubbing her forehead. They were in there now, acting all married. All Unique hoped was that Gina and Apple had been obedient and stayed in her room watching TV on the small set that Markey had given her. She had told them to go in there whenever Finest came over. She should have taken them down to Mrs. Newbury's apartment but that old woman watched them way too much as it was. Unique had been going to the church nearly every evening now. Praying was just part of her life. She now couldn't imagine what she had done without church. She was singing in the choir, so between choir practice and praying and all that, she was a busy woman with barely time for anything.

Well, except Markey.

Unique glanced at her watch that Markey had given her. He'd probably be coming by soon. He'd been like glue to her since they reunited. They needed to do some more talking about things though, she knew that. It's just that every time they were together, other things more important came up. Church, seeing Cammie, making love—it was always something that came up other than talking. She was fascinated; however, he knew her older brother Larry. "I wanna know about that. I wanna know everything about what Markey knows," she said, smiling to herself at the thought that maybe she'd actually found her soul mate in Markey. She'd envisioned the man of her dreams being somebody else—true. But Markey was her first. He was her son's father and so why not him? It didn't matter how it all started. It didn't matter that some people might call it rape. It was nothing like that. It was nothing even close to what Curtis had done to Cammie. Even as a child, Unique knew in her heart, even then, she loved Markey. If he hadn't gone to prison he would have saved her that day. He would have taken her away from her mother and all the evilness she felt there in that house.

Despite Mrs. Newbury's words of caution, Unique had no fear of being with Markey, none at all. God took little Marquis away and had given her big Markey in his place. *Maybe little Marquis was just holding his place in my heart*, Unique reasoned in her mind.

Markey had become her hero in a way. She believed that. He was her guardian angel too. After all the mess with Tanqueray died down, he assured her they would have no more trouble out of anybody in that hood. There would be no more threats to their safety and security, and so far it had been quiet all around.

Sinclair had her puppy love in Malcolm. She'd grow out of that soon enough, and Tanqueray had Finest—with his no-good useless ass—but Markey, what she and Markey had was so much more powerful than that ghetto loving she saw around her. Markey was a real man in her mind.

Sure, some people held his past against him but all that was over, right?

"Hey, baby," Markey said, pulling up in the passenger side

of a dark car. She wasn't good with the makes of cars so she didn't care what it was. He said something to the driver and then stepped out. He was handsome and all cleaned up. "What choo doin' out here? Folks run you outta yo own house?" he asked, looking upward toward her apartment window.

She stood. "Nah. It's just really nice out here, so I was just out here thinking."

"Well, I hope you were thinking about me," he said, touching her face. "I'm hungry as fuck . . . you cook anything?" he said then.

"No. I'm . . ." she paused. She'd never had to tell anybody that she was out of food before, but since he'd come into her life—eating like a horse—and both her sisters moving in, even with the extra hundred dollars in food stamps for Sinclair, Unique was out of everything. "I haven't been to the store," she explained. "I was gonna go to church and then stop by the store on my way back," she lied.

He nodded, turning back to the guy in the car. "Let's take baby to the store," he ordered.

The driver, who was different from the guy who had taken them to rescue Tanqueray, nodded.

Unique hesitated. She had no money. She didn't even have a purse on her. She was planning to lie again, after church and claim to have forgotten it.

"Get in baby. Let's go get some food," he said. "Cook it up, and then go to church. I'm planning to go wit' choo to church tonight. You know that," he said.

Unique hesitated and then finally shook her head. "I ain't got no money," she said in a low voice.

He grinned broadly. "Now, did I ask you if you had money? I asked if you cooked. Let's go get some food so you can cook for your man."

Looking up at him, Unique couldn't help but grin wide.

This man was all that and more. She hopped in the back seat before he climbed back in the front and off they went to the closest Safeway store.

Markey bought at least a hundred dollars worth of groceries before she insisted they had enough and they headed back to the apartment.

Yes, he was a real man. He was beyond just a booty call like Tanqueray had in Finest or a puppy love like what Sinclair and Malcolm had. Markey was the one, who after the end of all this summer madness, would be around forever. He'd made his mark on her heart. She was sprung.

Epilogue

"It was only ten dollars."

"That's not the point. The point is she owes you now and you can't let these little hood rats get away with owing you anything. How you supposed to be somebody if you let folks take you for a weakling."

"I'm not weak."

"Then why didn't you get your money from her."

"Because . . ." Robert's face felt hot. He didn't like where these questions were going. He didn't want to talk about his feelings. He didn't want to tell his brother Jamie that he didn't get the ten dollar from Sinclair because he liked her. That day he met her on the bus wasn't the first time he'd seen her. He'd seen her around the W.E. and liked what he saw. She didn't seem to be running with the gang bangers around there. It wasn't until she got dropped off in the P that Robert had second thoughts about her. But he got all that squared away when he ran into her a week later. She was looking really cute in some daisy dukes. She was walking home from the store with her niece in tow.

"Hey," he called out.

As if suddenly remembering, she slapped her forehead and quickly went for her pocket. "Oh my God," she exclaimed, digging deep. All Robert could see was her little breast jumping up and down as she wriggled into the pocket of those tight ass shorts. "I owe you ten bucks. God I hope I didn't start no war with this . . ."

"Crazy," Robert snickered. "Hell no. I don't need no ten bucks from you," he told her.

"Really?" she answered.

"Nah, I mean, I do, but like . . ." Robert looked around and then down at her niece who was all in the conversation now. "How's your arm anyway?"

"It's a'ight," Sinclair said, flailing it all around.

"So, did you start school?"

"Yeah," Sinclair rolled her eyes. "Not the school I wanted," she admitted.

"Where you go?"

"In the P."

"Why?" he asked.

"It's just easy," she answered.

Robert was surprised how easy she was to talk to and how pretty she was. Her eyes were green and her hair was hanging long and loose. She was kind of skinny but what the hell, she caused a boner to come and he liked that. "Easy isn't what life's about," he said, trying to engage her in a deeper conversation about herself. She just shrugged.

"So. Hey, you got a boyfriend yet?" he asked. She blushed. Yes he saw it. It covered her face. She blushed. He wasn't sure what that meant and she didn't really answer him so in his mind that meant no.

"What you mean yet? I never said I didn't have one before," she teased.

"Yes, you did. You said you didn't have one," he told her.

"Malcolm is her boyfriend," the niece said, listening to their conversation.

"Please!" she rolled her eyes.

That's what Robert wanted to see. That rolling of the eyes meant the denial of a boyfriend. Yeah, the summer had gone by and boy, it had been a rough one. His family had been in all kinds of shit. It was a war that had spanned from Southern Cali all the way up to Sacramento and it took all his mother's prayers to keep him out of it.

But the weather was cooling off again and things had simmered down now and Robert was ready for change. Maybe kicking it with this black girl would be too big of a change but what the hell, it was what he wanted to do.

Yep, just the thought of her was causing a boner to come.

"Because," Robert said to Jamie, coming back to the conversation. "I know where she lives. I know what's up with her. Plus, she's been moving some shit for me at the school where she goes in the P."

"What? You working the P? What chooo trying to do? Start a war with them niggas?"

"No. It's not like that. Don't worry man, I got this under control," Robert said. He wasn't sure if he really did or not, but he knew this, Sinclair dug him. She dug prescription drugs too. She liked being high, that was for sure, but that was the easy part. The hard part was getting her to dig him and he was sure in his heart she did. She dug him a lot and before Christmas he was going to have that choochie. She was going to be his woman. Even if he had to take on all those black guys in the P, this little light skinned black chick was going to be his before the end of the year—of that Robert made himself a promise.

Coming Soon

Chocolate Dream
A Sweet Treat

by

Lena Scott

Chapter One

How I used to love 9:00 A.M.

Why?

It was the time the mailman came—a tall dark and handsome piece of chocolate cake.

His name was . . .

Wait, what was his name? I can't remember anymore. Oh, well, it doesn't matter because I simply referred to him as my chocolate fantasy or Mail Man Guy . . . whichever.

He was about six five or six with a butt so tight that I swear you could bounce a quarter off it and arms that rippled with musculature and mass. How I used to pray that one day he would wrap them around me, pulling me into that bulge that sat between his pockets, pressing against that zipper . . . pardon my dramatic pause . . . I need to catch my breath.

My dreams were filled with him . . . and he did fill me.

Every night right before I would wake up, I would nearly feel his presence in my room . . . in my bed—his touch, so personal, so intimate . . . so deep. He would investigate my body with his thick fingers . . . probing, finding spots that I didn't even know existed until he discovered them. He would kiss my breasts and then teasingly tug at them lightly until the nipples stood high and firm. He then would move to my stomach, lingering around my navel until I felt the tickle in my spin that would start my libido stirring. Then he would move on to my inner thighs and then my . . . my lips.

Pardon my girlish giggles. Again, I digress.

Awakening, I would find my mouth wide open and my heart pounding with stifled ecstasy and unrequited desire.

I knew soon I would have to bring this nighttime rendezvous to fruition; somehow, I would have to get next to this chocolate dream or get him next to me, which was the preferred option.

Climbing from my bed on this warm summer morning, I went to the window. My mind soared. It was amazing what a dream could do. It actually felt as if I'd been thoroughly sexed and sometimes, although I'm embarrassed to admit, I smelled like it too. My body tingled. I often delayed my shower for just a few moments longer enjoying the sexual musk that emanated from my lower region.

"Hello there," Mr. Perkins, the yardman called, looking up at me from the gardening he tended to under my window. Mr. Perkins was a homely little man with a bald spot in the middle of his head. I mention that first as that's the first thing I noticed having only really seen him from the angle of my second story window, looking down upon him.

"Hello," I called out, sounding bored and disinterested, as always. I even think this morning I stifled a yawn.

"How did you sleep?" he called up, blocking the sun from his eyes.

Just fine old man, I wanted to call down. *Stop talking to me; I'm waiting for my mail to arrive . . . and my deliverer to cum . . . excuse the pun.*

"Fine Mr. Perkins . . . just fine thank you," I answered.

"Only fine," he frowned. "I'm sorry about that," he said. His comment although puzzling, annoyed me. His voice annoyed me. He annoyed me. I looked down at him again, barely able to see his face, but for some reason today, I found myself straining to make out the features. Broad nose, full lips . . .

The doorbell rang.

No time for Mr. Perkins now, my sweet escape was at the door. I had forgotten that I still smelled rather . . . raw, not too far from resembling the day's catch. However, I needed to see . . . what's his name . . . the mail guy. So, I ran to the door swinging it open wide. Again today, he smiled at me and again, my heart nearly burst from my chest. My stomach fluttered, my knees buckled and my eyes immediately swept his crotch in response to the throbbing I now felt in mine. I ached for this man and all he kept from me, under his postal blues.

"Thank you," I purred, allowing my hand to run along his as he handed me a box of Gevalia coffees.

"I see you like getting stuff. You get something every day," he said.

"Yes . . . and I would like to get more if I knew how to arrange it," I alluded. He simply smiled as if he got it . . . but yet . . . didn't get it all at once. I leaned back against my doorframe in one of my best Betty Davis starlet poses, pushing my breast forward in my thin gown hoping he noticed. I mean, at forty-forty double D's how could he not; right . . . that's what I'm saying.

His eyes did roam a little and if I allowed myself the license to dream with my eyes open, I would swear that he reached out to touch them. I urged them a little closer.

"Well, you have a good day," he smiled, tipping his little postal hat, covertly winking. The sigh left my lips before I could catch it. He then strutted that tight behind to the next door.

Maggie Stone lived there. She was an ex–supermodel, beauty queen, yaki-wearing, bimbo freak, *white girl*. Not that I had any jealousy toward her or anything, I just think "real" women eat.

I headed back to my bedroom, the shower called to me now, for real—really loud.

I dug through my toiletries . . .

What would I smell like today?

Ahh . . . chocolate, why not?

I worked at the Body by Godiva store in the mall. Everything you wanted in chocolate. My favorite was the body spray. It made you smell downright yummy. I used it every night before I went to bed. Today was my first time planning to use it during the day.

I lingered in the shower letting my mind wander onto Mr. Mail Man Guy and the package he'd yet to bring to me. That's when I heard it. Through the wall I swear I could hear Mr. Mail Man Guy and Skinny Ms. Bimbo Stone . . . they were . . . oh, my gosh . . . they were in her shower together. I listened closer; I even shut off the water to hear, which was hard to do with all that construction he was doing in there. Pounding on the wall with that anvil or else he was using a jack hammer or something, but either way it made it very difficult to hear what they were saying. It suddenly occurred to me . . .

I didn't realize that my mailman was also a plumber . . .

Good to know . . .

I'd have to let him know that my "drain was running a little slow" next time I saw him.

I left for my job, passing Mr. Perkins.

"You gon' make me need insulin," he remarked, in response to my decedent aura. My lips curled before I could catch them.

I turned to him and barked my words toward his back—he had quickly gone back to working in the flowerbed, "Then you besta be seeing your doctor, Mr. Perkins," I smarted off.

"I ain't eat no candy since . . . well, it's been a while. I'm diabetic. But I sure do crave it . . . I even dreama eating it . . .

every night. Sometime I even wake up with the taste of it on my breath," he continued speaking—not looking at me, but off into the air.

"Well, Mr. Perkins, I really think that's a personal problem . . . one that has nothing to do with me," I added, speaking rather sarcastically, then sashayed my ample rear to the bus stop. I could feel the heat of his stare . . . but I didn't look back.

How dare he speak to me in such a way. If I wanted to stretch my imagination, I could almost imagine it to have been a verbal sexual exchange between us.

Mr. Perkins—eating chocolate, well I never . . .

Oh, but I would. In a heartbeat if only, Mr. Mail Man Guy would take a bite. He could eat my chocolate all day long . . . and I was far from stingy in that area.

The day was rather uneventful at the store until Maggie Stone came in. She bore the markings of someone's affections on her neck, or else a really big mosquito.

"I didn't know you worked here," she said, sounding stupid. I rolled my eyes. I couldn't help it.

"Duh. What can I do you for?" I asked. It wasn't that I didn't like Maggie; I was jealous pure and simple.

"Well, I wanted to get a chocolate dildo," she giggled. My brain nearly popped out of my head. I know my eyes twitched.

"Maggie, I'm sorry, this is not a porn shop. This is a high-class establishment. We don't carry such nonsense here. Our sprays and body oils and candies are . . ."

"Whatever," she interrupted with her slender hand raised. "I just wanted something for a gag. Dude I was with this morning had a li'l ol' pencil dick and I wanted to show him what a real black man was supposed to look like," she bragged—as if she knew. She was a white girl who made it a point to sleep with black men, looking for love in darkest corners of the earth.

"Well, not all black men are well endowed," I informed her, "But then, I'm sure you know that," I added, trying to dig a little.

"Tell me about it . . . like the mail guy . . . little bitty . . . " she began. My mind ran back to the shower that morning . . .

I swallowed hard, unable to speak . . . unable to think. All I knew was this: I would never be able to dream again. I figured I would probably hate Maggie from that moment on. She'd taken all I had from me . . . my sweet, chocolate dreams.

That night I lay in bed for a long time unable to drift off. I was so upset. Who knows what I would dream about tonight? Probably some horrible nightmare, I figured.

I must have tossed and turned for a while longer until surprisingly enough I began to feel the familiar touch of my dream creeper. I attempted to wake up. I wanted to be a fuller part of this dream, but it was so good that I gave up the fight and just laid back and let him have my night. His tongue slipped between the folds into the core of my apple. I nearly leapt from my bed. I lifted my hips to make sure he didn't miss anything and had a good angle. He seemed appreciative and held my hips in place. It reminded me of someone eating a big piece of watermelon. I know I was smiling because the visual was just too clear in my mind.

I love watermelon.

The sounds of my dream man feasting between my legs brought my voice tonight. I'm certain, because he even responded by shushing me.

How dare he quiet me down in my own dream! I protested only to have him put a monkey bite on my neck—the punishment of lovers who disobey. That's what my mother used to call it. She and my daddy were so cornball.

Always slapping and tickling. Once when I was a little girl I saw him reach his hand down her blouse to pull out and squeeze her titty. I thought it was funny considering milk squirted out. My baby brother was only a few months old and seeing my mama's titty was a normal and regular occurrence—and seeing my daddy playing with my brother's "supper bag" was commonplace too. When the milk came, my daddy ran and got his cup of coffee, came back to her and did it again. She giggled while he put the milk right in the coffee and drank it. He said that chocolate milk was good in coffee . . .

I remember his smile when he said that.

They were so cornball.

Tonight my dream man kissed me on the mouth and invaded it with his tongue. It was a good kiss and I enjoyed it ever so much—his breath smelled of chocolate.

When I forced my eyes open, it was morning. I looked around my bed for traces of my visitor. There were none, unless you counted the dirt on the floor by my shoes. I didn't. I mean, I had been at the flowerbed that morning. Why would I notice a little dirt by my shoes?

I went to the window and looked out. Strangely enough, Mr. Perkins wasn't working this morning. It was funny not seeing the old man below my window, and I felt somewhat odd. It was weird not seeing his bald head, not hearing his greeting.

About that time, a young woman came with gardening tools—she looked about my age.

"Hey," I called down to her. She looked up at me.

She was short and kind of frumpy looking, "Yeah," she called up, blocking the sun, the same way Mr. Perkins used to. I couldn't see her face either, but the resemblance to Mr. Perkins was obvious.

"Where is Mr. Perkins?"

"The hospital," she called.

"Oh, gosh! What happened," I inquired. My heart was inexplicably racing. I was immediately upset.

"He went into a diabetic coma this mornin'. His sugar went way high. Don't nobody know how. I try ta hide sweets from him, but somehow he manages to get inta dem. I swear, my fatha would attempt to climb a mountain fa a Hershey bar. So I usually try to keep sweets outta his reach," she giggled. "He gon' be alright doe. It's not the first time he's done this," she smiled. "I think he's got a stash somewhere that nobody has figured out," she added.

"Well, you tell him he better stop. I'm sure he enjoys it, but it's gonna be the deatha him," I fussed.

"Oh, yes, ma'am. Hear him tell it . . . ain't nothing better on earf than a biggo bite of chocolate," she said, grinning all the while.

"Poor Mr. Perkins," I said to myself as I headed to my shower. I didn't care about even seeing Mr. Mail Man Guy today. He could just leave my box outside my door for all I cared. It was Mr. Perkins that weighed heavily on my mind.

As the water hit me and I rubbed the chocolate scented bubbles into my skin, my neck began to sting.

"What the heck bit me?" I screeched, pulling my shaving mirror to level so as to see.

My voice stuck in my throat. My heart nearly stopped. I couldn't believe my eyes—the monkey bite glistened red and tender.

Grabbing my robe, I ran to the window and called down to Mr. Perkin's daughter.

"What hospital is he in?"